UNEXPECTED

D0880416

By the Author

A Royal Romance

Heart of the Pack

Courting the Countess

Royal Rebel

Unexpected

UNEXPECTED

by
Jenny Frame

2017

Credits
Editor: Ruth Sternglantz
Production Design: Stacia Seaman
Cover Design by Sheri (graphicartist2020@hotmail.com)

Acknowledgments

Thank you to Radclyffe, Sandy, and all the BSB staff who work so hard to make our books the best they can be. I couldn't have had a better experience since joining Bold Strokes Books, and I couldn't hope to have a better editor than Ruth Sternglantz. Thank you, Ruth, for your patience and support. I really appreciate it.

To my friends Amy and Christine, I'm thankful to have your friendship and your support.

Thank you to all the readers who have supported my books and have given me such great feedback about George and Bea's love story. I hope you enjoy their latest installment.

Thank you to my family who support and help me every day. I'm always grateful.

My darlin' Lou, thank you for seeing all my oddness and weirdness as endearing qualities, thank you for understanding me without me needing to explain, and thank you for your fierce loyalty, no matter what.

You and our Barney boy are my happy ever after.

For my darlin' Lou,
always and forever.

CHAPTER ONE

The dulcet tones of Britney Spears echoed through the workshop area of McGuire's Motors. Dale McGuire had her head under the bonnet of a 1957 Jaguar and she sang along at the top of her lungs.

The weight in the car shifted and her best friend and mentor Sammy Brooks appeared at her side. "Do you have to sing along with Britney Spears, and do we have to hear her twenty bloody times a day?"

Dale glanced to her side and said in her low Scottish tones, "Hey, Britney was a big part of my youth."

Sammy crossed her arms and gave her a mock glare. "Don't I know it? When you lived with us, Britney and your other cheesy nineties pop were all I heard day and night."

Dale chuckled and stood up. "You love it, Sammy. That's my gift to you and Val. I keep you young."

Ten years her senior, Sammy and her wife Valentina were the combination of the parents and siblings she didn't have. They'd taken her in when she'd arrived in London, seventeen and still a moody teenager.

"Yeah, right. Of course you do, kid. More like you turn my hair greyer than it already is. How are you getting on with the engine?"

Dale took the bonnet off its stand and eased it closed. "All done. We should be ready for the race next weekend. She's going to purr her way around the track."

Sammy walked back to where she was working on the car door and said, "If we can just get her looking pretty too. That was some bump you took."

As well as owning McGuire's Motors in London, Dale ran a classic racing team along with Sammy, and spent most weekends tinkering with their pride and joy, a classic blue Jaguar XKSS.

"Yeah, well, the idiot wouldn't let me pass his piece of shit car. Don't worry, she'll look like the dog's bollocks in no time."

Feeling the heat of the workshop, Dale undid the top part of her overalls and tied the arms around her waist, leaving her in a black sleeveless T-shirt. She reached into her pocket, fished out one of the lollipops she was never without, and stuck it in her mouth.

"You're going to rot your teeth, you know that?" Sammy said.

Dale rolled her eyes and without taking the lolly out of her mouth said, "Yes, Mum. I've switched to sugar free so stop being so sanctimonious, and let's get this bodywork done."

Sammy walked to the workbench and gathered some tools they would need. "At least bloody Britney's finished."

Dale grinned, pulled out her smartphone, and restarted the song that played through the garage's Bluetooth speakers.

Sammy growled and looked up to the heavens. "Fuck me. If I hear that song one more time I'm going to scream."

Dale loved to infuriate her best friend, and loved to play the role of annoying younger sibling. It was part of who they were, and she knew Sammy secretly loved it.

"No thanks, you're not my type, mate."

They heard the door to the garage open, and the sound of heels echoed across the workspace. A broad smile spread across Sammy's face. There was only one pair of heels that made Sammy smile like that. The ones that belonged to her wife, Valentina.

"Lunch is here, if you two could stop playing with your tools for a second."

Sammy stood up and said, "We'll be there in a second, sweetie."

"You better be. I walked all the way over to the other side of the shopping mall, in heels, may I add, just to get your favourite, Sammy."

The look on Sammy's face was something Dale secretly envied. When she met Sammy and Valentina, they had already been together four years, and were utterly devoted to each other. In the years since, they had gotten married and had a little girl. They were Dale's idea of a perfect family unit.

Her thoughts were interrupted by the sounds of a car pulling up outside the garage and the door opening slowly. "Hello? Dale?"

Dale let out a sigh when she saw it was a woman she'd had a brief encounter with last Friday night. What was her name? Lesley, Lisa…?

Sammy slapped her on the back and said, "I'll leave you with one of your groupies."

"No, Sammy, wait—"

But it was too late, she was off and walking to the garage office, leaving her alone with the rapidly approaching woman.

Shit.

"Hi, Dale, you are hard to track down. I tried every other one of your garages and couldn't find you, but the last one I tried said you might be here."

"Lisa—" She took a guess and hoped she was right.

"It doesn't matter. I've got you now."

Lisa stepped close to her, ran a fingernail down her biceps, and swirled it around her Celtic band tattoo, then pulled the lollipop from her mouth and licked it. It was supposed to be seductive, but all Dale felt was a need to get away. Lisa had been aggressively pursuing her for weeks, and she had gotten her.

"Are you going to be at Belles tonight? I'm going with some of my friends and I thought we could hook up again?"

Dale cringed at the word *hook-up*. Her whole adult life had been filled with hook-ups, mutually beneficial encounters that ended before they even began, but her body was becoming less and less interested. What used to seem exciting before was now becoming routine and boring.

"So? Will you be going, Dale?" Lisa asked.

Dale desperately searched for an appropriate answer. Why was it so hard to say no? Why was this all people wanted from her?

These were the questions that had been rattling around her head recently.

"I…uh…"

"Dale?" She was about to agree to whatever Lisa wanted when Valentina shouted over to her from the office. "You have a call from the supplier you were waiting on."

Thank you, Val.

"Sorry, I really need to take this call, Lisa. Maybe I'll see you around? Bye."

Dale nearly ran over to the office and shut the door with relief. "Val, you're a lifesaver."

"You're welcome." Val got Dale's sandwich from the food bag and handed it to her.

Sammy was sitting on Val's desk laughing. "Your face was priceless."

"Aye, thanks for ditching me, mate." Dale took a seat at her desk and started to eat her lunch.

"It's your own fault. You will insist on having a gaggle of groupies following you about."

"Would you stop saying I have groupies?" Dale said.

Val took a sip of her tea. "Dale, you bring on these awkward situations yourself. Why did you sleep with her if you didn't like her?"

Dale shrugged. "I don't know. She wanted to?"

"But you have to think about it more deeply before you jump in. Some of these woman are going to think you want more, a relationship," Val said.

"A relationship? They don't want a relationship with me. I'm someone to have fun with for a few nights. They want Dale from the bar—they don't want the Dale you know." *Nobody does.*

Val gave her a pointed look. "That's because you don't show them the real you. You could easily have a lovely girl who would want to walk through life with you."

Dale's chest tightened in panic at the thought. "You know I don't like talking about this, Val. I give them what they want and I get something in return. It's simple. I don't even go looking for anyone. I just go for a drink and to unwind. I don't know what they see that's so exciting. I'm just me. A glorified grease monkey."

"I don't either," Sammy joked.

Dale glared at her. "Very funny."

"Behave, you two," Val said. "Dale, you have this cool brooding thing going on. Every woman thinks they can change you. Domesticate you, like I did to Sammy."

Dale stopped chewing on her sandwich and swallowed. "Domesticate me? I'm not a farmyard animal."

"Believe me, mate," Sammy said and looked at Val adoringly. "It's much better in the long run to be domesticated and tagged."

"Yeah, but Val's already taken, so I'm out of luck," Dale said.

Val was beautiful, warm, caring, and an all-round elegant lady, and Dale had always had a small crush on her. If she was to imagine a perfect woman, Val would come close, but she loved her as a friend and mentor, and Dale didn't believe there was anyone else out there like Val. Sammy was lucky.

Val looked at her seriously. "You can't be alone forever. Sammy and I know you have your reasons, but everyone needs love in their life."

Over the past year or so that's what had been worrying her. Being alone, forever. But there was no other option for her.

❖

After lunch Dale was in a reflective mood. Val's words resonated inside her and wouldn't shut up, so she decided to work on the books and lose herself in the surety of numbers, while Sammy went back to work on the car.

She scanned over the accounts quickly as she clicked from page to page on her laptop. Business was good. Since buying out her former employer eleven years ago, Dale had grown McGuire's Motors steadily. But as good a business brain as Dale had, she couldn't have done it without her best friends Sammy and Val.

When she bought the business, she asked her friends to help her. Sammy was her area manager floating between all the sites, and Val was her secretary, PA, and all round office angel. This freed Dale to handle all the business side of things.

The way the books were looking, they could afford to expand if they wanted to, but did she want to? Dale was never really driven by money. She wanted enough so that she and her friends didn't need to worry about month-to-month income or their futures. But she had no family to support, and as long as she was comfortable that was okay. The one thing that did drive her was the determination to succeed. She was self-made, and very proud of that fact. She came to London with nothing and now she had a thriving business. That did give her satisfaction, and yet she was unsettled.

Dale got up and walked over to the window. She leaned against the frame and let out a sigh. "There has to be more than this."

Val popped her head around the door and said, "Dale? Do you have a minute?"

Without turning Dale said, "I've got too much time."

"Dale, seriously. There's someone here to see you," Val said.

Dale turned around and was surprised at the worry on Val's face. "Yeah, who is it?"

"I'll let them explain."

Val opened the door and a young boy with a soaking wet blue jacket and red backpack walked in. Dale looked from him back up to Val again.

"What—?"

"Are you Mary Dale McGuire?" the boy asked.

Dale narrowed her eyes. "Yes, but I don't like to advertise the Mary bit. Call me Dale. What is this all about?"

"Yes." The boy did a fist pump. "I found you at last. I knew I could."

Dale walked back to the front of her desk, leaned on it, and crossed her arms. "Listen, what's your name?"

The little boy walked forward and held out his hand for her to shake. It struck her immediately that he was entirely too adult and formal for a child.

"My name is Jake Harper." He reached into his pocket and pulled out a sheet of paper.

"How can I help you, Jake? Are you lost? Are your parents around?"

"No, I'm not lost, and one of my parents is here."

Dale, on the other hand, was utterly lost, but somewhere deep inside she had a sinking feeling. "Where? What is this about?"

By now Sammy had joined Val at the office door and seemed equally perplexed when Dale looked to her for help.

Jake held out a document and said, "You're my other mum and I've been looking for you. It was hard but I knew I'd find you."

"Sammy, if you..." Her words died in her throat as she took the document and saw her details on a printout from the Orchard Fertility Clinic.

Dale's hands started to shake as she read. "No, no, this isn't real." She looked up at Sammy and snapped, "Sammy, is this some sort of joke?"

"No way, although I wish I had thought of it. Whoever did has made you go white as a sheet."

When Sammy started to laugh she got an elbow from Val. "Dale, what does the paper say?"

"This must be a fucking joke."

"You shouldn't swear, you know," the boy said. "Mummy says you should use your intelligence to create positivity with your words."

This was insane. A boy called Jake was standing in front of her, saying he was her son and giving her a lecture on swearing.

Dale had almost forgotten about the egg donation she had made eleven years ago. It had been done on a whim, and she hadn't given it too much thought since, although the clinic had warned her that any children resulting from her donation had the right to have her details at age eighteen. Which none of those children could yet be. And the boy in front of her was hardly in that age group.

"How old are you, Jake?"

"Ten. It was my birthday last week."

Dale felt her legs turn to jelly. "Val, could you take Jake outside. I need to make a phone call."

Val held out her hand. "Come on, Jake. Let's get some juice."

Jake looked between her and Val, weighing up whether or not to go. "You won't just disappear, will you?"

A surge of emotion welled up inside Dale, and she had to gulp it down hard. "No, I just need a few minutes and Val will bring you back."

"You promise?"

Dale knew what it was to feel unwanted and to have promises be broken, so she forced a smile onto her face. "I promise, and Val will tell you that I always keep my promises."

Val nodded. "She does. Come with me, Jake."

Jake smiled, seemingly happy with that assurance. "Okay. See you soon, Mum."

"Thank you." Dale ended the call and threw the phone across the desk.

She held her face in her hands and repeated over and over, "This is not happening. This is not happening."

Dale's whole body was shaking and she felt sick.

"Dale? What's going on?"

She'd been so engrossed in her own turmoil that she hadn't heard Sammy come into the office. She raised her head and saw that Sammy's previously jovial demeanour had disappeared.

"I don't know where to start," Dale said.

"The beginning is always a good place."

Dale let out a big breath. It was so hard to say it. She felt like if she said it out loud, only then would it become real.

"Remember when you were planning to have Mia? You had all these brochures from private fertility clinics."

"Yeah, I remember vividly. It was an exciting and scary time."

"You left them lying on the coffee table, and one day I started to flip through them. I was curious."

"And?"

"I came to the section about egg donation and it explained that there was a huge demand for women to donate."

Her friend's eyes went wide. "You donated your own eggs?"

She nodded. "It was a whim, but something about helping a couple have a baby together really resonated with me. I felt a need I didn't really understand, and the money came in useful when I was saving to buy this place. It wasn't much, but it helped."

Sammy looked flabbergasted. "You could have told us about it. That's a big, big decision to take on your own."

Dale got up and walked over to the window. "I don't know why—it just felt kind of personal. But I wanted to help someone have something I knew that I would never have myself, if that makes sense. And then as time went on I forgot all about it."

"Until today?" Sammy said.

"I called the fertility clinic and they said it was true. Their records were compromised at the weekend and they are having an investigation into it."

"So that little boy out there is your son?"

Dale whipped around angrily. "No, I'm just an egg donor. Nothing more than that."

Sammy got up instantly, crossed to her, and put her hands on Dale's shoulders. "Hey, I'm on your side, remember? I know this is a really difficult situation, especially for you, but that little boy is going to be confused and easily hurt. You need to deal with him carefully. Get him home, and then you can face what it means."

Dale scrubbed her face with her hands. "You're right. Okay."

"His parents must be frantic," Sammy said. "Maybe you should phone the police."

"No, I'll drive him home. There must be some reason he came to find me. I think I need to talk to his parents."

Sammy pulled her into to a hug. "You're doing the right thing. I know it's going to be really hard for you, but even harder for Jake. Be careful."

You were a mistake, you weren't supposed to happen. The words that haunted all her quiet moments floated across her mind.

"I'll be careful. I know what being unwanted feels like."

❖

Dale walked quickly to her car in the garage car park with Jake's backpack over her shoulder, and with the boy trailing behind in her wake.

"Mum, slow down. You're too fast."

Jake had insisted on calling her *Mum* from the moment he saw her, but every time he said it, the title hurt somewhere deep inside her.

She stopped by her car and opened the door for him. "Jake, you have to stop calling me that. I'm not your mum and your real mum and dad wouldn't like it."

He looked up at her with big, sad brown eyes, so much like her own, and said, "I don't have a dad. It's just my mummy and me."

Dale wasn't expecting that. She'd imagined a couple using a fertility clinic to conceive. "Oh, okay. Well, get in the car and I'll take you home to her."

Jake walked up and down the side of her car studying it. "I've never seen a car like this. It looks like an airplane."

"It's a 1957 Jaguar. I like classic cars."

That didn't seem to satisfy him as he went on to prod the soft roof. "Why does it have a roof like this and why does it only have two seats?"

This child was insistent in his quest for knowledge. She could tell he was intelligent, but she wasn't in the mood for questions.

"The roof comes down in sunny weather and it only has two seats because that's all I need. Get in the car please, before the rain gets heavy again."

Dale finally got him in and got in the driver's seat. While she entered his address in her satnav, she watched Jake touch all the retro car knobs and the wooden dash with reverence.

"It's like a cockpit," he said, awestruck.

"Sit back, wee man, before you break anything."

It would take about an hour to get him home to the village of Plumtun, Croydon, although with the rain now battering the roads, she would have to take them slowly and carefully. Her first thought had been to have him call his mother, but he didn't have his mobile phone, and his mother thought he was safe in school, so the best thing she could do was get him home quickly and walk away without looking back.

After they set off, Jake was silent for all of thirty seconds. Talking seemed to be his default setting. Dale gripped the steering wheel uncomfortably as she felt Jake's eyes bore into her.

"Why did you call me *wee man*? You speak really weirdly," Jake said.

"I'm Scottish, from Glasgow. That's why I sound different." Dale hoped that would be the end of the conversation.

"Scottish?"

But she was wrong.

Jake seemed to mull over the word in his brain for a few seconds before he said, "Do you play bagpipes?"

"No."

"Do you eat haggis?"

"No."

"Do you wear a kilt?"

Dale was starting to get annoyed by the incessant questions. She looked at him and tried to keep calm in the crazy situation this day had brought her.

"Are you just rhyming off every Scottish stereotype?"

"What's Glasgow like? Do you have family there?"

He didn't appear to filter his thoughts. If one popped into his head he just said it.

"Do I have a grandma there?"

"No!" Dale snapped. "No more questions." As soon as she snapped she regretted it, but he had touched a raw nerve. She let out a breath and tried to regain control. "I'm sorry, Jake. This is all a bit of a surprise. How did you find me? The clinic told me they had a breach in their files."

"I hacked into their database," Jake said matter-of-factly.

"You did what? Come on, you're ten years old. You can't do that."

Jake looked almost hurt she had said that. "Yes, I can. My mummy says I can do anything I put my mind to."

"Of course you can. I'm sorry."

Jake gave her the warmest smile. "That's all right, Mum. You don't know me yet, but I have lots to tell you as we get to know each other."

Dale decided just to humour him for the moment, so as not to upset him. "So you hacked and got my name, okay. Did your mummy have a husband or a partner—"

"No, she used a sperm donor. My mummy couldn't have kids herself."

Jake said it as if it was the most natural thing in the world for a ten-year-old to be saying. Dale's head was bursting with emotion and information. For the first time in ten years she ached for a cigarette.

She reached down to the glove compartment and popped it open. Her stash of lollipops, her cigarette substitutes, came tumbling out. She took a cherry one and said, "Help yourself, Jake. Oh, I suppose you're not allowed to take sweets from strangers, huh?"

Jake eyed the lollipops and grabbed one. "You're not a stranger, Mum."

Dale popped the lollipop in her mouth and tried to ignore the *M* word. "So…why did you try to find me?"

"My mummy needs help. She's not been well and can't work very much just now. I thought if I found you and the man who donated sperm, that you'd both help us."

Dale's mind was whirling with fear and panic. What on earth was she getting herself into?

"Did you find the other donor then?" Dale asked.

Jake pulled the lollipop out with a pop. "Yes, but he died two years ago. It's only you who's left, only you that can help us."

"How can I help you, Jake? I'm a stranger."

She caught Jake gazing at her with a look of complete certainty. "You helped my mummy make me. Who else would help us when we are in trouble?"

That innocent sentiment hit Dale like a kick in the guts. "What kind of trouble do you have?"

Jake lifted up his schoolbag and took out a notebook. "I made a list so I wouldn't forget."

Dale glanced to the side and saw a neat, numbered list of

problems. The facing page was filled with what looked like some complex maths equations.

"You like maths, Jake?"

"Yes, I love it. I'm working on some famous maths problems that haven't been solved yet. It's fun, like a puzzle."

This boy was either delusional or he was the brightest child she had ever met. "So, what's on your list?"

"The heating keeps breaking down, and the water's mostly cold. Mummy uses kettles of boiling water a lot. The car is broken down and the sink is leaking..."

As Jake went on with his list, Dale realized why Jake was so determined to find her. Clearly his mother was struggling, and he had taken action in the only way he knew how.

CHAPTER TWO

I'm sorry to have to let you down, Mr. Gregson, but my health…"
Rebecca Harper was in her home studio trying to placate one of her clients over the phone. Her studio was no more than the large bare attic of the eighteenth century vicarage she had recently bought, but with a desk, chair, computer, and excellent photographic equipment, it sufficed until she could decorate. If her client list lasted that long.

"Yes, yes, I know how hard it will be to get a photographer so late in the day but—"

Mr. Gregson clearly had enough and slammed the phone down. Rebecca sighed, then sarcastically said into the phone, "Remember and keep me in mind for next time!"

She laid her mobile down on the desk, and struck another name off her dwindling client list.

This was fast becoming a habit. As a freelance commercial photographer, Rebecca relied on getting out to her clients' premises. Building sites, restaurants, government buildings, all lucrative contracts, but now in her sixth month of pregnancy, and struggling to cope with high blood pressure and doctor's orders to stay resting at home, her contracts were leaving her thick and fast.

Very few were willing or able to wait until her health improved, and Becca couldn't blame them. Her problems were not anyone else's but her own. She sat back in her chair and gently stroked her baby bump, and feelings of guilt squirmed around inside her.

"It was never meant to be this way, little one," Rebecca said.

She looked up at the large plans of the house that she had pinned to the wall. Rebecca had designed them herself when she had bought the vicarage ten months ago. Everything had seemed so rosy then. She'd always wanted to make a home far from the hustle and bustle of the city.

Rebecca had been searching for a school that would be able to cope with Jake's learning needs. Jake had been labelled by psychologists and doctors as a gifted child at a very young age. Now ten, the local school he had been attending struggled to keep up with the pace of his learning, and when a place had opened up in a private school a few miles from here that specialized in teaching gifted children, it had seemed the perfect time to make the move to the farming community of Plumtun.

The once thriving village, which the vicarage had served, had long since died as people were forced to the city to find work. Now all that was left were a few farms and a handful of houses, with the nearest shop five miles away.

For Rebecca, who valued privacy above all, Plumtun was somewhere where they could live quietly, yet have a quick commute to London for her business clients. Then everything changed.

Rebecca gazed at the time on her computer and realized Jake was a few minutes late. Fear, always very close to the surface, spread through her body. She got up as quickly as she could and went over to look for his school bus out of the window.

Jake was meant to be a bit later this evening, as he had computer club after school, but he should have definitely been home by now.

Calm down. It's only a few minutes, Rebecca thought. The bus was probably stuck behind a tractor or something, a common problem in that rural area.

She checked her watch every few minutes, and the fear started to intensify. If only the car wasn't on the blink, she would have been able to pick him up as she always did, and would have known he was safe.

After a few minutes more, she picked up her mobile and called Jake, but soon heard his ringtone coming from his bedroom.

"Jake, how many times have I told you to remember your phone."

Jake had a basic phone she had given him for this exact kind of situation. She hurried downstairs and stood by the front door, hoping beyond hope that the bus would come careening around the corner any second.

Rebecca waited and waited, and after about twenty minutes, she dialled the number for Jake's school.

"Hi, this is Ms. Harper. Jake's bus still hasn't come. Was he kept back at school, do you know?"

The school secretary replied, "I'm sorry, Ms. Harper. Jake never turned up at computer club today. We were just going to call you."

Rebecca's stomach dropped like a stone.

❖

Dale pulled the car into the gravel driveway and saw a woman with light brown hair standing by the front door with a silver haired woman near her.

"Is that your mum?" Dale asked.

"Yes, that's my mum—Rebecca, but everyone calls her Becca, and Granny Sadie from next door. She's not my real granny but she helps Mummy and me a lot, just like a granny."

Rebecca started to hurry to the car and Dale was struck by how beautiful she looked. She had long golden-brown hair, which was perfectly styled with a slight wave to it, and her petite, curvaceous frame exuded femininity. "Your mum's beautiful."

"I know. She's really pretty. I wish I could make her happy. She cries a lot when she thinks I can't hear her."

"She does?"

Jake nodded. "When Mummy bought this house, it wasn't nice, and she was going to get it repaired so we could have a home in the country close to my school, but then the baby made her feel sick and she couldn't work much."

Dale's head snapped around. "Baby? What baby?"

"Mummy's six months pregnant with my baby sister. That's why we need your help, Mum. Mummy's not been well."

Dale saw the well-defined baby bump Rebecca's hand was resting on as walked purposefully towards them.

"Jesus fucking Christ," Dale said as the reality of the situation dawned on her. Was that child hers as well?

"Don't swear in front of Mummy. She'll be angry," Jake cautioned her. "Oh, and remember, you promised you wouldn't disappear."

Dale didn't know what to say. Her head wanted to drive off into the night and never look back, and her heart wanted to help, to know more about this unusual little family.

Rebecca pulled open Jake's door and pulled him into her arms. "Where have you been, Jake? I was so scared."

Dale didn't know if she should get out and interrupt this moment, so she sat and waited for them to get reacquainted.

"I went to get you help, Mummy. I found my other mum and she's going to help us."

Jake handed her the printout from the clinic, and Rebecca went silent. After a few seconds she said coldly, "Jake, go inside with Granny Sadie."

That was Dale's cue to get out and talk, she guessed. She walked around the car and Rebecca still hadn't looked at her once.

Jake looked anxiously at Dale, not knowing whether to comply or not. "But, Mummy—"

"Inside now, Jake," Rebecca repeated. "Sadie? Could you call the police and tell them it's a false alarm."

The older woman stepped forward and took Jake's hand. "Of course. Come on now, sweetheart. You must be starving. Granny Sadie will make you a sandwich."

Jake looked at Dale with eyes that tugged at her heartstrings. "Remember, you promised?"

Dale gave him a quick nod and said, "I remember. On you go, wee man."

Jake walked away with Sadie. Dale walked close to Rebecca and said, "Listen, Ms. Harper. I'm sor—"

Becca snapped her head up and her large expressive green eyes were full of anger. "You are not taking my child away from me. You don't have any legal rights over him."

Dale held her hands up in surrender. "Hey, I don't want your child or any legal rights to him. He found me, not the other way around. He walked into my business with that piece of paper and turned my world upside down, so don't be angry at me. I just brought him home to you, okay?"

Becca simply gazed at her as if she was taking everything about her in, and it wasn't an unpleasant experience.

Becca was well put together, her make-up flawless, her clothes elegantly stylish. And she had a sexy upper-middle-class accent that made Dale think she must have a rich daddy somewhere and a trust fund, which made Jake's assertion that they were in such difficulties all the more strange.

"Then thank you for bringing him home"—Becca looked down at the clinic details again—"Mary, but you have to go and don't ever think about seeing Jake again."

Dale was starting to get angry. All she had done was the right thing and she was getting grief for it.

"My name is Dale, and children and a family are the last thing I want, so you don't have to get all worked up. My life consists of working hard, driving my race car, and going out and having fun. Nowhere in that does a child figure."

Becca looked at her retro Nintendo T-shirt with the *I Scored with the Princess* logo and said, "Clearly."

For some reason she didn't want to explore, that comment hurt, but she didn't respond. "I called the clinic and the information is correct. I don't know how Jake got the information. He said he hacked into the database, but that can't be true."

Becca sighed and rubbed her baby bump, as if trying to soothe it. "He can do it. Jake is a special child. He has an IQ of one hundred fifty-five and is an expert in computers. He is one of the youngest children to pass the Microsoft engineer's exams, and he's done this sort of thing before."

"Jesus. What an amazing boy," Dale said.

"He is." Becca was sounding a little less hostile now. "I don't know where he gets it from. The maths and equations he does, I'm lost when I look at them."

But Dale knew, and it built another connection to Jake and this family in her heart. She had always found numbers extremely easy and had excelled in maths until she went to secondary school, and foolishly thought being cool was more important than her studies.

"You've done a great job with him—he's a polite and clever boy." Dale's gaze lowered to Becca's bump, and she was desperate to ask the question that was burning in her brain.

Becca must have felt her gaze because she immediately tensed. "I'm grateful for you bringing him back, but I think you should go now."

Dale scanned the once impressive, but now tired looking vicarage. "Jake said you needed help with some things around here. Is there anything I could help you with?"

"It's none of your concern. We are fine. I can look after *my* son myself."

Talk about independent. Rebecca Harper seemed to have a hard shell covering her beautiful body, and didn't appear as if she ever smiled.

"Okay. If you ever need anything, I'm Dale McGuire of McGuire's Motors. You've probably heard of my business."

Rebecca gave a sarcastic laugh. "Yes, one of your garages gave me an overinflated quote only a few weeks ago. Mechanics see a woman coming and take them for idiots."

Dale's business was one thing she didn't tolerate criticism of. She was proud of the service and professionalism she provided. "McGuire's Motors does not take advantage of women. I could work out a good deal for you if you'd like."

"No," Becca snapped. "We don't take charity from anyone. Please just walk away, Dale, and don't ever think about us again."

Something inside Dale told her she shouldn't walk away, but she had to. She nodded and walked around to the driver's door. Just as she was about to get in, Dale looked up at Becca and asked, "Will you tell me one thing before I go?"

Becca nodded.

"Is your new baby…" She wanted to say *mine* but knew that wouldn't go down well. "Are Jake and the new baby from the same donor?"

Becca took a few seconds and then said, "Yes, they're from the same donor."

Dale felt her throat tighten, and emotion churned in her stomach. She managed to croak a thank you before getting in her car and speeding off.

❖

Becca closed Jake's bedroom door and walked downstairs to the kitchen. Sadie was still there and waiting for her.

"I've made a pot of tea. Sit down and get the weight off your feet, sweetheart," Sadie said.

"Thanks." Becca sat and wrapped her hands around the steaming cup of tea, hoping the heat would seep inside her and reach the cold inside.

Sadie, who lived in the old farmhouse next door, was a great support to Becca and Jake. Neighbours were few and far between around here, so Becca had been really lucky to have Sadie right next door.

Sadie sat down and placed her hand on Becca's arm. "How's Jake?"

Becca sighed. "Angry. He's not speaking to me because I sent Ms. McGuire…Dale away."

Sadie let out a long breath. "That was a turn up for the books, eh? That boy of yours is a smart cookie."

My boy, thought Becca. She'd never thought about the donors she had used after she had chosen them. When she had looked through the clinic's database, she had been drawn to the egg donor who had a high IQ but was also a manual worker. She thought that would give her child a good chance of having a wide range of abilities.

The clinic had always cautioned that her child had the right to search for their donor when they were eighteen, but she'd promised herself she would deal with that if it ever came up. This was entirely different.

"I never thought this could happen."

"What was she like, this Dale?" Sadie asked.

Becca added some milk to her tea and stirred. "She scared me."

"Why? She didn't want to have anything to do with the Jake or the baby, did she?"

Becca gave a hollow laugh. "Going by the childish way she dresses for her age, I doubt it. She scared me because when I looked in her eyes I saw Jake in her."

It was the first time that she didn't feel like Jake was totally her child. Whether she saw Dale again or not, now Becca knew there was someone else who had a part in creating her children, and she knew she would never forget that feeling when she looked into Dale's eyes.

"I don't want you to worry, Becca," Sadie said. "You have to think of the baby just now, and I'm sure that's the last you'll see of Dale." Sadie stood up. "I made a casserole for you and Jake for dinner. I'll just go and get it from the oven at home."

Becca grasped Sadie's hand and smiled. "Thank you. I don't know what we'd do without you."

"Don't be silly. It was lonely out here before you and Jake came. This house stood empty for five years, so believe me it's wonderful to have you two a stone's throw away. I like to look after people."

Plumtun's remote nature had been what Becca longed for, but now six months pregnant, with what the doctor feared might become pre-eclampsia, it was becoming a problem.

"Thank you, Sadie. You're an angel."

When Sadie left, Becca looked around her half-finished country kitchen and felt the guilt that was always her companion at the moment. When they had moved in and she'd had the funds to start renovations on the vicarage, the kitchen had been the first thing she'd tackled. The walls were newly plastered but the builders had not painted or finished. The new kitchen fittings and cupboards were sitting still in their packaging in the garage, and not likely to be installed anytime soon.

As her pregnancy had progressed and she began to feel ill, she'd had to take on less and less work. Her funds dried up and the builders packed up, leaving them in an unfinished house.

Becca felt overwhelmed and tears sprang from her eyes. For Jake to go to the drastic step of finding Dale McGuire meant he knew how bad things were for them financially, and that was her fault. She had put their little family at risk because of her need to have another child, and Jake was suffering for it.

Everything was coming apart. Her career, her family, and her relationship with her son, and now Dale McGuire was an even bigger threat looming over it all.

❖

Dale drove into the car parking area in front of McGuire's Motors and shut off the engine. The garage was all locked up. Sammy and Val had obviously gone to pick up their little girl, Mia, from her grandma's.

She had always admired what Sammy had achieved. She had everything—a wife like Val, a child, and a family that loved her.

What did she have to hurry home for? Nothing, not even a pet. But although she had admired Sammy's life, her own had never really bothered her until the last year or so.

Dale was thirty-six years old, and her life was filled with working at the garage during the week, then going out the pub on Fridays and Saturdays, and she was tired of it. The only bright spot about her weekends—besides her racing—was having Sunday lunch with Val, Sammy, and Mia. She loved that.

Mia was her god-daughter and she loved her. Dale was great at being the cool playmate, but she wasn't the one Mia ran to to take care of her when she was hurt or scared. That was Sammy's job.

But Jake had run to *her*.

Jake and Becca had filled her thoughts on the drive home. Dale might have only known Jake for the best part of a couple of hours, but as she drove away, she felt like she was leaving a part of herself behind.

Dale reached down to her glove compartment to grab a lollipop, and found a photograph sitting amongst the lollies.

"How did this get in there?"

She pulled it out and stared at the image of a smiling Becca standing with Jake on what looked like his first day at school.

She turned the picture over and a read a message on the back. Dale read out loud, "To Mum, please don't forget about us."

On the last word Dale's voice cracked, her eyes filled with tears, and a memory floated across her mind as she looked at Jake's picture.

You were a mistake, Dale. I've got my own life now.

Dale wiped away the tears that threatened to fall. "Fuck this."

She stuffed the picture into her pocket, started her engine, and drove off at a high rate of speed.

Half an hour later, she dropped her car off at her flat in Islington and got a taxi to her regular pub hangout, Belles.

She nodded to the bouncers as she walked through the door, and headed straight to the bar of the trendy all-female club.

Dale could feel lots of eyes on her and lots of whispers as soon as she entered. She was well used to getting lots of attention from women. She didn't know why, but it had always been like that ever since she had first gone out in the London pub and club scene.

She took a seat at the bar and the owner walked over to her.

"You're early tonight, mate."

"I needed a drink, Mac. Can I get a lager and two shots of vodka, just for starters?"

Mac had worked at Belles ever since Dale had first sneaked in here age seventeen. She was part of the furniture and had been a good friend to her over the years.

"It must be bad. Give me a minute," Mac said.

While she waited, Dale looked around. It was only seven

o'clock. Far too early for the serious party crowd, but it was still pretty busy. As she looked around at all the youthful faces, she felt out of place.

Dale had always swaggered into Belles and felt at home, but recently everything that had been so appealing was becoming less so. The music wasn't as good, the laughter and chatter were too loud, the haircuts too weird, and the women far too young.

What is happening to me?

At the other end of the bar, a girl who looked barely eighteen met her eyes and smiled seductively, clearly trying to hit on her.

Mac arrived back with her drinks. "Here you go."

Dale immediately knocked back one of the vodka shots and said, "Mac, why do your punters look younger and younger? It's making me feel old."

Mac laughed. "You're right. We're the two oldest here. The last of the old crowd. Everyone got married and settled down, that's why. When you've got someone to go home to, a night out in a noisy bar doesn't appeal any more."

Dale knocked back another shot and took a sip of lager. It was true. Every one of her friends and acquaintances from the bar had dropped out of her life, as they each met a partner and settled down. Now it was just her, and her age only seemed to enhance the attention she got from the younger crowd.

Dale remembered being fresh out on the gay scene in her late teens and chasing the sexy, experienced older women. In fact the first woman she had slept with had been in her midthirties, and taught her everything she knew about making love to a woman. Now, Dale realized for the first time, *she* was the older, experienced woman in amongst the youthful crowd at Belles.

Feeling utterly depressed, Dale took a long drink of her lager. The young woman who had given her the eye across the bar walked over to her, flanked by her friends, some of whom Dale recognized.

"Hi, Dale. Would you come and dance with us?"

The way her friends whispered and giggled behind her made them appear like a gaggle of schoolgirls, and that made Dale feel even older.

"I don't really feel like dancing tonight, girls."

They looked perplexed, and Dale understood why. She always danced, she was always the life of the party at Belles, but tonight partying was the furthest thing from her mind.

"Oh, please, Dale, you always love to dance—"

"I'm sorry, girls. Not tonight." She shouted over to Mac, "Could you get these girls drinks on me?"

"Coming up," Mac said.

The girls looked disappointed but reluctantly left her alone with the promise of free drinks.

I feel like I'm at a high school disco.

Her thoughts turned to Becca and Jake and she wondered if they were settled for the night. Jake had said that his mum cried a lot, and she could believe it. When Becca had looked her in the eyes, she had seen sadness and loneliness in Becca's, as if she was carrying the weight of the world on her shoulders.

"Can I have another shot, Mac?"

Mac reached for the bottle behind her and filled shots for them both. "You don't usually knock them back like this. Is everything okay?"

Dale reached into her pocket, pulled out the picture of Becca and Jake, and put it down on the bar.

Mac looked at the photo and said, "Beautiful woman, and cute kid. Who are they?"

"That, Mac, is my family in a parallel universe. I've got one kid and one on the way, and I'll never know them."

Dale picked up her shot and downed it, desperately hoping it would calm the churning emotions inside her.

❖

Becca struggled up the last steps of the oak staircase with a bowl of apple pie for Jake. He'd refused to come down for dinner and so Becca hoped to tempt him with Granny Sadie's apple pie.

She knocked on the door and got no response. "Jake? I've got dessert for you."

Becca still heard nothing so she opened the door and walked in to find Jake working on his computers. He had his older desktop and Becca's own laptop she used for work sitting side by side. He needed much better equipment to meet his talents but it was the best she could do.

"Jake? I've got apple pie for you."

"Not hungry," Jake replied grumpily.

Becca sighed and walked over to sit on his bed. "Jake, I know you're angry, but please come and eat something."

"I'm coding a new game. I haven't got time."

"It's Granny Sadie's apple pie with custard."

The tip-tapping of Jake's fingers as they flew across the keyboard came to a stop. He looked around at the bowl and got up from his chair. The temptation was clearly too much.

He sat down on the bed beside her and took the bowl. Becca stroked his brown hair, and again thought of Dale's thick dark unruly locks, so much the same as her son's.

"I know you're not happy with me, but we have to talk about today."

Jake stabbed his spoon into his dessert and nodded.

"What you did was wrong, Jake. For one, you could get into a lot of trouble with the police for hacking into the clinic's database. We've had this talk before. Just because you can do it doesn't mean you should. That's private information."

Jake looked up at her with tears in his eyes. "I just wanted to get you help, Mummy. Why shouldn't the woman who helped you have me help *us*?"

Becca sighed. How could she explain something so complex to a child? Jake might have a higher IQ than most adults, but he was still a little boy, with the simplistic world view of a little boy.

When Jake started to ask why he didn't have a daddy or another mum like the other kids at school, she had considered not telling him the truth about his conception, but only for a matter of seconds. Becca knew what harm lies in a family could do, and she'd vowed she would never do that to her own child. But she'd never anticipated the steps he'd taken.

"Jake, things could have gone really badly today. You rode on the local bus yourself—anyone could have gotten you. I need to know where you are at all times. Remember, we don't ever, ever talk to strangers or anyone who wants to know about our family. If you ever go off somewhere yourself without telling me again, there will be no more computer club. Do you understand?"

Jake nodded solemnly. "I just wanted to help. Dale was nice. I liked her."

Becca gulped hard. It hurt to think Jake might want to have a relationship with his real mother.

As if reading her mind, Jake put down his bowl and hugged her. "You're my mummy, and I love you. That's why I wanted to help. I hate to see you sad."

Becca squeezed him tightly. "I know you love me, but you have to trust me to handle the problems we have. Ms. McGuire appeared to be a good person, but it could have been someone so different. They could have taken you and I'd never see you again."

Jake sighed in resignation. "I'm sorry, Mum. I wanted to help."

"You can help me by not making me worry, Pooh Bear," Becca said.

Jake kicked his heels against the bed and said sadly, "She called me *wee man*. I liked it."

Becca had to change the subject and get him off these new thoughts and feelings. She looked over to the whiteboard on his wall and noticed equations and coding language she didn't understand on it.

"So, tell me what game you're coding now."

"A game to help kids understand maths," he said sadly.

Becca couldn't be any prouder of Jake if she tried. Despite being an exceptionally intelligent young man, he had no arrogance and always thought of other people.

She gave him a squeeze and said, "That's a wonderful idea."

He shrugged and looked depressed. "I just want to help people, just like I wanted to help you and the baby."

Again, Becca felt the guilt eat away inside her. Her life seemed filled with trauma and drama. Maybe that was just her fate?

CHAPTER THREE

Dale opened her eyes and found herself in a vaguely familiar bedroom, and a feeling of dread bubbled up inside, not to mention the pounding in her head and sick feeling in her stomach.

She rolled over and saw an alarm clock displaying the day and time: Sunday, 11:00 a.m.

"Fuck me. I did it again." She groaned.

This was the second day in a row she had woken in someone else's bed. She hadn't been on a two-day bender like this in a long, long time. The last thing she remembered was downing some shots with a group of women she met at a club in town, and then…then she'd bumped into Lisa.

Dale rarely saw a woman more than once, but Lisa was persistent. Maybe Val was right—maybe Lisa thought she could be domesticated.

She pushed herself to sit on the side of the bed and her headache got worse. She looked around. Luckily she was alone in the room. Dale spotted a bottle of water on the side table and downed it quickly.

"I'm too old for this," Dale told herself.

As her head started to clear, more memories of last night came to the forefront of Dale's mind. She remembered dancing with some girls she met, then being pulled away by Lisa, who had appeared from nowhere. She'd been extremely drunk, and she hadn't put up much of a fight.

After some kissing in the toilets of the club, Lisa manoeuvred her to a taxi and home to her flat. From there Lisa was all over her, and the one thing that was clear in her mind was that she'd felt nothing. No excitement, no thrill, no nothing. So much so that she had feigned falling asleep to get out of the awkward situation, and that was a first.

Dale had always enjoyed sex, and it came naturally to her. She loved everything about a woman's body—the feel, the smell, the taste, everything turned her on—but last night and the night before, there was nothing.

She rubbed her face with her hands furiously. Maybe age was finally catching up with her.

Then the gnawing in her stomach, that she had been drinking to get rid of, returned with a vengeance. The image of Jake and Becca, standing outside their broken-down home, crashed into her head.

Dale could hear Jake's voice loud in her mind. *You won't disappear, will you?*

But she had, hadn't she? She had broken her word, even though she did it because his mother, Becca, had asked her to.

Becca. Something had happened inside when she looked into Becca's eyes. The sad loneliness she had seen there made her want to chase it away.

"Get a grip, for fuck's sake, man," Dale said angrily.

She grabbed her jeans and hurriedly gathered her clothes, and pulled on her boots. The only thing that was missing was her green combat jacket.

Dale headed to where she remembered the living room was, and found Lisa sitting on the couch with her jacket on her lap, staring at her picture of Becca and Jake.

"What do you think you're doing going through my things?" Dale said.

She made a grab for the picture, but Lisa ducked away, holding the picture up in the air.

"Who is she, Dale?" Lisa voice was ripe with accusations.

"Nothing to do with you. Give me the picture." Dale grabbed her jacket from her but Lisa jinked out of the way again.

"Look, stop acting like a child and give me my picture back."

Lisa's face was red and angry. "This is no way to start a relationship, Dale."

Dale couldn't believe what she was hearing. "We have no relationship. We've slept together once—last night didn't even count."

"Yes, funny that, isn't it? You fall asleep just when we fall into bed. That doesn't sound like the great lover Dale McGuire, does it?"

Lisa was clearly deranged, and she had to get out of here. "You don't even know anything about me. I've never said I'm a great lover. I'm just me. Give me the picture now or I'll take it from you."

"Tell me who they are first," Lisa demanded.

Dale had enough and used her long legs to cover the distance between them, catching Lisa by her nightshirt before she could move. She grabbed the picture and put in safely in the back pocket of her jeans.

"Don't ever get in touch with me again, and if you see me at Belles, don't come near me. I'm finished being nice."

Dale put on her jacket and marched towards the front door of the flat. She had to get out of there.

Lisa's tone changed and she came running after her saying, "Dale, I'm sorry. Please don't leave…"

But Dale walked through the front door and slammed it shut. The thought of Lisa looking at Jake and Becca's photo made her really angry.

She pulled out her smartphone and saw countless messages from Val and Sammy, worried about how she was.

When Dale got out to the harsh light of the street, she vowed never to put herself in a situation like the last two nights again.

Dale looked at her watch and realized she was going to be late for her weekly Sunday lunch with her friends, and that was one thing she never missed. She tapped out a quick text message to Sammy, jumped into a taxi, and headed home to get a quick shower and change.

❖

Ashley Duval was woken by a cold breeze coming from the open balcony doors of her penthouse apartment. Her lover Nika had a habit of taking her coffee out there each morning, even when the autumnal chill had descended.

She got up, pulled on her T-shirt and boxers, and gazed with smug satisfaction around the luxurious bedroom. Life was good. Ashley was chief investigative reporter at the country's biggest tabloid newspaper, on a fantastic salary, and she was sleeping with her editor, who also happened to be the daughter of the owner of the newspaper.

She had been offered the job just at the time when her career was starting to wane, after an early stratospheric rise in the media world. When she had seen Nika at a party, Ash saw her way back to the very top and went in for the kill.

She started to walk to the balcony doors and saw Nika grasping her coffee cup lightly and gazing over the London skyline. Nika was beautiful, but never quite believed it herself. Years of trying and failing to meet her father's unattainable standards left her with a certain vulnerability, and Ash, being an opportunist, prided herself on using that to get what she wanted.

Ash walked up behind her and put her arms around her waist. She immediately felt Nika stiffen, and that was not a normal reaction.

"Morning, angel. Is there something wrong?"

When Nika only sighed, Ash gave her little kisses on her neck. "You're not still angry about that girl from the mailroom, are you? I told you, she was lying. Do you think I would have sex with her when I have you? Come on, angel."

"No, it's not that. I know you wouldn't do that to me—that's why I fired her," Nika said as she turned in Ash's arms.

I'm so good, thought Ash.

She had indeed slept with the pretty new girl from the mailroom—a few times—with promises that she could help the girl get a leg up in the newspaper business. Women were so easy. It had given Ash such a thrill to fuck her in the empty office right next door to Nika's.

"Good, because you know all these rumours are just because they're jealous of what we have. Don't you?"

Nika gripped her T-shirt nervously. Something was clearly wrong.

"What's wrong then?" Ash asked.

"I need to talk to you about work."

She was beginning to have a bad feeling about this. "What about work?"

"Daddy's worried about the circulation figures. He says we may have to lose some people from the staff."

Ash dropped her arms from Nika and took a step back. Her lover looked really nervous, and whatever she was about to say was clearly coming from her father.

She crossed her arms. "And?"

"Daddy says that we need more from you. That you came with a big reputation and got a huge salary for it, but we haven't had any big stories from you yet. I've tried to keep him off your tail but I need you to find something soon. Just to placate him."

Ash couldn't believe what she was hearing, and replied angrily, "Does *Daddy* even have the first clue about how an investigative journalist works? I can't just produce a story out of thin air. I need to follow leads, wait on tip-offs. It all takes time."

Nika didn't take anger very well and started to retreat from her. "I tried to tell him that. Believe me, baby, I'm on your side. I know how hard you work. We just need something like the Carter story. That's what we hired you for, and I know you'll come good."

Ash balled her fists in frustration. The Carter story. The story that had made her as a young, green journalist, and the story that had also been a millstone around her neck, as she'd failed to produce anything as good as that since.

Nika reached out to touch her and Ash hit her hand away. "I'll get you your fucking story. Then I'll maybe be good enough for Daddy's precious girl. I want to marry you, and you doubt me like this?"

Ash walked off, ready to get out of there, and her lover chased after her, tears falling down her face.

"Please don't go, Ash. I'm sorry. He said I had to talk to you or he would. I want to marry you too—I want you to be part of my family."

She got dressed quickly and grabbed her coat. "I'll go and find you a story then, angel. Don't wait up." She slammed the front door and heard her lover's sobs behind the door. "Fucking bitch."

❖

Dale paid the taxi and walked up the path to Sammy and Val's suburban home. She spotted an excited face at the living room window. It was Mia, her ten-year-old god-daughter. Mia started to wave furiously and then ran off to meet her at the door.

Dale loved Mia and the special friendship they had, and it only made the guilt she had at leaving Jake intensify.

She rang the bell expecting Mia to answer, but instead it was Val, who immediately threw her arms around her neck.

"Thank God you're all right. We were so worried when we didn't hear from you."

Before Dale got the chance to explain herself, Val pushed away from her, and this time her eyes were filled with fury, not relief. Val pointed an accusing finger in her face and gave it to her both barrels. "Don't you ever make us worried like that again, Dale! You get some life-changing news, and you just disappear for two days, no phone call, no text. I hardly slept a wink."

"I'm sorry—" Dale tried to say, but Val just continued.

"No, I'm not interested in your *sorry*s. You were thoughtless." Val turned on her heel and walked off full of fury, leaving Sammy and Mia standing in her wake, looking as shocked as Dale felt.

"Mum was really mad, Dale," Mia said.

Dale walked in the front door and said, "I guessed that, munchkin."

Sammy clapped her on the shoulder. "Don't worry. She'll soon calm down. We were both worried, mate."

"I'm sorry. I had a lot on my mind." Dale was conscious of saying too much in front of Mia, and Sammy nodded.

"We can talk later. First you look like you could do with some food. Lunch will be ready soon."

"Do you think Val will feed me, or serve it on my lap?"

Sammy laughed. "She'll forgive you quickly."

Mia pulled at her jacket. "I've got a new game to play with you and I got this cool Zelda mod for Minecraft. Come on."

Dale lifted Mia off her feet and threw her over her shoulder. "Great, I can't wait. Hey, I've got a new joke for you. Why do cows wear bells?"

Both Mia and Sammy replied, "Because their horns don't work!"

"Your jokes are awful. You know that," Sammy said.

Dale winked at her friend and softly smacked Mia on the bottom. "No more laughing at me, munchkin."

Mia giggled as they made their way into the house. Dale was home, the only home she had now, and was ever likely to have. She had to stop thinking about Jake and Becca. This was her family.

Dale, Sammy, Val, and Mia sat around the kitchen table enjoying Val's delicious Sunday lunch. Val had seemed to warm up as the dinner went on and luckily Mia talked nonstop about her computer games.

"The Zelda mod I downloaded for Minecraft is so amazing."

"Cool, I can't wait to play it. The gaming expo is coming to London soon. We need to go to that," Dale said while wolfing down the last of her dessert. Val's Sunday dinner was a perfect antidote to a hangover.

Mia got down from the table, and asked excitedly, "Can we go and play now?"

Dale looked to Val, who shook her head. "We need to speak to Dale first, sweetie. Adult talk time."

"*Mu-um*," Mia whined.

Dale ruffled her hair and said, "You go and get the game started and I'll be there soon, okay?"

Mia gave her a big hug and walked off happily.

Sammy poured the coffee and said, "So? What happened when you took Jake back?"

Dale took a sip of coffee while Sammy sat down beside an expectant Val. "I met his mum, Rebecca Harper. Becca."

"What was she like?" Val asked.

Dale fished into her jeans back pocket, pulled out the photo, and showed it to her friends. "That's Becca. Jake left this picture for me to find in the car."

They both studied the picture. "She's beautiful," Sammy said.

Dale nodded. "She really is, and she's so elegant. She has a really posh accent, although they live in this run-down house."

Val took the picture from Sammy, to study it more carefully. "There's something familiar about her, but I can't put my finger on it."

"How did she react to you?" Sammy asked.

Dale sighed. "She was terrified I was there to take Jake away from her. She's a single mother. Jake told me Becca couldn't have kids herself, and used a sperm donor as well as an egg donor. The sperm donor is dead, so that just left me for Jake to find."

Sammy handed her back the photo and Dale stared at it.

"You did reassure her it wasn't your doing, didn't you?" Val said.

"Aye, I did. She told me that Jake had done this kind of thing before...computer hacking. He's a bit of child genius by all accounts. She asked me to turn around and forget they existed."

Val covered Dale's hand with hers. "And did you?"

Dale gulped hard, and shook her head. "I couldn't. I felt a connection to them...something deep inside. I mean, Jake, he loves maths, just like me and—"

"He has your big brown eyes," Val finished for her.

"Yeah, it's like I know him, and not just him. When I looked in Becca's eyes I saw sadness and loneliness, something I recognized. I offered to help, but she told me to leave."

"Maybe that's best," Sammy said. "This is an emotional and difficult situation—maybe you should just forget it ever happened."

Dale rubbed her forehead furiously. "I can't get them out of my head. That's why I went on a bender all weekend. I hoped I might forget these feelings if I drank enough."

"And did it work?" Sammy asked.

"Nope. It got worse. I feel guilty that they have no one to lean on and no one to look after them, and I broke my promise to Jake. I promised I wouldn't disappear, and I did. I lied to him just like I was lied to by my family. I promised I would never do that to anyone I cared about."

Val moved her chair closer to Dale and put her arm around her. "You have nothing to feel guilty about. You helped Rebecca have this lovely, clever boy. That's something to be proud of."

Dale closed her eyes and remembered the feeling when Becca told her that her unborn baby was hers as well. She felt a rush of emotions, and it brought tears to her eyes.

"It's not just Jake."

"What do you mean?" Sammy asked.

Dale looked at her two closest friends with tears in her eyes. "Becca is six months pregnant, and it's mine too."

Sammy and Val were stunned into silence.

CHAPTER FOUR

Becca felt the room start to spin a little as she took a seat in the waiting room of her lawyer's office. The Monday morning journey into the city of London had been horrendous. After putting Jake on the school bus, she walked a mile to the nearest bus stop, took the bus to the nearest train station, and caught a train to the city. Her stress levels were sky-high, and no doubt her blood pressure was too. She stood on the train for a while and then, thankfully, a young woman offered her a seat. Becca could have kissed her.

By the time she arrived at the offices of Trent, Trent, and Masters, she was ready to faint, vomit, or cry, possibly all three.

Becca gripped the arms of her chair tightly, trying to steady her dizziness, and said to the receptionist, "Could I have some water, please?"

"Of course, Ms. Harper." The staff at Trent, Trent, and Masters knew her well. They had been her family's solicitors for many years, and the firm was now run by the younger Ms. Trent.

The receptionist returned with a chilled bottle of water and a glass. "Trent won't be too much longer."

Trent, as everyone called her, was an old friend and ex-lover. She was the one person in the world who had always stood by her, and although their relationship didn't work out, they had remained friends. She trusted her implicitly with her business, just not her heart.

Becca took a sip of cool water and some big breaths of air to try and quell the sick dizzy feeling she was having.

Trent opened her office door and with a big smile and a welcoming gesture. "Becca, wonderful to see you. Come in."

Trent looked as smart and dapper as usual, with a pale grey three-piece suit and highly polished shoes. She was very good looking and always popular with the ladies.

Becca allowed Trent to give her a quick hug and kiss before she sat down.

"How's the sprog?" Trent asked.

The term immediately made Becca mad. "His name is Jake."

Trent held up her hands defensively. "I know. It's just an expression. How is Jake, then? Still on his way to becoming the next Albert Einstein?"

Becca sat down carefully and Trent sat on the corner of the desk with her arms folded. That was Trent. She always had to play these games, but she had lost the ultimate power game with her.

"Jake's doing well. His new school has really helped him grow."

"Hmm." Trent let out a long breath. "It's extremely expensive, Becca."

It was times like this that Becca wondered if having her ex as her lawyer was a good idea, but no matter what stupid things Trent might say, she could trust her with her personal business.

"Yes, and something you will never be burdened with," Becca said with a sharp tinge to her voice.

"Okay, okay. No need to get excited." Trent walked back around and sat at her desk.

Becca had been mulling over whether to ask Trent's advice about Dale McGuire, and decided it couldn't do any harm to get legal advice. "Trent, before we get started, I wanted to ask you something."

"Shoot."

"You know I used a donor egg and sperm to have Jake and this little one?"

Trent nodded, and Becca continued, "Is it possible for the donor to have any rights over any children that are born from the donation?"

"No. As I'm sure you know, the only ones who have any rights are the children when they reach eighteen years old. They are then free to try and track down the donor. Why? Has something happened?"

Becca thought carefully before answering. She was always careful with what information she gave anyone, even her oldest and most trusted friend. "Jake hacked into the clinic's database and brought the egg donor to my door."

"Good God. Are you okay? Did she threaten to take Jake from you?" Trent asked angrily.

"No, she said that she just wanted to bring Jake home safely and had no interest in having a family. To be honest, she didn't look like the type to want children."

"What was her name?"

"Dale McGuire. She owns McGuire's Motors. Have you heard of it?"

Trent looked surprised. "Dale McGuire? My God. Yes, I have heard of her. She's well known in the pubs and clubs. A bit of a player, so I'm told."

That description confirmed everything that Becca's first impression had given her. "Just what I thought. I doubt I'll have to worry then."

"If she comes back, just give me a call. I'll sort it out for you, okay?"

Becca felt better. She doubted that anyone fitting that description would want to interfere with her family. "I will. So, my father's estate?" This was the real reason why she was here.

Trent said, "Give me a second till I call up your records."

She was dreading this, but had to face it. The settlement of her father's estate. She watched a frown appear on Trent's face as she read over the details. It clearly wasn't good reading.

Eventually Trent leaned back in her seat and clasped her hands. "I've given this my personal attention, Becca. I want you to know that."

"I know. You always try your best for me, Trent. I've never doubted that."

Trent nodded and began. "After extensive investigation into your father's estate, we found huge debts. Most have died along with them, but as you know your father transferred his mortgage into your name, to try and hang on to the family home, and there's one creditor who is non-negotiable."

Becca nodded solemnly. "Eugene Hardy."

Most people coming from the London area knew of the Hardy brothers, and no one would ever want to be indebted to them, especially Eugene, the head of the criminal gang. Apparently her father never had those same worries.

"Exactly. He's been in touch, you could say," Trent said reluctantly.

"Was he here?

At Trent's silence, Becca's heart started to pound. "Just tell me."

"I have good news and bad news. The good news is that we found some money your father had in a slightly shady offshore account. Something that wasn't seized as proceeds of crime."

"Shady? Sounds like Father. Just how shady?"

"Not shady enough for you to worry about, especially with me as your lawyer. Besides, we need as much money as we can get."

This was what she was waiting for. The amount of debt her father, Thomas, and his recklessness had left her.

"So? How much is owed?"

"After using the funds we have secured, and some hard negotiating with Eugene and your other creditors…£500,000."

Becca felt her stomach drop and a million thoughts raced through her mind. How could she pay for this? How could she afford to pay Jake's school fees? How would they even live? Tears welled up in her eyes, but she called on the control she had learned as a teenager, tamped down her panic under a steely barrier.

"I see," Becca said in a monotone.

Trent picked up a pen and tapped it repeatedly on the desk. "My advice, as your lawyer and your friend, is to declare bankruptcy, and I can give you—"

Becca's shock and panic turned to anger. "No. My father might have run away and dodged his responsibilities, but that is something I will never do."

Trent threw down her pen on the desk in frustration, and walked over to the windows overlooking the London skyline.

"Why did I know you were going to say that? You're so stubborn—you'll be saddled with debt for the rest of your life."

Trent turned around and looked directly into Becca's eyes. "Things could have been so different. I wanted to marry you. We could be living in my beautiful apartment, you with your successful business, and me, owner of my family's prestigious law firm. Instead of that comfortable, stress-free life, you put your needs above mine and walked away."

"My needs being having a baby? I'm not having this argument with you again, Trent. If I didn't have Jake, I would be empty, unfulfilled. Is that what you wanted for me? Remember, you were putting your needs above mine too, and gave me an ultimatum. You tried to shape my life for me, and I said no."

The reason why they broke up was still a touchy subject, and anger still bubbled beneath the surface.

"I never wanted children in my life. I think what we had together was enough."

"I know you didn't, and there's nothing wrong with not wanting children, but it made us incompatible. We're different people, Trent. You were there for me at a time when no one else was, but you know we were never going to work. We wanted very different things. You know that. Besides, you don't lack for female company."

Trent nodded. "I don't understand why you got pregnant again, a few months after your father died. Wasn't one enough? Now you're so ill because of it, you can't work as much, you're losing clients, and you're in big financial trouble."

Becca had heard enough. She got up as quickly as her body would allow and placed a hand on her baby bump. "She's going to be a lovely little baby girl, Trent, not an it. No, you would never understand why I did it, Trent. That's why we could never have a future. I think you should stick to being my lawyer and stop giving out personal advice."

"Becca, wait, I'm—"

"I'll go over my accounts tonight and email you with my plan."

That was why Becca knew she would always be alone. Trent was the only one she had ever trusted with her past, since her life had gone out of control, but they didn't want the same things in life. She couldn't imagine trusting anyone else with her heart or her secrets.

❖

Jake looked so peaceful and content as he slept. Becca had given him thirty minutes to read in bed before lights out, and he had fallen asleep quickly. She kissed his forehead and pulled his covers up to his chin, so he wouldn't get cold. There was some heat coming from the room's radiator but not much. Yet another thing on her to-do list—or, rather, to-pay-for list.

Like this, Jake looked peaceful and secure, but in reality things still weren't good between them. He was convinced in his naivety that getting his egg or sperm donor to help them was the answer to all their ills, but of course he didn't understand the risks of allowing someone to help you.

Becca did.

She picked up the iPad that had dropped onto the covers as he fell asleep and said, "Goodnight, Pooh Bear."

Becca took the tablet down to the kitchen, where the heat from the cooker range would keep her warm. She picked up a notepad and paper from the countertop and sat down, then opened her banking app with great trepidation and let out a sigh at the account balance displayed there.

"Okay, stay calm. We can find a way out of this."

Becca started to write down the figures and sums, listing Jake's school fees, and the utility and tax bills, and it all came out to not enough money to pay back her father's debt. Being self-employed and unable to do much work, she had been living on her savings, and the little left over from a trust left by her grandmother. The trust fund had bought this house, and paid two instalments of Jake's school fees, but now between that and her savings there was barely a thousand pounds left, which would hardly cover two months of utility bills. While the central heating was not working properly, it was hugely inefficient and still costing a fortune.

She felt queasy and shaky. How was she going to get out of this mess? It was no wonder her blood pressure was through the roof.

Tears started to well in her eyes and only now that she was alone would she allow herself to cry at the situation she was in.

In desperation, she opened the browser to run a search for rates for re-mortgaging the house, and found herself staring at the website for McGuire's Motors.

Jake had still been looking up info about Dale, and there she was on the homepage of her business.

Dale McGuire was standing with two other women—one very beautiful woman, whose picture was captioned with the title *Admin Manager*, and the other a butch-looking woman in overalls like Dale, whose title was *General Manager*.

Becca touched the screen and let her finger trace Dale's good-looking, warm face, while she stroked her baby bump. If Trent was right to think that she was a player who would have no interest in Becca's family, then why did she feel warmth when she looked in her eyes?

❖

Ash had taken up residence on a bar stool at her favourite cocktail bar, O'Henry's, and was drowning her frustrations in vodka martinis. The bar was surrounded by many newspaper offices and was a popular hangout for journalist and media types. She had called every informant she had in her phonebook and turned up nothing but minor celebrity scandals. She needed something big, something to keep hold of Nika, slip a ring on her finger, and get her hands on the family fortune.

The truth was—and she would only admit this to herself—she had been lucky to get her first big break, the Carter story.

One of the biggest governmental financial scandals to hit the

United Kingdom in years, and she just happened to be attending the same university as the daughter of one of the main players, Dr. Thomas Carter.

There had been a resurgence of interest in the Carter case when Thomas hanged himself in jail recently. Ash's publisher had contacted her about a new book, but she had no new information. Victoria Carter had disappeared after the trial, never to be heard from again.

Ash swallowed the last of her drink and walked to the bar to order another. The dark-haired woman next to her was looking at a picture on her smartphone, and something about the woman in the picture rang a bell. She'd need to get a closer look.

She turned to the girl. "Hi, I saw you from across the room and I just knew I had to come and speak to you. I'm Ash."

The young woman looked at her quizzically and then broke out into a smile. "I know you. I've seen you on talk shows. Are you the famous journalist?"

Ash got a ripple of pleasure through her body as her ego was stroked. She gave her biggest smile and said, "Guilty as charged. And your name is?"

"Lisa. It's great to meet you at last. I'm actually a junior reporter at your newspaper."

Ash smiled. "Lisa, can I get you a drink?"

Lisa unlocked her door and led Ash into her flat. "Can I get you a drink, Ash? I've got bottles of lager, white wine?"

"I'd love one. A lager, please."

Lisa dumped her bag on the side table and left her phone on the arm of the couch. "Take a seat."

Ash sat right beside the smartphone. "Thanks, Lisa." She eyed the phone and wondered if she had enough time to look before Lisa got back. Ash had had to listen to her whine about being dumped by some woman, and be sympathetic, for two hours to get as close as this. She had a hunch about the picture she'd glanced, and she always followed a lead, no matter how tenuous, till the very end.

When Lisa went into the kitchen, she quickly grabbed the phone and tried to open it, but it had a fingerprint lock on it.

Fuck! This isn't going to be easy.

Lisa came back with her drink and sat down. Ash took her drink and moved closer. She was in full-on seduction mode.

"I wouldn't waste your time being hurt over this Dale woman." Ash put down her bottle and stroked her fingers tenderly down Lisa's face. "You're too good for her."

Lisa gulped hard and her lips parted in response. Ash moved in to kiss her and thought, *Women are so easy.*

After kissing her for a minute or so she pulled back. "You see? You're too good."

"Why didn't Dale think that?" Lisa said sadly. "She blew me off completely. All she cared about was a stupid picture."

Bingo. "A picture?"

Lisa reached for her smartphone and opened it up. "This one. I snapped it while she was sleeping."

Ash grabbed the phone from her hand, and a smile spread across her face as she looked. *Victoria Carter. Hello again.*

CHAPTER FIVE

McGuire's Motors's biggest branch in Lambeth, East London, was busy with customers on Monday afternoon. Dale felt like getting her hands dirty, and so was helping out with the repairs.

Her other mechanics were busy all around her as they worked in their own car bays. Dale wanted to work on her own and lose herself in grease and motor oil, and yet all she could think about were Jake and Becca. She had been staring absently into the engine of this Porsche Cayenne, and somehow didn't know where to start.

Dale felt a slap on her back, and she jumped. "Hey…oh, it's you."

Sammy had brought her a cup of tea. "You've been staring at that car for twenty minutes. What's wrong, mate? You look miserable."

She sat back against the car and sighed. "What do you think?"

"Jake?" Sammy offered.

"Jake, Becca, and the wee yin she's having. I can't get them out of my head. Even though Becca wanted me to leave, I feel like I've abandoned them."

"Like you were?" Sammy offered.

Dale nodded and took a sip of tea. "Aye. I mean, I never imagined in a million years that I'd want children, but now I've met Jake, I feel…"

"Responsible for them? Like I do with Mia?"

"Yes, exactly. I feel like it's my job to take care of those problems Jake told me about, even though Becca doesn't want me there."

"There's no right answer here, Dale. This is a really unusual situation. I mean, you read stories like yours occasionally in the newspapers and on the web, but to have it actually happen to you against all odds..."

"But it did happen to me. What should I do? I can't just do nothing," Dale said.

"Val and I were talking. She's afraid you'll get hurt, but I think you should go back and try again. Maybe fix her car at least. Then you can say you've tried. What do you think?"

Excitement immediately started to build inside Dale. "I'd love that. You think I should? Really?"

"Yeah, take tomorrow off, and go while Jake's at school, so you don't make his mum too mad about it."

Dale smacked her friend on the shoulder, "Aye, I'll do it. Thanks, mate."

❖

Dale stood in only her boxers and sleeveless compression shirt, staring into her wardrobe at the hangers of T-shirts and jeans, and wondered at the wisdom of what she was doing. Her friends had advised her that the only way she could put these feelings of guilt and interest to bed was to visit Ms. Harper again and talk properly. Maybe Rebecca would let her repair her car at least, even if she wouldn't take anything else from Dale.

So here she was agonizing over what to wear to visit a woman who had asked her never to return.

"I must be crazy," Dale said, before pulling out one of her most understated designer T-shirts and looking at it carefully.

The thing that had most annoyed her during her brief encounter with Becca was the way she had looked at her clothes, had made her feel like she was immature. Dale was a small business owner, and a successful one at that, and did not like to be painted as a child.

She thought about her visit to Belles and how she'd felt old amongst all the bar patrons there, for the first time. Maybe she did dress too young, but it was just part of her personality.

Quickly she grabbed her black suit, the one that she only ever wore to her lawyers or accountants, and held it up in front of herself. Maybe if she dressed smartly, Becca would take her seriously.

Decision made, she got suited and booted and looked in the mirror. Her white shirt was crisp and smart, but her black tie hung loosely around her neck. She had to keep some part of her personality on show.

Dale waxed her hair so it was perfectly neat instead of her usual messy look. "I look like an extra from a bloody gangster movie."

She got her car keys and checked her tie for the last time. "Well, Ms. Harper, you wanted mature, you've got it."

❖

Dale drove slowly up the country road that led to the Harpers' house. She squirmed every time her precious Jaguar hit a rock or pothole on the unkempt road. Could Becca have lived anywhere more remote?

She pulled in to the vicarage driveway, and everything looked quiet. Good. She had thought it best to go during school hours, so as not to get Jake too excited.

Dale parked her car and walked up to the front door. There was a big lion-head door knocker, and as she went to use it, it fell clean off the door and fell into a bush beside the door frame.

"Shit!" She quickly reached down into the bush to pull it back out. It seemed to be caught on something, because it wasn't budging.

"Come on, come on. This is a great way to make a serious impression."

She manoeuvred it around the branches and gave it a good pull. Then she heard a rip. She'd torn her jacket sleeve. "Brilliant, fucking brilliant." Dale shook her head and sighed.

She looked at the screws hanging from the knocker and knew she would need a screwdriver to fix it, so she stuffed it in her pocket out of sight and knocked on the wooden door.

Dale waited for a few minutes and didn't get an answer, so she started to walk around the house, looking in the windows as she went. The only sign of life was a lit fire in what looked like a sitting room.

She eventually walked around to the back garden. It was large, but all very wild and overgrown. The grass was high and weeds were allowed free rein.

Not a good place for Jake to play.

As she walked closer to the back door, she was surprised to find Becca trying to drag a heavy looking bin bag through the kitchen door.

Dale immediately ran over to her and took the bag from her. "Hey, hey, why are you lifting heavy things in your condition?"

At first Becca looked stunned that she was there, but her expression soon turned to anger. "What are you doing here? I told you not to come back."

"Aye, I know, but I just wanted to talk to you." Despite the current circumstances and how angry Becca was, all Dale could think was how much more beautiful she was than she remembered. She was a perfect lady.

But Becca wasn't in the mood for her it seemed, because she replied, "Leave now or I'll call the police. I told you to forget about us—you have no rights over Jake."

Becca was extremely frustrating. "And I told you that I didn't want any rights over him. Listen, I know this is a frightening situation for you, but it was a big shock for me too. I know about Jake now"—Dale's eyes lowered to Becca's baby bump—"and the wee yin there. I can't un-know it, and it's been hard thinking about it all weekend. I can't just leave it like this and never think about you all again. I'm not like that, Becca. Would you please just give me ten minutes to talk to you? Please?"

Becca sighed. "Ten minutes then. That's it."

Dale pumped a fist inside herself. She couldn't quite explain why she was so excited at getting this one little chance to talk. The only thing she could say was that when she looked at Jake, at Becca, and at the baby bump Becca kept her hand on protectively, she felt connected. There was no other way to describe it.

"Thank you," Dale said and lifted up the bin bag. "Where can I put this for you?"

"Over there by the garage. The outside bin's over there. Thanks."

"No problem. I'll just be a minute."

As Dale walked over to the garage she thought, *Don't mess this up. Don't mess this up.*

Becca stirred the tea in the pot and lifted the tray to bring it over to the table.

Dale was immediately on her feet. "Let me get that for you."

Becca's defences came up straight away. "No, I can manage." As much as the debt that was hanging over her head was a huge, almost insurmountable worry, nothing was as frightening as the woman sitting at her kitchen table. Although Becca kept telling herself that Dale McGuire had no legal rights to her children, she was still a threat. Jake had taken to her straight away, and he was still angry that she'd sent Dale away.

But most of all, Dale McGuire scared her because just looking at her reminded Becca that Jake, and the baby inside her, weren't biologically hers.

She plonked the tea tray down and poured out a cup. "Milk? Sugar?"

"Just milk. I'm sweet enough," Dale joked.

The joke and Dale's broad grin were totally lost on her. How could she joke in a situation like this?

Dale's smiled faltered when she got nothing back, so she cleared her throat and rubbed her palms together awkwardly. Becca handed over her cup of tea and noticed the big rip on Dale's suit jacket.

"What happened to your sleeve?"

Dale blustered nervously for a few seconds and then said, "Eh, I lost a fight with your rose bush at the front door."

Becca gripped her cup tensely and took a sip of tea. "Do you have somewhere important to go after here?"

Dale furrowed her eyebrows. "No, why?"

When she'd first seen Dale in her rugged jeans, computer game character T-shirt, and classic sports car, she thought she looked quite immature. She didn't look like a successful businesswoman, and yet she was. She'd given Becca the impression that she was irresponsible, probably a player, not a cultured, sophisticated woman like Trent. Trent lived in suits, and the look fitted her to a tee. Dale looked as if she had borrowed her dad's suit for a job interview or for court. She wore it like it didn't fit her somehow, but although it didn't seem her style, it was sweet in a way.

"You don't seem like the suit type."

"No, I don't have anywhere to go, but I can look smart if I want to." Dale looked at her exactly like Jake did when he was mad about something, and that made her stomach clench with fear, nervousness, and something else. Something she couldn't identify.

"If you say so. So? You have ten minutes. Say what you came to say."

Dale tapped her fingertips on the table, trying to find the right words. She knew Becca might be unhappy at seeing her again, but she was downright frosty. Dale normally charmed those she met with a joke and a smile. Becca was going to be a tougher nut to crack. She was not only beautiful, but so cultured, and so far out of Dale's league.

Becca looked as if she should be on the arm of a doctor, a lawyer, someone like that, certainly not a grease monkey like her, but yet here Becca was in a run-down farmhouse, pregnant, on her own, and in the middle of nowhere. There had to be a story behind Rebecca Harper.

"I'm on the clock? Wow, this is hard to put into words." Dale drummed out a beat with her hands on the table. "This is a weird situation, I know that. I was told when I went to the clinic that there was a possibility a child might look me up at eighteen, but I never really took it seriously. When Jake turned up, it knocked me for six."

"I don't know why you came back today," Becca said. "If you never really cared or wanted a child to contact you at eighteen, why are you here now? I gave you a perfect get-out clause. I told you to go."

Dale ran her hand through her short hair, and loosened her tie even more. "A mixture of things really. I like Jake—I really do. He's great kid. You must be really proud."

"I'm his mum," Becca said sharply. "Of course I'm proud."

Dale felt the sharp reminder that Becca was his mum. And she was nothing to them.

"Listen, I'm not here to upset you, and I want you to trust me that I don't want to come between you and Jake."

Becca rubbed her baby bump. "I don't trust anyone, Dale, and I don't know you."

"Okay, okay, that's understandable. Let me just say this. I profited from your need for a child. I was saving up to buy my first garage from the guy I worked for. I nearly had enough, but not quite. So the money the clinic gave me, your money, got me over the line. Once I got my first garage, it just kept growing into the business it is today, so I owe you."

"You don't owe me anything, Dale. You would have gotten the money some other way."

"Maybe," Dale said. "But I didn't. You helped me at a time of need and now I'd like to help you. Jake gave me a list of problems… Give me a second."

Becca gazed at her silently as she rummaged around in her jacket. She finally found Jake's list and started to rhyme off the problems.

"The central heating, the car—"

Rebecca stood and Dale stopped her list. "Dale, I'm sorry Jake came and disrupted your life, and gave you all these problems that you now feel you need to solve, but you don't. You are not obligated to me or us for anything, and I do not take charity."

Becca walked over to the kitchen door and held it open for Dale to leave.

"It's not charity. I just want to help." Dale couldn't believe how calm and cold Becca was being, and it was beginning to annoy her. "You promised to give me ten minutes, so sit back down, hen."

"Did you just call me *hen?*" Becca marched back over with the red flush of anger spreading from her neck up to her cheeks.

To Dale that marked progress—at least she was provoking some kind of emotion.

"Aye, I did. Now please, sit down. I'm not here to hurt you or upset you, believe me."

Becca seemed to consider Dale's words for a few moments, then sat.

"Thanks, Becca. I know this is difficult for you."

"Do you? Could you imagine how it would feel to long for children all your life and not be able to have them? To make your dream a reality and then come face-to-face with the biological parent of your child? I have nothing against you, Dale, but I wish Jake had never found you."

Dale could feel the strain and stress in Becca's voice. Jake said her mum wasn't feeling good, and if she was making Becca feel worse, maybe she should go.

"Yeah, I understand. I'll go, but before I do, will you tell me what's wrong with you? Jake said you were ill. Is the baby okay?"

Becca sighed. "I have very high blood pressure. I collapsed at work on a job. I'm a commercial photographer, and I was on a construction site. It was not the best place to faint, and the doctor advised for my own safety that I give up work. He's worried about pre-eclampsia setting in. I get monitored every week. I had problems when I had Jake too, but now I'm a lot older this time around, so things are harder still."

Dale closed her eyes briefly. *She's stressed and I'm making everything worse.*

"A commercial photographer? That really interesting. Have you always worked for yourself?"

"Yes, ever since I left university and I—well anyway, it's not a safe environment for me or the baby at the moment, and I have to turn away clients."

"Then let me help you. Let me take your car into my garage to be fixed and I can help with the other things. You'll be less stressed and start to feel better."

"No," Becca said without hesitation. "I don't take help from anyone. I look after my family, myself. I don't need anyone."

There was a lot of history and bitterness behind that statement, Dale surmised. Whatever had made Rebecca Harper emotionally closed off and such a stubborn individual must have really hurt her badly. Dale wasn't the most emotionally switched on herself, but she lived, she loved her friends and Mia, and she laughed. Becca didn't even crack a smile.

I'm going to make you laugh, hen, eventually, Dale promised herself, but first she had to get Becca to trust her, get one foot in the door.

"Becca, I'm going to be straight with you. I made a promise to Jake that I would help you, and that I wouldn't disappear. I don't ever break my promises. I would understand if you didn't want Jake to see me again, but at least let me help in some way. Just so that I'm not failing him completely. Let me repair your car, here on your property if you like, and then I'll know you have a way to get to doctors' appointments and stuff."

"Why is this so important to you?"

You were a mistake, Dale.

Dale looked down at her tapping fingers on the table. She had her secrets as well as Becca, and she wasn't ready or able to tell that story.

She stood up and walked the few paces to Becca's side. "Let's just say, I don't want to let Jake down the way I was."

Becca sighed and rubbed her baby bump soothingly. "Okay, the car and that's it, but you do it here, and during school hours, so Jake doesn't see you."

Yes, yes, yes! Dale cheered inside. It might not be her foot in the door, but it was at least a toe, and she could work with that, because one thing Dale knew for certain. She wanted to know Becca and Jake better.

"Oh, and I need to fix your door knocker." Dale pulled it out of her pocket sheepishly.

"I hope you don't do that to my car—it's bad enough as it is."

Dale winked at her. "Don't worry, hen, I'm good with my hands."

❖

Becca watched Dale drive off and heard her name being called. It was Sadie coming through the gate between their two properties.

"Becca, is everything okay? Was she bothering you?"

When Sadie got up close, Becca threaded her arm through Sadie's for support.

"I'm fine. Dale McGuire just turned up out of nowhere wanting to help. She said she's not been able to stop thinking about us."

"And are you worried she's getting too interested?" Sadie said.

Becca nodded. "I told her to go but she wouldn't. She insisted on helping, and so I gave in and said she could fix the car, but only during school hours so Jake doesn't see her."

"That's not like you, Becca. To let someone close, I mean."

Becca sighed and they started to walk back to the house. "I know. There's something about her that I can't say no to. Maybe it's because she's the first one, apart from you, obviously, to show an interest in Jake. Trent doesn't even use his name."

Sadie patted her hand. "Maybe you should trust your instincts then. Perhaps she is genuine. What's the worst that can happen? Your lawyer told you that you have the law on your side, and Jake will never know."

Becca knew only too well what the worst that could happen was, but she wasn't going to talk about that. As much as she liked and trusted Sadie, even she didn't know Becca's past. Only Trent did, and she wanted to keep it that way.

"Perhaps you're right," Becca said to Sadie.

All she could do was hope that she didn't live to regret this chance she was taking.

Chapter Six

The next morning Becca was getting Jake ready for school while he finished breakfast. She closed up his sandwich box and popped it in his backpack.

"Is there anything special you would like? Granny Sadie is going into town."

Jake let his spoon crash down into his cereal bowl and said, "I'd like some lollipops, just like Dale."

"You know I don't like you to eat sweets, Jake. They'll rot your teeth."

Jake didn't reply but just got down from the table and took his backpack from Becca. "Mummy, I was sure Dale would come back. She promised me she wouldn't disappear."

Becca saw hurt in Jake's eyes. This was exactly what Dale had been talking about, the promise she'd made that Becca wasn't allowing her to keep. Yet another thing for her to feel guilty about. She'd sent Dale away.

"I'm sure she's very busy, Jake. She runs a big business. Besides, I think it's better this way."

Jake hugged her and placed his hand on her baby bump. "I thought she would help us, Mummy."

Becca let out a sigh. She couldn't do right from doing wrong these days. "Let's get you on the bus, Pooh Bear."

Jake got his things and they walked down to the end of the driveway. After a hug and a kiss, Jake got on the bus and it drove off. Just as Becca waved the school bus away, a van pulled around the corner into her driveway. On the side it said *McGuire's Motors*.

Becca's heart started to beat faster. *Why did I agree to this?*

Dale jumped out of the van with a huge smile on her face. "Morning, hen. I waited around the corner until I saw the school bus leave."

"Thank you." Dale was back to her jeans and T-shirts today, but in a way Becca preferred that to her formal shirt and tie. This suited her much more. It was just Dale.

"I wanted to prove I could follow your rules," Dale said.

"I appreciate that. I'll unlock the garage for you, and you can drive up."

"Nae bother, I'm going to fix the door knocker I broke too. Do you want to get in the van and I'll drive you up?"

Dale was much too full of energy and smiles for this time in the morning. "I'll walk."

Dale's smile faltered, and then she said, "Oh, okay. Speaking of knockers, you'll like this one. Knock, knock."

"Excuse me?" Becca had not heard someone say that to her since she was a child, and it certainly wasn't appropriate now.

"A knock-knock joke. You're supposed to say, *Who's there?*"

"Why?" Becca said flatly.

Dale sighed. "Because it's funny. You do laugh, don't you?"

"No, I don't have a sense of humour," Becca said coldly. *I've never needed one.*

"Well I'll say it for you. Knock, knock. Who's there? Cows go."

Dale was completely insane. Becca gave in.

"Okay, I'll play. Cows go who?"

"No, silly. Cows go moo!" Dale started laughing, but Becca was unmoved. Dale seemed to have the maturity of an eight-year-old.

"Get it?" Dale said. "Cows go moo."

"I'll unlock the garage for you," Becca said and turned to walk away.

But Dale shouted behind her, "Oh, come on. That was funny."

Becca was annoyed that Dale thought this was all a big joke. Letting Dale come here was the biggest risk she'd taken in years, and she was not going to laugh about it.

"I'm not going to give up until I make you smile, Becca," Dale said before getting into her van.

Good luck with that, thought Becca.

❖

At eleven, Becca made a mug of tea, took a packet of biscuits from the cupboard, and went out to the garage. As much as she was uncertain if Dale should be here or not, she wasn't ungrateful.

When she approached the garage, she could hear Dale before she saw her. Was she really singing what Becca thought she was?

Becca opened the door, and Dale was in mid-dance with a wrench in place of a microphone.

She had to physically stop herself from laughing.

Dale, caught in the act, stopped dead and lowered the wrench slowly, while her cheeks went pink. "Uh…I *was* working, it's just my favourite song. I like Britney's music. It makes me want to dance," Dale babbled.

Dale had on blue oil-stained overalls tied off at the waist, and her T-shirt revealed a Celtic style tattoo on her biceps. Her whole look was dishevelled and sexy, and Becca had the insane urge to go over and run her hands through her thick messy-styled hair.

Get a grip, Becca told herself. "I brought you tea and biscuits."

Dale looked delighted that she was being kind to her, and that made Becca feel guilty. Was she that cold to people? But then she reminded herself what being open and friendly had cost her once before.

Never again.

Dale took the tea and looked at the packet of chocolate covered biscuits with a smile. "You're giving me the posh biscuits? You must have liked my joke this morning."

Becca didn't quite know what to say to that. "Posh biscuits? They're just biscuits."

"When I was wee, we called the chocolate ones posh biscuits, cause my ma only brought the chocolate ones out if the priest was coming to visit, or for visitors. Me and my sister used to steal them off the plate and blame Father Benedict."

There was something so innocent and childlike about Dale McGuire, it was hard to keep her distant persona intact without laughing. All of the adults she had ever mixed with were serious professionals, Dale was something completely new to her.

"Well I can assure you that it's just the biscuits I had open and that's why you're getting them."

Dale leaned against the car and took a sip of her tea. "I suppose for a posh girl like you, posh biscuits are an everyday thing."

That name annoyed Becca a touch. After all, she was sure Dale had much, much more money in the bank than she'd had in a long, long time. "I'm not posh. Look around you. The place is falling apart at the seams."

"It doesn't matter what your surroundings are or how much money you have—it's just who you are, and you, Becca, are a classy lady."

Becca didn't quite know how to respond to that, so she changed the subject. "How long do you think this will take?"

Dale shrugged. She didn't particularly want to give a time frame, because then Becca would know when she would be leaving, and she wanted to spin this out as long as she could and get to know Becca a bit better.

"Depends on how often I can get here to do the work. My manager Sammy is covering for me, but there are some things at work I need to do."

"Please don't neglect your own business on my account," Becca said.

"I won't. Sammy is my best friend and more than capable of running most things without me. No, I need to change the exhaust and get a few more parts, possibly a few weeks?"

"Okay, just remember you don't have to do this."

Dale put down her mug on her closed toolbox and took a step towards Becca. She was dying to ask about the baby. The baby bump that Becca rested her hand on attracted her like a beacon, and she wanted to know everything about it.

"How are you feeling, Becca? You know, with the baby and everything."

As soon as she motioned the baby, Becca started to physically clam up and pull away. "I'm fine. I just need to look after myself. If you don't mind, I need to get back to my studio."

"Studio?" Dale asked.

"I have a photography studio in my attic. If you need anything, just let me know, but you need to go before Jake gets home after three."

"I will, I promise. Thanks for the tea." Dale was going to have to work really hard to get through the hard outer shell Becca kept around herself, but she would, no matter what.

❖

Over the next few days Dale got into a pattern of arriving just after the school bus left, and each day the pull to see Jake again was bigger.

Before starting work on the car, she would head to the kitchen and leave a sticky note on the kitchen door with a joke written on it. Since Becca didn't come to talk to her often, it was the only way she could think of to build up some kind of communication with her.

It appeared that it started to work after a few days, because by the third day, there was a note waiting for her in reply, attached to a bag with a sandwich and a flask of tea.

It read, *If I give you lunch, will you stop telling me bad jokes?*

Dale laughed to herself, and then took out her pen to write back. *Nah, hen. It'll only make me try harder...Why couldn't the pony sing himself a lullaby? He was a little hoarse.*

"She's got to laugh at that one."

Dale went to the garage and started working on Becca's exhaust. She could be doing everything a whole lot quicker, but she was trying to drag things out as long as possible. She wanted to get Becca to trust her. Perhaps it was a good thing that Jake wasn't around just now. It gave Dale the time on her own at the vicarage to try and figure Becca out, which wasn't a straightforward project.

She was clearly a very complex person. Becca was kind and at the same time cold towards her. Obviously this situation was a big shock to them both, and Dale could understand her being scared, but it wasn't just that—Dale sensed great sadness and fear in Becca. That made Dale sad, and she wish she could help her in some way. Whatever it was that made Becca so skittish, it must have been something desperately painful for her.

Dale took her lunch and went to sit on the pile of tyres at the front door of the garage. Just as she was about to bite into her ham and cheese sandwich, the lady from next door came through the gate between the properties, carrying a basket of eggs. Dale stood politely as she approached.

"Dale, isn't it?"

"Yeah, nice to meet." Dale shook her hand. "It's Granny Sadie, isn't it?"

Sadie chuckled. "Yes, it is, but you can call me Sadie. You're helping out Becca, I see."

"Aye, the car has quite a few problems. Becca was reluctant at first, but she's allowing me to fix it for her."

Sadie took a step towards her and gave her a serious look. "I hope you are genuine, Dale, because Becca has too much on her plate to deal with extra stress. She's a kind, loving woman, and she deserves so much more than life is giving her at the moment."

That was definitely a warning, and Dale was secretly pleased Becca had someone looking out for her.

"I swear, I just want to help Becca and Jake. I don't want to upset them, or take Becca's kids away. I promise."

Sadie nodded. "I'll take you at your word then. Don't let me down. I'll just get these eggs up to Becca."

About five minutes later she saw Becca come out of the front door of the house, carrying a camera and tripod.

Becca set up her equipment next to a garden bench that looked over the fields and trees on the land next door.

It struck Dale how lonely Becca looked—yes, lonely was

exactly how she would describe Becca. No one came to visit her, no cars were ever there, no family or friends except Sadie next door.

On impulse she took what was left of her sandwich and flask and walked over to the other side of the large garden.

Becca appeared so engrossed in setting a shot that she never heard Dale approach.

"Uh…hi, Becca."

Becca grasped her chest in fright. "My God, you could have warned me you were there."

"Sorry, sorry. I just wanted to thank you for leaving me lunch." Dale held up her bag.

"You're welcome. It's the least I can do. How is the car going?"

"It's going okay. I'm fitting a new exhaust today and waiting for some other parts to be delivered."

Becca looked panicked all of a sudden. "How much are all these parts costing? I don't want charity."

Dale held her hands up in defence. "Hey, don't worry about it, hen. The parts I can get for next to nothing. This is what you agreed to let me do to help, so I am." Dale sensed that Becca was getting ready to argue, so she quickly changed the subject. "You're taking pictures?"

"Yes, since I can't work as much, I'm trying to stop myself getting rusty. There's a lovely tree next door with some beautiful birds attracted by its berries."

"Can I see?"

Becca looked surprised at her request, and unsure of what to say. "I suppose."

Dale put her lunch down on the bench, and then went to look through the camera lens.

"It's straight ahead, next to the fence," Becca said.

Dale saw it and saw all the birds feasting on the berries there. "They are beautiful. How do I zoom in?"

Becca put her palm on the small of Dale's back and leaned in to move the lens.

Dale was afraid to move and lose the touch Becca had initiated, obviously without thinking. But after a moment, she took her eyes off the lens and looked into Becca's eyes intimately. There was so much going on in the look Becca returned—confusion, fear, but also, Dale was sure, a spark of attraction. It was only there for a second or two, but it was there.

Then Becca recoiled and turned to open up some other of her camera bags.

The atmosphere between them immediately frosted up, and Becca said, without turning around, "I won't keep you. I'm sure you have a lot to do."

That was her cue to leave. "Yeah. If you need me for anything, just shout."

When Dale was walking away, she heard Becca say, "I don't need anyone."

CHAPTER SEVEN

Two weeks passed with Dale continuing to try to break the ice with Becca, but her usual charm wasn't working as fast as she'd hoped. It was Friday and she couldn't drag out the car repair any longer, especially since Becca said she really needed the car for food shopping in the next few days.

Dale walked reluctantly to the kitchen door and knocked. Knowing it was going to be her last day, she'd bought some things she hoped would help Becca and show her she cared. Dale held the bag and lifted her hand to knock on the door, but she heard Becca shout, "Oh, just work! Please?"

Whatever it was, it was making Becca angry. Dale knocked on the door and entered. She found Becca looking flushed, hot, and bothered. "Is everything okay?"

"Yes, everything's fine. Can I get you something?"

"No, I just wanted to let you know the car is finished, and you'll have no more problems."

"Okay, thank you. I appreciate it." Becca picked up her bag and quickly took out her purse. "I want you to take this. I know twenty pounds isn't near enough for the job, but I want to pay you something."

Dale pushed her hand away. "I don't want your money, Becca. This was about helping you. We agreed—I was helping you."

She could see Becca's stress rising. As Becca crushed the note up tightly in her hand, tears came to her eyes, which really surprised Dale.

"I don't like to be beholden to anyone," Becca said.

"Look, please, stress isn't good for you. Everything is okay, and you're not beholden to me. Twenty pounds means a lot to you and Jake."

"It didn't use to," Becca said, tears rolling down her face.

Dale couldn't believe it. The so far frosty, stubborn Rebecca Harper was breaking down in tears.

"Hey, it's okay. Don't be upset," Dale said. She had the biggest urge to pull her into a hug, but she resisted and instead escorted her to the kitchen table and got a box of tissues from the countertop.

Becca cried into a tissue and said, "I'm sorry, I don't do this. I don't cry in front of people, but the dishwasher not working is just the last straw."

Dale took a chance and took her hand. "I'm not people. We might have only known each other a few weeks, but, well, we share…stuff."

Becca dabbed her tears. "Stuff?"

Dale searched around for some appropriate term that wouldn't offend Becca. "You know? Egg type stuff."

Out of nowhere, Becca started laughing and said in her very upper-middle-class accent, "Egg type stuff?"

Dale was just as unsure how to react to the laughing as to her tears. "I tell you some brilliant jokes all week and *that* is what gets you laughing?"

Becca nodded. "Your jokes are terrible, by the way, but I smiled when I read them every morning, especially the one about the pony."

"You did?" Dale felt like she had won another small victory. She'd made the beautiful and remote Becca laugh and smile. That was no mean feat.

Becca nodded and smiled, wiping away her tears.

Dale felt she had to explain herself better. "I meant you have part of me. You know?"

Becca hurriedly dried her tears and blew her nose. She did know what Dale meant. There was something about her—perhaps it was having Dale's child inside her—which made Becca feel connected to Dale. Then she realized what price her emotional breakdown could cost her. "I do. I'm sorry you had to see that."

"Don't be daft. Everyone gets upset from time to time. You've got so much on your plate."

A feeling of dread spread through Becca. She had trusted someone with her emotions and secrets before, and it had nearly destroyed her.

Becca's calm steely reserve came seeping back. "I suppose you have all the ammunition you need now?"

"What do you mean?" Dale asked.

"To take Jake away from me. You have plenty of money for a good lawyer, and now you've got the evidence of an emotionally and physically unfit mother who can't afford to take care of her children."

Dale pulled her hand back from Becca's and looked shocked. "Is that really what you think of me? Have I not shown you these few weeks that I just want to help? I've done what you asked, I've kept to all your rules, and I wish you would trust that I don't want to take the kids away from you. I'm not the mother type."

"What are you then?" Becca said.

Dale sat back in her chair and crossed her arms defensively. "A good friend, a playmate for my god-daughter Mia."

Becca was surprised. "You have a god-daughter?"

"Aye, Mia is the daughter of my best friends in the world, Sammy and Val. They're kind of like parents and siblings, rolled up together, to me. They took me in when I ran away from home to London, penniless and homeless."

Dale had so many hidden depths and stories, and Becca wanted to know them. "You ran away from home?"

She watched Dale squirm uncomfortably in her seat. It was clearly a touchy subject. "It's a long story. Anyway, I wasn't wanted, so I came to London to start a new life. I met Sammy at a garage where I was looking for a job, and they took me in."

"And Mia?"

A bright smile covered Dale's face when she talked about Mia. "Yeah, she's ten years old, just like Jake. Sammy and Val used a sperm donor from the clinic you used. That's where I got the idea to donate. Do you want to see a picture?"

Becca nodded and couldn't help but smile at Dale's enthusiasm. There was something about Dale. She clearly had confidence and charm that made Becca certain women flocked to her, but there was something else, a vulnerability that she presumed came from whatever she had been running from, and it was so endearing.

Dale took out her wallet and handed her a picture. "This is Sammy, Val, and Mia together."

Becca gazed at the couple she had seen on the McGuire's Motors website, and was envious of their closeness, and the little brown-haired girl beside them was just beautiful.

"Mia is a sweet little girl," Becca said.

"She is, and so cool. We play computer games and watch films. I just have so much fun with her. Here's another picture."

Dale opened up her smartphone and showed her a picture of Mia up on Dale's shoulders, at the park. They were laughing and having lots of fun. The strange thing was, this Dale whom she was getting to know and who was beaming with pride, showing her pictures of her god-daughter, was not the one Trent warned her about.

It struck Becca that Jake didn't have someone in his life like that. She took care of his needs emotionally and physically, but she wasn't a parent who was going to kick a ball at the park or chase around in the garden with him. Dale would have been that.

Dale cleared her throat and said, "So will you trust me that I'm not going to try and take away your kids?"

Trust was a huge thing for Becca. She didn't trust anyone except Trent, and even Trent didn't see her emotional side. But something told her to trust Dale, on this issue anyway. She would miss Dale's bad jokes waiting for her every morning, and even just her presence working in the garage relaxed her so much. She wasn't always on her guard with Dale around, like she normally was. Having another person around was nice.

"I don't trust anyone, Dale, but I am starting to hope I can trust you."

"I'm going to make you trust me. I always keep my word, and

I give you my word I'm not here to cause trouble. So tell me what's wrong with the dishwasher and I'll fix it."

❖

Dale screwed on the back of the dishwasher and jumped to her feet. "Okay, moment of truth time."

Becca watched her as she pressed the power button, and it lit up straight away.

"Yes!" Dale shouted. "You're going to need a new one soon, but that should keep it going."

"Thank you. That's such a relief, I can't tell you. Let me make you tea before you go. I'll even give you posh biscuits."

There was no way Dale was going to turn down that. "Great. That would be nice."

Once Becca made the tea, Dale carried the tray over to the table and sat down. Dale's bag of things she had bought was still sitting on the floor and she was waiting for the right moment to bring it up.

When she was nearly finished her tea, she lifted the bag onto the table and prayed this would go down well.

"Before I go, I wanted to give you something. I was doing some research on the net about high blood pressure and I picked up some things that might help."

She rummaged in her bag and brought out three bottles onto the table.

"Potassium, vitamin C, and magnesium. I checked with the pharmacist that they were okay for a pregnant woman. It says on the internet that these vitamins can really help."

"Dale, that's really thoughtful, but—"

"There's more, hang on."

Dale took out a box and placed it on the table before rubbing the back of her neck bashfully.

"I know when Val was pregnant, getting massages from Sammy always made her feel better, so since I can't do that for you, I got you this neck massager."

Dale handed over the box to an astonished Becca.

"The guy in the shop said it was really good. You put it around your neck like a scarf."

Next she brought out a digital music player. "I made up a special relaxation playlist for you on here. I thought you could listen while you had the neck massager on. Oh, and I got a pack of my favourite lollipops for the wee man. You can just pretend you bought them."

Becca started to feel emotional again. Despite the fact that Dale could have thrown money at her, she took the time to find out what little things would make life easier, and bought her those. No one had ever taken such an interest in her pregnancy. In fact Trent saw it as an inconvenience, something that had ruined their plans, but Dale was almost like an excited kid about it.

Becca tried to remind herself that she barely knew Dale and could never trust her intentions. A little paranoid voice inside her said, *She's just using you to get close to Jake.*

"Dale, I don't know what to say. This was very kind."

Dale put the empty bag down on the table and looked sad. "Well, this is my last day with you. The car's fixed and I didn't want to leave without helping in some wee way."

Becca wanted to hug Dale then for her sweetness and for being sad. It was insane, and so unlike Becca's normal behaviour, but each day Becca saw Dale, and every bad joke she heard, something softened inside her.

Just then the baby made itself known and gave Becca a sharp kick. When Becca cried out in surprise, Dale was on her feet in panic.

"What's wrong? Is it the baby?"

"She's kicking. Come here and feel." Becca was astonished at herself. Why had she said that? She always kept people at arm's length, and here she was inviting Dale to feel the baby.

Dale was over like a shot, kneeling down in front of her, full of excitement. Becca took her hand and placed it on her stomach.

The baby didn't disappoint and gave her a few strong kicks. Dale gasped in wonder. "Wow. I can't believe it. She's really in there. Hello, wee yin. I can feel you kicking."

Becca couldn't help but feel excited at sharing this moment

with Dale. When she was pregnant with Jake, she'd never shared anything like this with anyone. It was nice.

Then Dale looked up at her with eyes full of emotion. "Thank you for sharing this with me, Becca."

Becca's heart started to beat fast as this moment began to feel rather intimate. She had to stop herself from running her hands through Dale's short messy hair.

"Dale?"

"Yes?" Dale said breathily.

She couldn't understand why she was about to say this, but she did anyway. "Do you want to come back next week and do some more repairs from Jake's list? Whenever you're free, of course."

The biggest smile imaginable broke out on Dale's face. "I'd love to. Thank you so much, Becca. I promise I'll follow any rules you want to give me. I just want to help you."

"It's so hard for me to trust, Dale. I hope I'm doing the right thing," Becca said.

"You are. I promise." Dale reluctantly took her hand off the baby bump and stood up. "I better go, I suppose."

Becca walked her out to her van, and Dale asked, "What do you and Jake do on a Friday night?"

"We usually watch a film, if I can drag him away from his latest coding project. He's coding a game to help children with maths at the moment."

Dale smiled with what Becca could only describe as pride. "He's such a great kid."

Becca nodded, "Sometimes we get a pizza, if I can manage it. Pizza is Jake's favourite food."

"A boy after my own heart," Dale said, but clearly realized how it could be taken and corrected herself quickly. "It's just a turn of phrase—I didn't mean he was mine."

But he is, Becca thought.

"So what does Dale McGuire do on a Friday night? I'm sure the ladies are lining up waiting for you." Becca regretted saying it as soon as the words came out of her mouth, when she saw Dale's face fall.

"I go out to the pub because I don't have anything else in my life, not because I go on the hunt for women. Your kind of Friday night sounds much better. Take care of yourself and the wee yin. I'll see you Monday."

❖

Dale almost skipped with happiness and excitement as she walked into the headquarters branch of McGuire's Motors. The garage was full of noise and shouts as cars up on the ramps got fixed or serviced. Some the mechanics called out to Dale as she passed. One man said, "Hey, stranger, where have you been hiding?"

His workmate said, "Somewhere getting some of what you can't, Mike. A woman."

Dale laughed and left them to their banter. If only they knew she *was* with a woman, having no sex whatsoever, and happier than she had ever been. If only she could see Jake too, it would be perfect, but Dale hoped she could work on that. She never ever wanted to take Jake away from Becca, that was the truth, but she would like to see him again.

Dale went into the reception area where the customers waited for their cars, and walked up to the desk manager, Ted, a retired mechanic who was really good with the customers.

She waited until he was finished and leaned on the desk.

"Dale, what can I do you for?"

"I have a list of car parts I need for the Ford I've been working on."

Dale handed Ted the list and he sucked air in through his teeth, before saying, "New tyres, new engine, paint job? For all this year of car is worth, you'd be as well buying a whole new car."

"I know, but that isn't an option for my friend. So I have to just make the best of it."

Dale would have gladly gotten her a car, or given them one of McGuire's Motors's courtesy cars, but she knew Becca would never, ever agree to that.

Even though the car was fixed, it was in bad condition, so Dale thought if she could give it a complete overhaul that would be a safer car for Becca and the children.

Ted nodded. "I'll get them ordered up. It should just be a couple of days."

"Thanks, Ted, are Sammy and Val here?"

"Yes, they're stock-taking in the back office."

"Thanks, mate."

As she walked back to the offices her head was full of ideas to make Becca's house more liveable. She had enjoyed being around the house, helping Becca out and trying to break down her walls.

Becca's initially frosty reception had given way to a reserved and careful woman who didn't give anything away, except today. Today she had seen the Becca underneath the reserved exterior, and she wanted more.

Dale found Sammy going through the stock lists and Val working on the computer.

"Hey, mate," Sammy said. "How did you get on today?"

Dale threw her jacket on her chair and sat down in front of her computer.

"It was fantastic. She let me feel the baby kick," Dale said excitedly.

Val and Sammy looked at each other, before Val said, "Wait, the same woman that didn't want you there and would hardly talk to you let you feel the baby."

"Aye, I think my excellent repertoire of jokes finally got through to her. She was upset because the dishwasher broke and I comforted her, and the wee yin kicked inside her and—"

Dale stopped and relived the moment. It brought tears to her eyes, and she quickly had to get herself under control.

"Dale? What was it like?" Val asked.

"It was the best moment of my life. I couldn't have imagined feeling like that—the feeling that a part of me was growing inside a beautiful woman like Becca."

Before she completely broke down, Dale logged on to her computer.

Sammy cleared her throat. "Listen, mate. I know what it feels like to experience something like that. I couldn't stop touching Val's baby bump when she was pregnant with Mia, but…"

"But what?" Dale said sharply.

Val patted Sammy on the hand and answered for her. "You're not her partner, and you're not the baby's parent. Rebecca is."

Dale was starting to get really angry. "Why are you saying this to me? You were the ones that said I should try to help her out."

"Yes, help her, Dale, but it sounds like you're getting attached, and when Rebecca decides she's had enough of your help, you are going to be hurt."

Dale sat back in her chair and tried to look as nonchalant as possible. "Me? Hurt? No way. I just want to help, that's all."

Val made an exasperated noise and slapped the desk, making both Sammy and Dale jump.

"Don't give me any of that Dale-from-the-bar patter. I helped bring you up, I held you when you found out your first girlfriend was married, and then again when your mother wrote you that letter, so don't try and tell me you couldn't care less."

Dale sprang up and walked to the window. "Okay, okay, I care. I want to know them. I want to get to know Jake, I want to help Becca. I think she's beautiful and I want to break down her walls. I want more than a life of going to the pub, drinking, dancing, and waking up in some stranger's bed, some woman I don't even like. I'm ready for something more now."

After receiving a push from Val, Sammy walked over to her and put an arm around her. "Mate, do you not think it's a bit soon to feel this way?"

"I felt my child move inside her, Sammy. How could I not? I need to try. If I'm hurt, then at least I tried."

"If that's how you feel," Val said, "then we'll be here for you."

Dale managed a smile. "Thanks, and thanks for covering for me with the business. I know I've been preoccupied."

Sammy laughed. "So preoccupied, you haven't even changed the month on your precious Britney Spears calendar."

Dale's eyes went wide and she hurried over to the other side of the room and took the calendar off the wall before flipping the page to the next month. She put it back up onto the wall and spoke to it.

"I'm sorry I forgot about you, Britney. There's another wee lassie in my life now, and she might not know it yet, but I'm going to wear her down and make her like me."

CHAPTER EIGHT

Since the car was fixed, Becca thought she would meet Jake when school let out, then pick up some things for dinner. So she called ahead and asked the school to not put Jake on the bus. As she drove down the country roads, she thought how wonderful it was to have her car back in full working order. In her current condition, it meant independence and freedom.

Without the car, Becca had been too reliant on Sadie, and as willing as Sadie was, Becca didn't like to put so much on the elderly woman's shoulders. Now she didn't have to be a burden to anyone, and that was all thanks to Dale McGuire.

Dale had bounced into her life without warning, with her bad jokes and big smiles, and despite the cold reception she had given her, she kept smiling and trying.

Becca pulled through the gates and parked in the parents' and visitors' area. The Westview School's building was beautiful, a former eighteenth-century estate house that served the once bustling village. It was similar to the school Becca had attended as a child, although she had boarded, and Westview took both boarders and day pupils. Becca couldn't imagine not having Jake come home at night. He was her little miracle and meant everything to her.

She turned off the engine and sat back in the seat.

Becca looked over to the group of parents also waiting for their children. They chatted and laughed, no doubt sharing stories and the difficulties of family life. Becca had never walked over and joined the group. She always stayed on the periphery, trying to go unnoticed. Not that she was shy or inhibited, but she had learned through experience that protecting her anonymity meant never making friends and never letting anyone in.

She closed her eyes and unexpectedly an image of Dale on her knees, feeling the baby kick, floated across her mind, along with a feeling of warmth.

Her eyes snapped open. That moment had replayed over and over in her mind since it had happened.

Becca had no idea why she had acted so spontaneously and let Dale experience what her baby felt like. She never allowed anyone that close, far less someone potentially dangerous to her family. Yet she had, and every time she had a quiet moment the tenderness they'd shared when Dale gazed into her eyes with genuine wonder was something she couldn't forget.

Becca kept trying to remind herself that she couldn't trust Dale, no matter how genuine she appeared. Someone had slipped behind her defences before and destroyed the last vestiges of her family.

Angel, trust me with your heart. I love you, and I'll take care of you...

Becca was disturbed by a knock on her window, and she jumped in fright, but turned her head and saw the smiling face of one of the teachers. She rolled down the window and said, "Good afternoon, Ms. Chester. Is everything all right?"

"Yes, nothing to worry about. I just wondered if we could have a quick chat?"

Becca followed the teacher to one of the school offices.

"Take a seat, Ms. Harper. My classroom assistant is getting the children ready, so I thought I'd take the opportunity to get a quick word with you about Jake."

Becca was immediately on alert. "Why? Did something happen?"

"No, don't worry. I simply wanted to discuss his behaviour. We've spoken before about Jake being slightly withdrawn from the other children, liking to work himself on projects and other class activities. Well it's getting worse, I'm afraid. I do understand Jake is working at a much higher level than anyone else, but learning to work together is important."

"I understand, Ms. Chester, and I've been encouraging him to interact more. That's why I sent him to computer club after school."

Computer club was an expensive extra at Westview School, but if it meant Jake would benefit from it, Becca would do anything.

"He loves computer club, Ms. Chester, and I'm sure it must be helping—"

"Ms. Harper, he doesn't work with the other children there either. My colleague who runs the club contacted me because she had similar concerns. Jake works on his own projects, not group activities, and in the last few weeks he's been a lot worse. He won't even go outside with the other children at break time."

This new information was hitting Becca hard. "I had no idea. I just assumed that computer club was helping."

"I'm afraid not. Does Jake have friends outside of school that he regularly plays with?"

"No, not really." Becca hadn't really thought about that aspect of her son's life. She was so used to hiding and covering her tracks that it never occurred to her that Jake would be learning the same patterns from her. She had never discouraged friendships, but never encouraged them either.

Ms. Chester leaned forward. "We think Jake should start sessions with the school psychologist."

Becca felt an intense feeling of panic. Everything was going wrong in their life, and she knew the blame should lie at her door. She had lost control.

Dale answered the doorbell and Mia jumped into her arms. "Dale!"

"Hey, munchkin. How are you today?"

"Great, I can't wait to play with you. I brought all my favourite games."

Sammy appeared at the door a few seconds later and said, "Are you sure about this, Dale? Val's mum couldn't watch Mia, but we could change our dinner plans. I know you always go out Friday nights."

Dale took Mia's bags from Sammy and shook her head. "No, I don't want to go out. There's nothing I want or need at Belles any more."

Sammy looked at her seriously. "They've got inside your head, haven't they?"

Dale gulped hard. Inside her head, inside her heart…Jake and Becca were all she could think about. She had this need inside her that she'd never known could exist, or that she even had a name for, but it was pulling her heart to that run-down vicarage in the country. It had gotten even worse since she had shared that special moment with the beautiful Becca and the baby.

"Yeah, but I'll handle it. You and Val have a good night, okay?"

Sammy gave her a soft punch on the shoulder. "You know we're here for you, mate."

"I know, thanks."

Once Sammy left, Dale put Mia's bags in the spare room and walked back to the living room. "We'll order pizza soon. You get the game set up and I'll get some juice, okay?"

When she came back through to sit down, Mia was sitting on the couch looking at her picture of Becca and Jake.

Shit!

She had forgotten to put it back in her wallet. "Hey, Mia. Here's your juice."

Dale put both their drinks on the table and down beside Mia.

"Dale, who are these people?"

What could she say? She couldn't tell her the truth, but Mia knew already that Dale didn't know other kids.

"Um…"

As she searched for some explanation, Mia looked from the picture to Dale and back again a few times.

"He looks like you," Mia said.

Dale's throat dried up instantly. "Just some new friends I met. The woman is called Becca and the boy is Jake. I'm helping his mum with a few repairs to her house."

Mia smiled, seemingly happy with that answer. "They look really nice. What's Jake like?"

Dale had a huge sigh of relief, and got up to switch on the games console. "He's ten, just like you. He likes computers, maths, and—" She knew nothing about him. Her own flesh and blood, and she knew virtually nothing about him.

"What else?" Mia asked.

"He loves pizza. I know that."

Mia smiled and handed her back the photo in exchange for one of the games controllers, and Dale put it back in her wallet.

"He sounds really cool."

"He is." Dale sat down and picked up her iPad to order pizza delivery.

"Okay, munchkin, what do you want on your pizza? Cabbage, onions, and anchovy?"

Mia made a puking noise. "No way, you always say that. You know I love just cheese pizza."

Dale laughed and started to tap their order into the takeaway app. "I know. Okay. One large cheese, one large meat feast, garlic bread, cheesy nachos, potato wedges with dips, and, never forgetting, ice cream. How's that?"

Mia bounced up and down. "Yes! Oh, can we eat the leftover pizza for breakfast?"

Dale gave her a wink and a smile. "Yep, breakfast of champions." Then in a stage whisper she added, "Just don't tell your mummy. 'Cause she'll kill me."

"Yes!" Mia gave Dale a high five. Mia suddenly looked serious. "It's a shame your friend Jake can't share our pizza and play with us. I bet he'd like that."

Dale jovial mood was gone. She remembered Becca had said that Jake loved to have a movie and pizza, if she could manage it.

Jake and Becca were all on their own on a Friday night, in the middle of nowhere with no one to take care of them.

Mia must have noticed the change in her demeanour because she said, "Are you okay?"

Dale needed a moment, and gulped down the emotion. "Yeah, just give me a sec, okay?"

She made for her bedroom, placed her iPad down on the bed, and held her head in her hands.

I'm going insane.

These new emotions were so confusing and so hard to deal with. It hurt that she had a child and one on the way that she would never know. Maybe it would have been better if she had never found out about them.

Dale opened up her bedside cabinet and took out her mum's Bible. It was the one thing of her mum's that she most treasured. Her mum had been a devout Catholic and never missed chapel. Her Bible had been one of *her* most treasured possessions, and was full of keepsakes. There were bookmarks with Bible verses on them, religious poems, and one special card that said, *To the best mum in the world, love, Dale.*

"Fuck this," Dale said angrily. She wasn't going to ever give up on her children, like she had been, whether they knew about her or not.

Dale dialled the number of her favourite pizza chain. "Hi, I just placed an app order and want to place another large order, but first I wanted to check if you can deliver to the village of Plumtun."

Dale sighed at the response. "I don't care if it'll cost a boundary charge, can you do it?

"Yes. I'll give you my credit card number."

❖

Jake sat at the kitchen table completing his homework while Becca put away the few bits of shopping she had gotten, before making dinner.

Jake had been quiet on their way home. She had tried to get him to talk, but he just didn't want to engage. It was such a worry having to do this by herself. Being a single parent meant she had no one to bounce ideas off of, and she needed ideas quickly. She wanted Jake to grow up and have normal friendships and relationships, but at this rate he would be closed off from everyone, and that would be her fault.

Of course he had been down in the dumps since she'd sent Dale away. Maybe Jake was telling her in his roundabout way that he was missing something from his life?

More guilt, to pile on top of the rest.

Becca's mobile beeped with a text message, and she jumped. She rarely got texts except from Jake's school or, on occasion, Trent.

She picked up the phone and her heart thudded unexpectedly. The message was from Dale. Becca had given her the number so she could make sure Jake was safely off to school before she arrived.

"Who is it, Mummy?"

"Oh, just…Trent." Becca cringed inwardly at the lie.

Jake immediately scowled. "She doesn't like me."

"That's not true, Jake." Trent didn't dislike Jake, but she did probably resent his place in Becca's life. She'd barely acknowledged him whenever she'd seen him over the years.

Jake didn't argue and went back to his schoolwork, giving Becca a chance to look at Dale's text.

The message contained a picture—a selfie of Dale and the pretty little girl Dale had shown her a picture of before.

Hi, Becca, Mia and I are having a pizza and games night sleepover. We wanted to share with you, so you should be getting a pizza delivery any moment. It's my treat, and I hope you'll accept it. Just tell the wee man that you bought it. Have a good night, and look after yourself and the wee yin. Dale

Becca's hand went straight to the baby. For the first time she felt care and concern for her and the kids, from someone apart from Sadie. Normally if anyone asked to help, or offered her anything, she would immediately panic and refuse, but with Dale's message all she felt was warmth.

Becca couldn't believe Dale was having a sleepover with her god-daughter on a Friday night. The ladies' woman Trent had described was getting further and further away from the reality of who Dale was.

There was a knock at the door. "I'll get it," Becca said quickly.

She hurried to the front door as quickly as her baby bump would allow, and opened it to find a young delivery driver, laden down with pizza boxes and other food parcels.

"Ms. Harper?"

"Yes, that's me." Becca took the two pizza boxes from him to help him out.

"Thank God. I thought I'd never find this place."

That's the point. No one can. We're safe here.

"Here's your order, hope you enjoy."

Becca couldn't refuse it. The thought was so kind, and she knew how much it would have cost Dale to get this food out here.

"Jake? Can you help me?"

Jake came running from the kitchen, and his eyes lit up with joy. "Pizza! Mummy, did you get us pizza?"

She had to lie. Again. "Yes, I thought we'd have a treat for movie night."

Jake hugged into her side. "Thanks, Mummy. I love you."

This was the first time Jake had smiled in a few weeks, and it was all because of Dale.

"I love you too, Pooh Bear. Let's get these things to the kitchen."

❖

Belles was alive and bouncing as usual on a Friday night. Over at a corner table sat Ash and Lisa. They had been there two hours now, and still no Dale McGuire.

"You told me she'd be here, Lisa. I hope I'm not wasting my time," Ash said.

"No, she's always here, every Friday and Saturday. She starts here and sometimes goes on to another club."

Ash tapped her fingers on the table. She was starting to get restless. "Maybe we missed her coming in?"

Lisa laughed. "Nobody misses Dale McGuire coming in, believe me. She has a posse of girls around her in seconds."

Ash grabbed Lisa's wrist without warning. "Listen, this is not a joke. I need to find McGuire and, through her, Victoria Carter. I have a lot riding on this, and you have your career."

She let Lisa go and embarked on a softer approach. Ash stroked her cheek and whispered softly. "Now tell me, does she have a friend here that knows where she lives?"

"The only one she really talks to properly is Mac, the owner. She's working behind the bar."

"Okay, I'll go and see if I can get her to talk. You stay here."

Ash sauntered over to the bar and tried to catch Mac's eye.

She eventually saw her. "What can I get you, mate?"

Ash gave her a friendly smile. "A white wine and a vodka martini, please."

As Mac got the drinks, Ash tried to engage her in conversation. "It's a great place. Are you the manager?"

"Cheers. I'm the owner," Mac said.

"It's a good crowd too. You must have a lot of regulars."

Mac looked at her suspiciously. "Some, yeah."

"I heard Dale McGuire comes in here a lot."

Mac handed her drinks. "She does. That'll be £15.90."

Ash got out her wallet and handed over the money. "Has she been in yet? I'd really like to see her."

Mac looked her up and down. "I think it's safe to say you're not her type, mate."

Ash laughed. "Oh, don't worry. I'm not one of the girls looking for that kind of attention. No, you see, I'm looking for someone, and I had information that Dale knew her."

"No, she's not been in and she normally is by this time," Mac conceded.

This was becoming one big waste of time. She'd given up an awards dinner with her lover for this. "Maybe you've seen the woman I'm looking for then?" Ash took out the photograph she had of Victoria Carter and showed it to Mac. "She has some connection to Dale McGuire, so you might have seen them together."

Mac looked and Ash saw a moment of recognition in her eyes, but she replied. "No, sorry."

That was all Ash needed. There was definitely a connection, and she just had to be patient and find her. Her next stop was clearly going to be McGuire's Motors headquarters.

I will find you, Vic, and you'll make me a big story again.

CHAPTER NINE

Dale couldn't wait to see Becca again, but work commitments meant she couldn't get back to the vicarage till Tuesday.

She got out of her van, grabbed her tool bag, nearly ran to the back door, and knocked. When Becca opened the door, her heart fluttered and her mouth went dry. Every time Dale saw Becca, she saw something different and more beautiful in her.

"Morning," she said.

"Good morning, Dale. Can I get you coffee?"

Dale was surprised at how open Becca was being. "Yeah, I'd like that. I could do with one."

"Take a seat," Becca said.

Dale sat down at the kitchen table while Becca poured the coffee.

"I wanted to thank you. The food you sent on Friday night, it was really kind."

"You're welcome. I hoped you would accept it but I wasn't sure."

Becca brought over her coffee, and sat at the table with her. "I normally wouldn't but it was such a kind thought and it was from you and your god-daughter. Then Jake saw the delivery and I got his first smile for a few weeks."

As soon as Becca said that she clammed right up, as if she'd said too much. Why was Jake unhappy, Dale wondered?

She was about to ask that question when Becca quickly changed the subject. "I was surprised you were babysitting on a Friday night. I thought you told me your life consisted of going out and having fun on the weekends? That's what you told me, anyway."

I couldn't stop thinking about you, Jake, and the baby.

How could she explain to Becca without freaking her out? "I always love to have Mia to stay, and maybe I'm just getting old, but in the last year or so pubs and clubs are looking less appealing. I've just been going through the motions really."

"You can't be that old."

"Thirty-six," Dale volunteered.

"Oh my, I'd have guessed twenty-eight, thirty tops. You look after yourself then?"

"Not really, I suppose it's genetics, but it helps if you've always had—"

"Boyish good looks?" Becca offered out of nowhere. The phrase stunned Dale, and Becca's cheeks went a bright shade of pink.

She's noticed me. Yes!

"I mean...um..." Becca faltered.

Dale decided to let her off the hook. "My regular hangout, Belles—I don't know how or when it happened, but suddenly the women started to get younger and the music more likely to give me a headache. I mean, what's wrong with Britney Spears and cheesy pop?"

This got her another smile from Becca. She was on a roll today. So far, she'd gotten smiles and no standoffish attitude.

She spotted the vitamins she had brought and the neck massager, out of its box, on the other side of the kitchen.

"Did you try the massager?"

"Yes, it was lovely. I've used it every night, while I read my book."

Dale was so happy at the progress she was making. Becca was relaxing around her at last. "So, how are you and the wee yin?"

Becca smiled at the use of the baby's nickname. "We're fine. I get some headaches and dizziness now and again, but it hasn't been as bad as it was."

"That's good," Dale said. After a few moments of silence, she decided she'd best not test the limits of this new phase of their relationship. "Well, I thought I'd make a start on patching the roof for you, as best I can on my own."

"Will it be safe to do?" Becca asked.

"Aye, I'll be fine. Can you show me where the rain is coming in?"

Becca hesitated for a second, and then said, "Up in my studio is the worst. I'll take you up."

❖

Becca led Dale upstairs to her studio. Why was she doing this? She'd never even brought Trent up here, but there was something about Dale that made her want to open up, no matter how wrong her mind told her that was.

"This is my photographic studio. It's not perfect yet, but I hope one day when I can get the work done, it'll work well for me. You can see the buckets and where the drips are coming in from the roof."

She watched Dale walk through the attic room gazing at everything and anything.

"It's a great space, and that's all you need to start with. My business started from one lock-up. It had enough space for three cars at a time, and I built up and up, and bought the land around it eventually." Dale turned around and gave her a wink. "Great things can happen from little beginnings."

Becca's stomach flipped, and she couldn't blame the baby this time. It seemed like Dale was talking about more than business, but maybe she was just imagining it. She could almost feel an electricity sparking between them the more time she spent in Dale's company. She tried to tell herself it was probably some biological urge to find a mate while she was pregnant, but she never, ever had that urge when in Trent's company.

Dale picked up one of her business brochures and started to flick through.

"Man, you do a really good job. These pictures are excellent. You're making me realize how bad McGuire's Motors's website is. It could really do with an upgrade and new photographs like this."

Maybe that's a way I can pay her back for everything? Becca thought.

Dale walked over to the plans she had hanging on the wall. "Are these the plans for the vicarage?"

Becca went over and joined her. "Yes, this is…was my dream until I had to halt work on the house. When I first viewed the house, I thought I could finally give Jake a proper childhood. Somewhere with wide-open spaces to play, somewhere we could have chickens, ducks, goats, somewhere to show him there's more to life than a computer screen. I get frightened sometimes…"

Becca let her voice trail off. She couldn't believe how open she was being or what she had been about to say. She was not going to be led down this road again.

"What?" Dale asked. "What frightens you?"

"Nothing."

Dale groaned in frustration. "Look, you don't have to censor everything you say to me. I'm not going to use it against you. I'm not here to hurt you, or steal Jake away. I'd love to know both you and Jake better, but that's it. That's the honest truth, but I accept you won't let Jake see me, and I'm following every rule you give me. Why can't you just trust me?"

That was the simplest question Dale could ask, and one to which she could give a truly honest answer.

"Because I trusted someone once, and they destroyed everything that I had. I'm never going to do that again."

The simple honest answer silenced Dale.

"Shall we go back downstairs and I'll let you get on?" Becca said.

Dale nodded and they walked towards the attic staircase, but Becca turned around and realized Dale wasn't beside her. She had veered off to a corner of the room where she displayed all the pictures she had taken of Jake as he grew.

Becca walked over to join her and found Dale staring at one

particular photograph of her holding baby Jake in her arms in the maternity ward.

Dale reached out and almost touched the picture. She was clearly having a deeply emotional response to a simple photograph, and seeing her reaction to newborn Jake was something that touched her heart deep inside.

"That was taken by one of the nurses, when I came back from theatre. I had to have a caesarean section because my blood pressure was getting too high. I wanted to remember that moment forever."

"Was anyone with you when he was born?"

"No, no one," Becca said sadly.

Dale took Becca's hand.

She was stiff at first, but then she relaxed somewhat into Dale's warm touch. "I took these photos, at all his different stages. First word, first step, first day at nursery, and then school."

"Wow, he's just so perfect," Dale said, the emotion resonating in her voice.

"I can't wait to add this little girl to the pictures."

Dale turned to her then and gazed at her baby bump like she was fighting not to touch it.

"I suppose I better get started in the roof," Dale said, making her way to the stairs.

"I'm going to be out this morning. I hope you don't mind if I leave you for a while—I have a job to go to, but I'll leave the kitchen door open so you can make yourself a cup of tea."

Dale's head snapped around. "What do you mean, job? I thought the doctor ordered you off work?"

"He did, but it's nothing too arduous. I've been feeling a lot better anyway. It's just a small art gallery in the next town that needs some new pictures for their website. I'm not doing the big contracts, just some small ones to keep some money coming in."

Dale scowled. "Becca, I don't think that's a good idea—"

"This is none of your business, Dale. I'm doing what I need to do for my family, so just keep your opinions to yourself." Becca left her standing in the attic while she walked off angrily.

❖

Dale finished putting the last patched tile on the roof and looked over her handiwork. She was no roofer, but she was handy enough to turn her hand to most practical jobs. That was the way her dad had brought her up. The McGuires never called in a tradesman when they could do it themselves. To her dad, it was letting your family down if you couldn't repair, decorate, or build something yourself, and Dale had taken that into her own life.

She was happy with the job, but the house would probably need a whole new roof whenever Becca could do the proper refurbishment.

Dale looked at her watch and wondered when Becca would be back. It had been a few hours since she'd left.

Becca.

What a mistake she had made earlier by questioning her sense in working. After their chat today, she had felt they had crossed a bridge, that they were getting closer. Becca had let her guard down.

Dale knew money was tight for her, but working when the doctor had told her not to was crazy as far as she was concerned. Especially since Becca had told her about Jake's difficult birth only a few minutes before.

She walked down the ladder and started to pack her tools into the box, and then carried the ladder around to the garage.

Dale had no idea when Becca would be back, but she hoped she had the chance to see her before Jake came out of school She had to make it right with her, because despite Becca's determination for independence and trust of no one, Becca and Jake needed her. They needed someone on their side to take care of them, and Dale was determined she would be the right one for the job.

She got out her notepad and looked down Jake's list of jobs. She had managed quite a few in her time at the vicarage, but the one major problem she had yet to get fixed was the central heating. The quick look she had had at the outside boiler told her that it needed to be replaced, and long term she was sure it could be dangerous, but

Becca didn't have the money to cover the work and equipment and would be horrified if Dale offered it to her. She'd need to handle it carefully.

Dale heard the sound of a car pulling into the driveway, and hurried out hoping it was Becca, but it was in fact a truck with the car parts she'd asked to be delivered.

By the time she and the driver got them off the van and safely packed into the garage, Becca's car was coming up the driveway.

Dale signed the delivery driver's paperwork. "Thanks, mate."

She then hurried over to Becca, who was taking bags out of the boot. Dale wasn't quite sure of the reception she would get. "Can I get these for you?"

Much to her surprise, Becca smiled and said, "Yes, thank you. If you could put them on the kitchen table, please."

Dale grabbed the bags and set off for the kitchen before Becca had a chance to change her mood or mind. She put the things on the kitchen table, and switched the kettle on. When Becca finally caught up with her, she was still smiling. This was not the Becca Harper who'd left here earlier. In fact, the change was unnerving.

Dale pulled out a chair for her. "Sit down. I put the kettle on for you."

"Thanks." Becca sat and let out a sigh. "If you look in that brown paper bag, you'll find some sandwiches I brought for lunch."

"Oh, thanks." *Weird.* "Um...Becca, about earlier? I didn't mean—"

"No, Dale. I want to say sorry. You've done nothing but help me, and I've done nothing but scowl at you most of the time. I was thinking while I was away at my appointment, and I need to apologize."

"No, you've got every right to feel threatened by my presence, Becca. I understand that."

"I've been under a lot of stress, and feeling guilty about everything."

"What do you have to feel guilty about?" Dale asked.

"Everything. Bringing another child into the world when I don't have the means to support Jake, far less the new baby, when

I knew my age and pregnancy problems would be difficult. And making Jake so worried that he went to find you. All I can tell you is something happened to me last year that made making a bigger family the most important thing in the world."

Dale took a seat beside her, and again took a giant risk by covering her hand with her own. Luckily Becca didn't run. "You don't owe me or anyone else any explanations."

"I do. You've been so kind to me, and you're right, you have followed all my rules. If you are waging some secret plot to take my children away, then you're hiding it well, but still I can't trust anyone. That's my problem not yours."

Dale said sincerely, "I would feel the same as you, if our positions were switched."

Becca gave her a soft smile. "I don't think you would. You are warm, open, kind."

Dales heart started to flutter. *Please tell me I'm not dreaming. Am I actually winning her over?*

"All I can tell you is that there are reasons why I am like I am, why Jake and I are out here trying to hide from the world. I don't know if I'll ever be able to talk about it. There are just two people who know everything, my ex, who's also my lawyer…"

Dale suddenly went on alert, and a tight knot clenched in her stomach. An ex, she hadn't considered that.

"And one other person, who put the final nail in the coffin and destroyed my family," Becca said sadly.

Dale tapped her fingers on the table restlessly. "Was your ex part of Jake's life? Did you have him together?"

"God, no. Trent never wanted children and I did, desperately. So we went our separate ways."

Dale had no right to, but she felt such relief when Becca said that. She didn't want to think of Becca and Jake ever being claimed by someone else.

"I'm telling you this, Dale, and taking a risk for the first time in years. I haven't even told Sadie these things before."

"I promise you're safe. I would never hurt you, the wee man, or the wee yin. I promise."

Becca smiled and it warmed Dale's heart. "You know, you're the only person who's ever been concerned about their welfare before. I've been alone for a long time."

"You don't have to be."

Becca's eyes widened and Dale realized she'd said too much.

"I mean…alone with Jake and the wee yin. I can be your friend."

Becca sighed. Everything told her not to, but her heart said yes. "I've been on my own for such a long time. So long that I didn't realize I was teaching Jake not to trust, and to fear others, just like me. I had a meeting with his teacher last night. He won't socialize, make friends, or even go out at break time, and it's my fault."

"No, Becca—"

"It is. I'm teaching him to distrust the world. I need to change if he is to change too. But God help me if you're not sincere."

"I'll prove to you that I am, Becca. I promise."

"Only time will tell. I just wanted you to know what a huge ask it is for me to trust," Becca said truthfully.

They both said nothing for a few seconds and then Becca asked, "What was being delivered when I arrived?"

Dale looked apprehensive to tell her.

"Just tell me, I'm not going to snap at you or anything."

"Parts for your car. I got it working, but I thought I could give it a few upgrades for you, to make it run better and be more comfortable."

Becca had to practice some of that trust she was talking about. "That's very kind of you, but I have one condition."

"What condition?" Dale said.

"In exchange, I'll take photos of you, your staff, and your business, to upgrade your website. What do you say?"

"Deal."

Becca reached into one of the shopping bags and pulled out a brown envelope. "There's one more thing."

"What?"

She handed over the envelope and said, "Open it."

Dale opened it and found a set of Jake's baby pictures. "Oh my God. It's the wee man's pictures."

It made Becca feel wonderful to share this with Dale. "You gave me the chance to have a child, and I'll always be grateful for that. I saw your reaction when you looked at my pictures, and no matter what happens, I wanted you always to have something of him."

Becca was sure she saw tears in Dale's eyes. She just prayed she was right to let Dale this far in.

CHAPTER TEN

Ash had been waiting in her car from before McGuire's Motors opened. She had her camera sitting on the passenger seat waiting for a glimpse of Dale McGuire, but she never arrived with the rest of her staff. After weighing up the pros and cons, she decided to go inside.

She walked into the reception area and stood at the desk waiting for the silver-haired member of staff to look up.

"Good morning. My name is Ted. How can I help you today?"

"Morning, Ted. I'm looking to get my Mercedes serviced and some new tires put on. Would you have any appointments free?"

Ted quickly checked the computer, and said, "I'm sorry, ma'am, but we're all booked out till Friday. Would that be suitable?"

"Listen, I'm an old friend of Dale's. I'm sure she could do it more quickly. Is she in today?"

"No, I'm sorry. She's off today."

"Could you give me a phone number for her? As I say, we're old friends."

Ted looked her up and down slightly suspiciously, and replied, "Give me a moment, will you?"

When he went through to the back, Ash leaned on the reception desk and looked around at the motoring prints littering the walls. She recognized Dale in the pictures from the McGuire's Motors website. Going by the pictures, Dale must take part in racing, as she was sitting on the bonnet of a classic Jaguar with winner's laurels around her neck, and a huge bottle of champagne.

She walked over to look at the pictures more closely. *So, you're the one Lisa and the others are fighting over? I bet you're one arrogant prick.*

Ash knew her type well, but what connection did she have to Victoria Carter? Vic was never the kind to be attracted to that type, although she was sure that lawyer friend of hers was more than an acquaintance.

"Excuse me," a voice behind her called.

She turned around and a grin spread across her face. This woman was beautiful. Older—in her forties, probably—and completely fuckable.

Ash walked back over to the desk and turned on the charm. "Hi, there, and you are?"

"Valentina Brooks. I believe you want to put your car in. Did Ted tell you we have no appointments till Friday?"

Ash leaned on the desk, and must have moved her hands a bit too close, because the sexy Valentina took a step back.

"He did, but I thought Dale could fit me in a bit earlier since I'm an old friend. Could I talk to her?"

"I'm afraid she's not in today. How exactly does she know you?"

"Oh, we go way back," Ash lied.

Val crossed her arms. "Funny, I've known her since she was seventeen and I don't ever remember you."

Fuck. "Well we probably moved in different circles. Could you remind me of her telephone number."

"I'm sorry. We don't give out staff phone numbers. Now do you wish to make the appointment for Friday?"

"No, thanks. That's not a good day for me. I'll catch Dale around."

Ash walked back out to her car. This wasn't going to be as easy as she thought.

❖

Ash came back later that night and waited for the staff to pack up and leave.

One man left on foot, rather than driving, so she drove her car around the corner and caught up with him. She stopped her Mercedes and lowered the window to talk to him.

"Mate, have you got a minute?"

"Why? What do you want?"

Ash parked and got out. "I'm from the *Tribune* newspaper and I wonder if you could give me some information?"

The man looked at her ID then back to her. "What information?"

"On your boss."

"Dale?" he said with surprise. "What would a newspaper be interested in her for?"

"You'd be surprised. So will you talk?"

"No way. Everyone already got their balls booted for giving out her whereabouts to some girl who tracked her down." He started to walk off and Ash caught up with him.

"Believe me, I'm not interested in her romantically, and I'm willing to pay." Ash took out her wallet and showed him some notes.

He stopped and eyed the money hungrily.

"Come on. It won't hurt anyone, and it'll be to your benefit. Let's go back to my car."

He thought for a second and then followed her back to the car. When he got in, he said, "You won't tell anyone, will you?"

"Of course not...What's your name?" Ash asked.

"Mike."

"Okay, Mike. I've got one hundred pounds here that's yours if you help me out, with more to come if you get me some information."

"What do you want to know?" Mike asked.

Ash took out her picture of Victoria Carter and showed it to him. "Have you seen this woman before? Maybe with Dale?"

Mike shook his head. "No, you never see her with any of her women. I don't recognize her at all."

"Has Dale being doing anything unusual recently?"

Mike nodded this time. "Yeah. Dale never misses work. She goes around the different McGuire's Motors branches, depending on the day, but she's always at one of them."

"And what's different?" Ash asked.

"She's hardly been at work, and she's never done that before. When she does come in, it's usually just for a few hours and then she leaves again."

Ash thought she might actually be getting somewhere. "Does anyone know what she's doing?"

"Nope. There's a lot of talk, but no one knows. Except—"

"Except what?"

"I heard she asked for a lot of parts to be ordered for some personal project, but they weren't for her race car like usual. It was for a twelve-year-old Ford. Dale doesn't drive old cars, unless they are classics."

"Could you get me the address they were sent to?"

Mike shook his head. "No way. I don't have that kind of access. Only Ted, or my bosses Val and Sammy, can get that kind of info."

Ash took the hundred pounds she had and put them in his shirt pocket. "There's five hundred more if you get me the address they were delivered to."

Mike took the money from his pocket and squeezed it in his hand. He was obviously tempted.

"Come on, Mike. It's easy money."

"If I do, you won't ever grass me in, will you?"

Ash smiled and said, "Cross my heart."

❖

Becca was in her studio working on the prints she had taken earlier in the week. The job wasn't a lot of money, but it would be enough to pay some household expenses. If she could just hang in there with these smaller jobs until the baby was born, maybe then she could find her way out of the financial hole she was in by winning a few big contracts. If Eugene Hardy could wait that long. She had an excellent reputation, and hopefully that would help towards the contracts she'd had to break.

She saved her work and looked at the time. Two o'clock, time to take some tea and biscuits out to Dale. Becca had to admit that after being alone in this big draughty house for so long, it was comforting to know Dale was out in the garage pottering away with her car and singing along with Britney Spears. In fact it was more than comforting. Dale's presence made her smile.

Becca had never met anyone like Dale before. Her first impressions had been completely wrong. They were from different sides of the tracks, true, but Dale was highly intelligent, and an extremely good businesswoman. She was a diamond in the rough, and someone who had run from her past, much like she did. Whatever that hurt and pain was made her determined to do the right thing by Jake and the baby she was carrying.

Becca sat back in her chair and soothed the baby, as it moved around, with tender loving strokes. "Shh, little one. You're hyperactive, just like Dale."

She gasped when she realized what she'd said. There'd been a moment when she'd begun to think that she was carrying Dale's baby, and not just hers. It was probably when they'd shared the special moment of feeling the baby kick.

The way her body and mind were reacting to Dale was so out of character for her it was scary. Maybe Jake and the baby were trying to tell her something. Maybe it wasn't wrong to ask for help and maybe Dale was meant to be the one to do it.

Becca was just about to leave the desk when her mobile rang. It was the school, and she answered with a feeling of dread.

"Hello?"

The school secretary must have heard the panic in her voice because she said, "It's Westview, Ms. Harper. There's nothing to worry about. We've had a power cut at school. There are roadworks going on outside the school and they seem to have gone through the mains supply. We're asking that all day students be picked up and taken home for their own safety."

Becca let out a sigh of relief. "Oh? No problem. I'll come straight to get him. Thank you."

She took her time going downstairs and out to the garage to get the car. The garage door was open and all she could see of Dale was a pair of overall covered legs.

"Dale? Could I steal the car for a bit, I—"

Then she realized all four tyres were off the car and piled in the corner, and her heart sank.

Dale pushed out from under the car and smiled at her first, but then saw the look of worry on her face.

"Hey, hen, what's wrong?" Dale said, jumping to her feet. "Are you and the wee yin okay?"

"Yes, we're fine, but I have to go and pick up Jake from school. There's been a power cut. But my car has no wheels. Can you put them on quickly?"

Dale looked a little sheepish. "Ugh, no, not really. It doesn't have a battery in either—I'm fitting a new one."

Becca shook her head with frustration. "How am I supposed to get Jake? Can I take your van? I'm insured for any vehicle."

Dale walked over to her. "Becca, you can't drive my truck in your condition with no experience. It's a heavy vehicle to drive. Let me take you."

"No!" Becca snapped. "Jake can't see you. He'll get too involved with you and—"

Dale grasped her lightly by the arms. "Look at me, Becca. I swear to you, I won't hurt Jake or try to come between you if you let me see him. You said you would try to trust me. Please let me help?"

Becca's panic and stress were making her angry. "You're using this as an opportunity to see Jake."

Dale threw her hands up in the air. "Oh, for fuck's sake, Becca. What I'm trying to do is help and take care of you. The same as I have been trying to do since I came into your life. I care, okay? I care about you, I care about the baby, and I care about Jake. So shoot me. Is that a crime?"

Becca instantly regretted what she had said. Dale had done nothing but be kind to them, and hadn't she just told herself in the study that maybe Dale came into their lives for a reason? She probably would have great difficulty driving Dale's van too.

She looked at Dale square in the eye and said, "You can't swear around Jake and the baby."

A smile broke out on Dale's face. "Yeah? I won't. I promise, no swearing in front of them."

"Let's go and get Jake then."

Out of nowhere Dale engulfed her in a hug. "Thanks, hen. Thank you for letting me see him. I know how hard it is for you, and I promise I won't let you down."

Becca closed her eyes and allowed herself to enjoy the feeling of being held in someone's arms. It wasn't just anyone though. It was Dale, and the crook of her neck smelled warm, safe, and thrilling.

Her body felt like it was waking from a long slumber, and where she'd previously felt nothing, she suddenly felt everything. Dale's smell, the urge to taste, the desire to run her fingers through that thick, dark, messy hair.

She pushed back from her before she did just that. "Let's go and get Jake then."

❖

Dale tapped her fingers on the steering wheel nervously. She was waiting in the parking area of Westview School, while Becca went to get Jake and explain that Dale would be taking them home.

She never thought she would be this nervous. This was what she'd wanted since she'd offered to come back and help Becca out. To see Jake, and help Becca and the baby any way she could. Now that was happening and she was a bit scared.

What if Jake was angry at her for leaving them? What if he had decided this situation was all too weird for him?

She let out a breath. *Calm, keep calm.*

The school looked really impressive. Becca had told her about all its facilities and the program for gifted children. It was night and day to the school Dale had gone to in the East End of Glasgow. She was proud that her child was getting better opportunities in life than she had, but how long could Becca keep up with these school fees? Who knew? What she did know was that she didn't want to disappear. She wanted to be a friend to this family and help them. Maybe give some meaning to her own life at the same time.

Don't blow it.

At last she saw Becca and Jake coming out of the school reception area. She got out of the van, and when Jake spotted her, he ran as fast as he could towards her.

As he got nearer he slowed up, looking a bit unsure of himself. "Hey, wee man. How are you?"

Becca walked up behind him and said, "It's okay, Jake."

Now filled with confidence, he jumped into her arms. "You didn't forget about us. You came back!"

Dale hugged him tightly and said, "I told you, I always keep my promises."

She looked over to Becca and mouthed, "Are you okay?"

She nodded, but looked tense. Dale hoped she didn't mind Jake giving her this sort of affection. They would need to have a proper talk when they were alone.

Dale never wanted to step on Becca's toes. Becca was Jake's mummy, and she had to make her believe that role would always be hers. "Okay, wee man. Let me get you in the van and then I'll help your mummy, okay?"

Jake nodded enthusiastically.

The van had three seats in the front, and so she strapped a smiling and excited Jake into the middle one. The she went around to help Becca, who had gotten up into the high van cab with great difficulty when they'd left the vicarage.

Becca appeared pensive, and Dale understood why. It would be hard enough for any parent to all of a sudden have someone else competing for their son's affections, but even harder given Becca's trust and emotional issues.

"Are you sure you're okay with this?"

Becca gave a forced smile. "It's fine."

Dale reached out and lightly touched Becca's hand. "Look, I get it. You don't have to pretend or put a brave face on it. It's frightening having me in your lives, and although we've made some progress, you don't completely trust my intentions."

Much to Dale's surprise, Becca squeezed her hand back and simply said, "I want to."

Those three words hit Dale full square in the chest. Coming from someone so cautious and guarded as Becca, *I want to* meant the absolute world.

"Thank you. I know what that means, and I won't let you down."

They hadn't let go of each other's hands and were simply gazing into one other's eyes. Dale wondered if Becca was feeling as many new emotions as she was.

She studied Becca's plump rosy lips and had the biggest urge to lean in and kiss them. She jumped out of her skin when Jake knocked on the window to get them to hurry up.

"We should get going," Becca said. She was helped up into the cab with the greatest care, and Dale even put her seat belt on. It felt wonderful to Becca to be taken care of in this new way.

Despite all her outward tough signs, Dale was so gentle with her, and in those few seconds Becca wondered if Dale would be equally gentle making love to her.

Anyone who saw Dale McGuire would assume that she liked fast cars and equally fast women, but so far Dale hadn't been what she expected. Everything about Dale was unexpected, and that was what made her so interesting, and exciting.

Dale got into the driver's side and said, "Okay, let's go."

As they drove, Becca was astonished at how much Jake was talking. He was so excited about having Dale there, but it wasn't just Dale—he was talking to them both equally, and enjoying the fact that they were all here together.

"I'm so starving, Mummy. What's for dinner?" Jake asked.

"Oh no!" Becca smacked her forehead. "In all the hurry I forgot to turn on the slow cooker. I had a casserole prepared for us. It'll never be finished on time."

Jake's shoulders slumped. "It's okay, Mummy."

"I'm sorry, Pooh Bear. It'll need to be scrambled eggs on toast."

"Becca?" Dale interrupted. "I'll have to get some dinner from somewhere anyway, so could I take you both to dinner? My treat?"

Jake was practically bouncing out of the van. "Yes, *please,* Mummy. Let's have dinner with Dale."

Becca should have been angry at Dale for putting her in that position. In fact she would have been incandescent before she and Dale had had their brief discussion outside the van. But what she had said to Dale was true. She wanted to trust her, and to do that, she had to give a little.

"That would be very nice, Dale. Thank you."

"Aye?" Dale was nearly bouncing with as much excitement as Jake. "Where do you want to go, wee man?"

"Somewhere with pizza," Jake exclaimed.

Dale looked over to her, unsure. "Is that okay, Becca?"

"Sounds wonderful."

CHAPTER ELEVEN

Dale drove them to a popular pizza restaurant about thirty minutes from Jake's school, as there were no restaurants anywhere near Becca's vicarage.

When they arrived at the restaurant car park, Dale lifted Becca down from the cab and whispered to her, "Thank you for this."

"Don't worry about it. The baby is craving hot peppers anyway." Becca smiled.

Dale couldn't count how many feelings she was experiencing as she led Becca and Jake into the restaurant—warmth, love, pride… being a part of something.

The waiter who met them at the door said, "Family of three?"

Dale glanced quickly at Becca to see how she reacted to that, and she just smiled at her.

Dale answered, "Yes, family of three." Her heart could have burst as she led them to the table. She helped Becca with her jacket and pulled out her chair. She noticed Becca's cheeks were a bit red.

"Are you okay?"

"Just a bit hot and flustered. I'll be okay in a minute."

Dale said to the waiter, "Could you bring a large glass of ice water immediately, please."

"Of course."

When Dale sat Becca squeezed her hand. "Thank you for noticing and thinking of me."

"You're welcome. Is the baby feeling okay?"

"Yes, the wee yin is fine," Becca said, using her turn of phrase. Dale laughed at the way it sounded in her upper-middle-class accent.

"I just get this way sometimes with my blood pressure. I can feel light-headed, headachey, and a bit dizzy. I just need to sit down and drink some water."

"Mummy, look, this place is so cool. Look over there."

They both looked behind them and saw a big screen on the back wall of the restaurant playing movies for the kids.

"Wow, this place is cool, Jake." Dale was on cloud nine.

"Can I go and watch?"

"After we eat," Becca said.

Dale ordered for them, and after about ten minutes the food arrived. When the server arrived with Becca's hot and spicy pizza with extra chillies, Dale was surprised.

"That looks so hot—are you going to be able to eat that?"

Becca smiled. "Oh yes. Chillies are my baby craving. I go through jars and jars of jalapeños. I love them on dry crackers."

"I love hot food, but even that would be too hot for me," Dale said.

As they started to eat, Dale laughed as she watched Becca and Jake eating their sliced pizzas with a knife and fork.

"What's wrong?" Becca asked.

"You eat pizza with a knife and fork? You really are posh, Ms. Harper."

Becca put her knife and fork down, and politely dabbed her mouth with her napkin. "Oh, and what is the correct etiquette for eating pizza, pray tell?"

Dale held up her hands and wiggled her fingers. "With your hands, it's the law."

Jake and Becca laughed as they watched Dale demonstrate pizza eating. Jake copied her straight away.

Then Dale said with a wink, "Come on, posh girl. Live a little."

She did and they enjoyed the rest of their food with Jake talking insistently and filling Dale in about his life so far.

While they waited on dessert, Jake went to sit with the other children and watch the movie on the big screen, giving Becca and Dale a chance to talk.

"Thanks for letting me do this. It's meant the world to me, honestly," Dale said.

Becca took a sip of water and said, "Thank you for inviting us. I'm sure you'd rather be out on a Friday night."

Dale took Becca's hand. "There is nowhere on earth I'd rather be right now."

Becca glanced down at their entwined hands and was silent for a few moments before saying, "I know you want to spend time with Jake—"

"No," Dale said quickly, "not just because of Jake, because of you too. You are a really special woman, Becca."

Becca laughed. "I'm nowhere near special. I'm distrustful, secretive, and I've taught Jake to distrust the world. Look at him."

Dale turned around and saw he was sitting at the other end of the screen, away from the other children.

"What's he going to be like when he grows up? He'll have no social skills, and the most meaningful conversation he'll be able to have will be with his computer."

"Becca, you're being too hard on yourself. He's a wonderful boy who knows how to love and to be kind to others. He was comfortable with me from the moment he met me. He talked to me like he'd known me all his life. He was polite and even gave me tips so I wouldn't get into trouble with you for my language. I could never have done the job you have, been a mother like you have. I would be proud to call him my son."

Dale pulled back, thinking she had gone too far. "I'm sorry. I shouldn't have said that."

"That's okay. I understand what you meant." Becca sighed. "I need to help him with his social skills and have him mix with other children, but yet protect him. I told you there was a reason we were out in the country, away from the world. I'm trying to protect him from what I went through."

Dale didn't expect an answer but asked anyway. "What did you go through, Becca?"

Becca shook her head. "I can't, Dale. I just can't." Then she added, "Not yet anyway."

That one little phrase gave her hope that Becca might one day trust her enough to let her in. "I understand. We all have our secrets and hurts."

"Even Dale McGuire?"

Dale noodled. "Aye, me too."

They sat quietly for a few minutes, both equally unable to talk about the things which made and moulded them.

"Let me pay the bill and I'll get you both home."

❖

Jake fell asleep on the way home, and Dale carried him into the house and up to bed. Becca's heart fluttered as she watched Dale be so gentle and lay Jake on his bed. She should probably have felt jealous of the attention she was getting from Jake, but it was the opposite. She enjoyed seeing them interact and talk about things that Jake wouldn't talk about with her—video games, movies, and toys. She could see why Dale was so popular with her god-daughter.

Becca lifted the covers and put Jake's hot water bottle under. It was cold in the bedroom with the heating playing up.

When they got downstairs, Becca said, "Have you got time for a coffee before you go?"

"I've got all the time in the world for you."

Becca gulped, feeling the flutter of excitement in her stomach again. "Why don't we sit in the kitchen. It's much warmer there." She walked in, pressed on the kettle, and said, "Tea or coffee?"

She turned around to find Dale pulling off her hooded jumper. The T-shirt rode up and gave her a tantalising glimpse of her well-honed body. Becca's cheeks started to get hot again, and the heat intensified when she saw the Celtic band tattoo coiled around her defined biceps.

It was such a long time since she had felt turned-on by someone, like a sexual being. Those urges were just something she pushed deep down and didn't think she'd need again. Dale made those feelings come out of hibernation with a bang.

"Are you all right, Becca?"

"What?" Becca had been caught staring. "Sorry, I was miles away. Tea or coffee?"

"Tea, please."

Becca prepared two cups of tea and brought them over to the kitchen table.

"Can I ask you something, Becca?"

"Yes, what is it?"

Dale tapped her fingers nervously on the table. "You said you only trusted your ex, Trent. How long since you've been with her?"

"Oh, a long time. About eleven and a half years. Trent's a good friend. She helped me and took care of me at a time in my life that I needed someone to trust. She was the daughter of my family lawyer. She runs her family firm now."

"Were you in love?" Dale looked down immediately. "I'm sorry, that's a really personal question."

Becca smiled. "Yes, it is, but I'll tell you. Yes, we were in love, but we didn't want the same things. Trent liked city life. Going out to restaurants, socializing within our group of friends. Whereas I wanted to settle down and have a family. We weren't compatible in the end, but I know she did love me, just not the way I wanted. I suppose you'd understand that. Your social life is important to you."

"It doesn't mean I never wanted a family," Dale snapped.

Becca realized quickly she'd said the wrong thing. "I'm sorry, Dale. I didn't mean—"

"No, I'm sorry. I should never have snapped like that. It just gets frustrating sometimes. People make assumptions about me, because of the way I dress, my personality, and because I've never been in a relationship, like I'm some kind of love 'em and leave 'em type. But I've never wanted to make notches on my bedpost. I just have never wanted to trust and let someone know me. So sex is really all I can give women I meet. They want Dale from the bar, the life and soul of the party, but that's not the real me. The only people who know me are Val, Sammy, and Mia."

Becca could feel that Dale desperately wanted to be understood, and that she had so much to give a woman.

"There's nothing wrong with being the life and soul of the Party, Dale. You're the first person to make me laugh in fifteen years," Becca joked.

"I guess that's a badge of honour I should get then?"

"Exactly," Becca said. "Awarded to Dale McGuire for achieving the seemingly impossible task of making Becca Harper laugh."

Dale gave her a wink. "See, you do have a sense of humour."

Becca cupped her hands around her mug of decaf tea, hoping the heat would seep into her body. "I haven't needed it for so long, I didn't think it worked any more. Amongst other things."

Why did I say that? Becca chastised herself, knowing Dale would probably get her inference. She tried to change the subject quickly. "Tell me about your friends, Mia's parents. You talk so fondly about them. They sound like lovely people."

"They are. They took me in off the street when I came to London. They understood why I ran away."

Becca heard Dale's voice crack, and her heart hurt for her.

Dale covered her eyes with her hands. "I'm sorry. I never talk like this with anyone."

"You can talk to me anytime, Dale. I can see you've got some painful memories."

"You could say that. Anyway"—Dale pulled herself together in seconds—"that doesn't matter."

"You have a really sensitive side to you. Why don't you show it more often?"

Dale looked at Becca like she was crazy. "Me? Sensitive? No way. I'm Dale McGuire the joker, happy go lucky, nothing can keep me down."

"That's only because you don't allow people to see under that bravado. I can see past it."

Dale shifted uncomfortably in her seat. She was starting to feel a bit defensive. "Yeah? Well good for you."

"Why are you annoyed? It's a good thing to be sensitive," Becca said.

"No, it's fucking not. It might be good in your little protected upper-middle-class bubble where everyone is in touch with their feelings, but not in the real world. Where I came from, being in touch with your feelings got the shit kicked out of you. Besides, you have no right to lecture anyone. You're so far away from your own feelings that you're positively frosty."

The look of shock on Becca's face made her understand she had messed up and possibly blown a whole evening of getting Becca to trust her. *Run!*

Dale had to get out of there before Becca told her to go and rejected her. She stood up quickly and said, "Thanks for tonight. I'll come back and put your car together tomorrow."

Still Becca said nothing, so she left as quickly as she could.

"You are a fucking idiot!" Dale told herself as she stood looking into her bathroom mirror.

She'd had one of the best nights of her life, spending time with her son, her own flesh and blood, and his beautiful mother, and she ruined it.

Dale looked at her reflection accusingly. "Why did you do that to yourself?"

She shook her head in disgust and walked out of the bathroom to her bedroom, and sat on the bed. She stared at her smartphone, trying to summon the bravery to text Becca and tell her she was sorry.

Dale picked up one of the photos Becca had given her of Jake. It was the one taken of newborn Jake with Becca, right after he was born. She ran her finger over Jake's little head and then Becca's smiling face.

It was crazy and she hadn't known them long, but there was no doubt in her mind that she wanted to be part of their lives. She wanted more nights like last night—well, except when she had done her level best to mess things up.

Why had she?

I was scared.

Becca was so guarded that she had no idea if she would ever be able to mend what she had broken, but she had to try.

Dale picked up her phone and texted an apology. She got into bed and waited for a reply. She put on the TV in the background and continued to wait. Half an hour went by and nothing.

"Oh, come on, Becca. Give me a chance," Dale pleaded with her phone.

As she waited she must have fallen asleep, because she woke up to the alarm on her phone buzzing insistently. "Oh, give it a rest, man."

Dale pulled the covers over her head and turned over to go back to sleep, before she remembered last night and what she had said. Now she was wide awake with a knot of worry in her stomach.

She sat up and looked at her phone. No message from Becca, just one to phone Sammy when she could.

Thinking she could do with the advice she called Sammy. "Hi, mate, it's Dale."

"How are you doing? Did you get on okay fixing Becca's car?"

"Aye, I had great day. Becca let me see Jake, and I took them to dinner, and—"

"Whoa, slow down. She let you see Jake? How did that come about? I thought she was really wary of you?"

"She was." Dale ran her hands through her messy hair. "Probably still is now, but yesterday we talked and then Jake's school was closed for the afternoon, and I had her tyres off, so she kinda had to trust me a little bit."

"How did it feel to see him again?"

Dale got up off her bed and picked up one of the pictures of Jake. "Unbelievable. I can't describe what it feels like to spend time with him, knowing he's part of me."

"But he's not yours, Dale. He's Becca's child," Sammy said firmly.

"I know that," Dale snapped. "You don't have to remind me."

"I think I do. You're getting more and more involved with this family, and I'm frightened you'll get hurt."

"Sammy, listen, I know there's a probability I'll get hurt, but that's worth it just to have spent time with him, and maybe the wee girl that's coming. I'm not going to tell any kid of mine that I don't want to know them. That's just not happening."

Sammy sighed. "Okay, I understand your reasons. Just be careful."

"Cheers, I will. I won't be working on the race car today. I need to put Becca's car right."

"No problem. Oh, by the way, Val remembered where she knew Becca's face from."

"Where?"

"Google Victoria Carter and the Carter fraud, and you'll find all the information you need."

Just then a text came through from Becca's phone.

"I need to go, mate. I'll call you later."

A bad man came and frightened Mummy, now she's not well. Mummy needs help.

Dale's heart sank like a stone. She grabbed her clothes and got ready as quickly as she could.

Chapter Twelve

Dale pulled up outside the vicarage with a screech. She saw Sadie at the front trying her best to clean out all the wood and splinters from the broken front door.

"Sadie, are they okay? What happened?"

"I'm so glad you're here, Dale. Becca won't let me call the police. They're both upstairs. Becca's feeling under the weather."

"How did the door get broken?" Dale asked.

Sadie leaned the broom against the wall and said, "I woke up with a start. It was about quarter past one, and I heard some loud bangs. I got myself up and looked out of the window, but I can't see the driveway from my bedroom, so I phoned over to Becca's to make sure they were all right. Little Jake answered and told me two men broke in."

"I need to see them." Dale went into the house and ran upstairs. She saw Jake standing outside the main bathroom, looking worried.

"Jake?"

He looked up and ran into her arms. "Mummy's not feeling well. The bad men scared her."

She squeezed Jake tight and kissed his head. "It's okay, wee man. I'm here now. I'll take care of everything. You don't have to worry any more. Okay?"

His tears started to fall. She guessed it was pure relief that someone was here to take charge and protect them. Jake was too young to bear that worry for his mother.

Dale wiped away his tears with her thumb. "I'll go and talk to Mummy. Why don't you go downstairs and get Sadie to give you a glass of water for Mummy."

He nodded and ran downstairs. Dale knocked at the bathroom door. "Becca? It's Dale."

"Don't come in," Becca shouted.

Dale sighed. "I know I'm not your favourite person after last night. I was wrong and I'm sorry. Besides I'm the only option you've got right now."

"I don't want you to see me like this."

Dale walked in the door and found Becca in her nightdress, leaning against the toilet and looking as white as a sheet.

"Becca, what's wrong? Is it the baby?"

She knelt down beside her and, without thinking, began to rub her back.

"I was so dizzy. I felt sick, and then I was sick over and over."

"Are you still feeling like you're gonna puke?"

"Yes, but I think it's stopped."

"Right, come on then, hen." Dale lifted a surprised Becca in her arms.

"Dale, I don't smell very good. Let me walk myself."

Dale continued to walk out the bathroom door, with Becca cradled in her arms, and made for her bedroom. "Who cares? I stink. I had to run over here without a shower, so we can stink together."

She carefully laid Becca down on the bed and pulled the covers over her. "It's too cold in here. Once I've got you settled, I'll get you a hot water bottle."

Becca moaned, and Dale knelt by the side of the bed. "I told Jake not to contact you. We're not your responsibility."

"What if I want you to be my responsibility?"

Becca didn't answer and an awkward silence hung in the air.

"I'm sorry about last night," Dale said softly. "I got a bit scared. I'm not used to being so open."

"It's okay. I got your text. I'm not used to being open and taking help either. Let's forget about it."

"What happened then?"

"Two men showed up to remind me that I owed their boss money."

Dale felt a burning anger deep within her gut. "What is this, the Mafia?"

Becca pulled the covers under her chin to get warm. "Something like that."

Dale put her hand on Becca's forehead and stroked her thumb along one of her eyebrows in a soothing fashion. "They didn't touch you, or Jake, did they?"

"No, they aren't at that stage yet. They just wanted to scare me, so they kicked open the door, knocked things over, and made a lot of noise. Of course I was anxious and I just began to feel ill later."

"You don't sound too surprised," Dale said.

"Nothing surprises me about Eugene Hardy."

Dale sat back on her heels, feeling a bit shocked. "You owe money to Eugene Hardy? Eugene Hardy of the Hardy brothers?"

Becca nodded, and Dale said in surprise, "Fuck me. This is serious then."

The Hardy brothers were well known gangsters in the London criminal world, and everyone knew that the last thing you wanted to do was owe them money.

She never heard Jake come in, but he appeared at her side with a glass of water, ready to get Dale into trouble. "Don't swear, Dale. You'll upset Mummy."

Dale took the glass of water from him. "You're right. I'm sorry, wee man. Here, Becca, drink some water." Dale didn't want to talk any more about Eugene Hardy in front of Jake, so she left that subject for now. "Becca, give me your doctor's number and I'll call him out to check you over."

"No," Becca said with alarm in her voice. "I don't need the doctor. I just need some rest."

"Oh, come on, Becca. Your blood pressure must be through the roof to make you so sick and dizzy. Why wouldn't you want to be checked over, for the baby's sake?"

Becca said nothing and closed her eyes, bringing the conversation to an end.

"Okay, you want to play it that way? Jake, go and get me Mummy's cell phone."

He immediately ran to his mother's dressing table and came back with the phone.

"You wouldn't dare," Becca warned.

Jake handed her the phone, and she began to look through the address book.

"Oh, I would. Let me see, Dr. Thorpe? Is that him?"

"Dale, I'm fine. You're making a mountain out of a molehill."

The sheer panic in Becca's face made her feel guilty. She was doing the right thing, wasn't she? "Give me one good reason why not."

"Because he might tell me I can't work at all, even the small jobs, and I can't afford it."

Dale pressed the doctor's number and it started to ring. "Not a good enough answer."

❖

Becca sat up in bed and watched Dr. Thorpe write her out a prescription. She was still mad that Dale had ignored her and gone ahead and called him. She would do anything to protect her unborn child, but if she couldn't even take some of the small jobs, then there would be no money coming in.

The doctor ripped the prescription off his pad and brought it over to her. "I've adjusted your blood pressure medication. This new strength should help you almost immediately, but no more working. You need complete rest."

Becca started to protest, but Dr. Thorpe silenced her. "No, no arguments, Rebecca. If you want to keep your baby healthy, then you follow my instructions. Remember, things could get a lot worse."

What could she do? She was in an impossible situation. "If you insist, Doctor."

Dr. Thorpe started to pack his things back in his suitcase, and said, "Who's your new protector out there? Is she related?"

"No, not related."

"Funny, she looks so much like Jake, I thought she must be related in some way."

It was strange. This was the first time Becca didn't feel bad about thinking that, and her heart skipped a beat. She decided to have a little fun with the doctor. "Yes, well, that makes sense, since she got me pregnant."

Dr. Thorpe nearly swallowed his tongue. "Oh? Um...yes. Very good. Well I'll leave you all to it."

Becca laughed inside at his blustering. He was an older man but had never questioned her about having a baby on her own, about being gay, or anything, but that statement had caught him off guard.

"Well, I hope you feel better, Rebecca, take care."

Becca chuckled as he hurried out of the bedroom. Dale popped her head around the door. "Hi, can I come in, or are you still angry at me?"

"Come in."

Dale stood by her bed, hands in pockets and looking quite nervous. "That doctor gave me the strangest look when he left."

Becca grinned and said, "I told him you got me pregnant."

"Oh, thanks a million, hen. He probably thinks I've got hidden extra parts now."

Becca giggled. "You deserved it for taking charge and giving me no choice."

"I suppose so. At least you're putting your new-found sense of humour to good use. So what did he say?"

"He's changed my prescription and, as predicted, told me not to work until I'm feeling better."

"Good, that sounds like a plan."

Dale clearly had no idea how bad her finances were, and she wasn't about to make it clear for her. There was no way she would accept charity and that would probably be what Dale would try to offer her next.

Either Dale really, truly cared about them, or she felt guilty, and Becca didn't want to contemplate either.

Dale picked up the new prescription. "I'll go and get this for you."

"Thanks, Dale, I appreciate it."

Dale ruffled her hair, and rocked back on her heels nervously. She was desperate to ask this question but sure Becca would clam up.

"Before I go, will you tell me how and why you could possibly be indebted to the Hardy brothers?"

"I don't want to talk about it, and anyway, it's not your burden to carry."

"Oh, for God's sake, Becca. Is it not clear by now that I care? I might have met you and Jake in a weird way, but it doesn't change the fact that I like you and want to help make things easier for you. Stop talking about burdens. I've got no one in my life to worry about but my friends and Mia. I have no real family. No one, Becca. What's wrong with me caring? Tell me?"

Becca sighed. "There's nothing wrong it."

Dale sat down on the edge of the bed. "Listen, Becca. We've both got our secrets. I think we have to be honest with each other. I'm not going to go away unless you look me in the eye and tell me to go. Do you want me to go?"

She could see the tension clearly written on Becca's face. Becca's head probably wanted her to go, but her heart? Well, Dale prayed she was burrowing her way slowly in there.

"Do you want me to go? Becca?"

"No," Becca said quietly.

Dale moved closer and took Becca's hand. "I'll tell you mine if you tell me yours?"

Again Becca seemed uneasy. "I don't think I can. It's such a long time since I've told anyone. And one person I trusted completely betrayed me."

"You think I'd betray you? Why would I want to do that when I'm spending every moment I can trying to help and make things easier for you?"

Becca took her hand out of Dale's. "The very first person I told my story to, opened the heart of my family to, I thought was trying to help me."

This was so hard. She was trying everything she could think of to secure Becca's trust, but it wasn't working. Maybe if she took the first step? Taking that step was easier said than done.

"How about I go first?" Dale clasped her hands and looked down at the floor. "Only Sammy and Val know this, and now you. It's hurt me for a long time, but without Sammy's and Val's understanding, I don't know where I'd be."

"Dale, you don't have to do this to prove a point," she heard Becca say.

But she did. As scary as it was, she wanted to tell her story to Becca. No, she needed to.

"I came from a pretty normal working-class Scottish family. My da taught me everything I know about tools, decorating, repairs, anything manual. He was a tough man's man, but he loved his family, and surprisingly he didn't seem to mind having a daughter like me, who was more masculine than feminine. My ma said I was the son he never had."

"Did you have any brothers or sisters?" Becca said.

"Aye, one sister, Nora, but she was much older than me. She was out of the house and married when I was about twelve. She moved to Aberdeen with her husband, and we only saw her once a year if we were lucky. Da died when I was sixteen, and that just left me and my ma."

Dale felt the bed move and Becca move to sit beside her. "I'm sorry to hear that."

"Yeah, well, we managed okay. I went to college to be a mechanic, and Ma was a cleaner at a local doctor's surgery."

"Were you really close?" Becca asked.

Dale laughed softly. "You could say that. My wee ma was the best ma in the world to me. Then…"

Becca slipped her hand onto Dale's knee. "What happened?"

Dale gulped hard trying to keep her emotions in check. "She had a stroke and died when I wasn't quite eighteen. It came right out of the blue, and it hit me so hard. I was in a daze and I just couldn't take anything in. Luckily my sister came back and handled everything. The funeral, lawyers, papers, all that kind of stuff. In fact she was really insistent that she be the one to handle everything, despite the fact that we didn't see her much. I just didn't know why then."

Reliving it and saying it were so much harder than she anticipated. Dale clasped her hands together when she felt them start to tremor.

"Dale," Becca said, "I know how hard this is. You don't have to do it just to prove yourself to me."

Dale knew then she would just have to find the extra strength to be honest. "Yes, I do, because you don't trust me, so I have to show that I trust you."

She took a breath and continued, "The night after the funeral, I was looking through my ma's things, looking for her Bible. She was very faithful to the church, and it was her most precious item. I found it eventually and then everything, my whole world, just fell apart."

"What did you find?" Becca asked.

Dale couldn't believe she was actually going to say this. "Tucked away at the back of the Bible in an envelope was an adoption certificate for me, and a picture of my sister Nora, in a hospital bed, holding a baby, just like the picture of you and Jake."

Becca gasped. "Oh my God, you mean…"

"I mean my ma was my granny, and Nora was my mother."

Becca slipped her arm around Dale's shoulders. Dale closed her eyes and experienced a warmth and comfort that she hadn't felt for a long, long time.

Becca's fingers somehow found their way to Dale's nape, and she gently stroked the soft, short hairs there.

"Did you talk to your mum about it?"

"Nora," Dale corrected her. "She was not my ma. I did, a few days later, after I'd been on a bit of a bender. I felt like my whole life was a lie, but at the same time everything started to make sense. Nora and I were never close as sisters, and anytime I tried to show her affection, she pushed me away."

"She was trying to keep her distance and not bond with you?"

"Aye."

"What did she say to you when you confronted her?" Becca said.

"I went to her house, and she was shocked that I had found out. That's why she had taken care of all the funeral paperwork, so that I wouldn't find out. Even after my ma had died, and I had no one else in the world to care for me, she didn't want me to know I did still have a mother."

Dale started to tell her story and get lost herself in her thoughts.

Nora stood with her back to Dale, gazing out of the living room window. Dale got up from the sofa, tears rolling down her face.

"You watched me breaking my heart at Ma's funeral, and you never said anything. You left the funeral without a word of when I would see you again. Knowing I had no one left in the world but you. No clue how I would pay the bills or rent on my own. A sister would never do that, but you did, and worse, because you were my mother and had been lying to me my whole fucking life!" Dale screamed.

Nora turned around said calmly, "Don't shout or swear, Dale. My children are asleep, and I don't want them to hear you."

"You don't want your children to be disturbed? Well one of your children is standing in front of you, and I'm fucking disturbed. Why did you do this? Why did you do this? Why didn't you want me?"

"I was fourteen years old and in no position to have a baby. The mother that you thought was so wonderful made me feel ashamed."

Dale was more hurt by the almost disinterested way in which Nora was reacting to her fury.

"Why are you so cold, Nora? You had choices. Everyone has a choice—you could have kept me if you wanted to."

Finally Nora snapped. "You were a mistake, okay? Is that what you want to hear? You were a drunken mistake I made at a party. I had to drop out of school, I messed up my exams and nearly my whole future because of it, and I didn't want to be reminded of it or held back any more. Mum offered to take you, and it was the best thing for all of us."

Dale felt like her heart had been ripped out and thrown on the floor between them.

"I was a drunken mistake? Who says that to their child? You are a fucking cold-hearted bitch."

"Get out, now," Nora said.

"Don't worry. I will. I hope your children never feel the pain I'm feeling now."

Becca felt the tears roll down her cheeks. It was heartbreaking to hear a mother rejecting a child like that.

Dale wiped her eyes on her sleeve, and Becca rubbed her back. It was obvious now why Dale was so determined to help her and Jake.

"I'm so sorry she hurt you, Dale."

"Yeah, well. I wasn't good enough apparently, unlike her other children. I have a brother and sister that I've never met and I never will. I promised myself when I left that house that if I was lucky enough to ever have a family, I would never turn my back on them, no matter how hard it was. When I met Val, she convinced me to write Nora a letter, give her one last chance. She wrote back and told me never to contact her again. She wanted nothing to do with me."

Finally, Becca lost that part of herself that had doubted Dale.

"I believe you, Dale. I understand why you want to help us. Thank you for coming back, even though I've distrusted you. And I'm here for you too. I would never have Jake or the wee yin on my own."

Dale turned around and cupped Becca's face tenderly. "You are their mother, the mother I would have chosen to have my children with, if I'd known you."

The intensity of the moment made it difficult for Becca to breathe. Her lips parted slightly, anticipating that Dale would kiss her.

Dale moved slowly towards her lips and breathed, "I'll always be here for you if you let me. If you tell me your story, I'll do nothing but help you."

It was so tempting. The last woman to say that to her had

proved to be the worst mistake of her life. But Dale was different, wasn't she?

Dale got closer to her lips and her heart started to pound. Becca hadn't been kissed in such a long time, but still she knew that this felt special and different. At the last moment Dale rested her forehead against Becca's instead of kissing her and whispered, "I know who you are, Victoria Carter. But I don't know your story, only the media's."

Becca gasped. "You know? How?"

"Val saw the pictures and recognized you from somewhere, and then it finally came to her. Sammy told me last night to Google your name."

Becca started to speak but Dale put a finger to her lips.

"Don't say anything. I'll go and get your prescription, and you can have a think, but the truth will set you free."

Becca was utterly stunned and shocked. Dale got up and picked up her jacket.

"I won't be long. Relax and we can talk when I get back."

❖

Becca heard doors open and close downstairs, and then Jake come running up to her room.

"Mummy, Trent is here to see you. She's in the kitchen." Jake's face showed how much he wanted her there.

"Okay, sweetie, I'll come down." Becca had called Trent earlier to get her advice about the debt.

Jake's scowl did not dissipate quickly. "I told her Dale would be back soon to look after us, but she still wanted to come in."

Jake didn't like Trent and he never would, it seemed. Trent didn't talk to him like she was interested, and Jake picked that up. Dale was very different—she was very different in every aspect.

"Why don't you go and tell Trent I need a few minutes to freshen up, and then you go work on your computer?"

"Okay, Mummy. Tell me when Dale gets back. I want her to come and see my computer project."

"I will, Pooh Bear."

After freshening up Becca went downstairs and found Trent in the kitchen with a huge bunch of designer flowers. Trent always was flash.

Trent rose and immediately came to her. "Darling, are you all right? You must have had a terrible shock." Trent guided her to her seat and sat down beside her.

"I'm all right. I didn't feel so good a few hours ago, but the doctor's been to see me and prescribed me some different blood pressure medicine, and the baby is fine."

"The main thing is that *you* are all right, Becca," Trent said pointedly.

Yes, you would think that wouldn't you?

Trent lifted the flowers and said, "Oh, I brought you these."

Becca took the large bunch and gave them a sniff. "Thank you. That's very kind. You didn't have to come all the way out here. I just wanted to let you know what had happened."

"I think now you'll understand why you have to declare bankruptcy. You need to pay Eugene Hardy as soon as possible. If you dispense with your father's mortgage debt, we can use the remainder from the offshore account to pay the Hardy brothers."

Trent put her briefcase on the kitchen table and clicked it open. "I took the liberty of preparing the documents. All you have to do is sign."

Trent placed the document in front of her and handed her the gold fountain pen from her top pocket.

Becca couldn't believe how controlling Trent was being. It was infuriating. She thought she had left this behind her years ago. "No."

"What do you mean, no?"

Becca pushed the papers back to her and said, "Who do you think you are, coming here and telling me what to do? I told you I will not declare bankruptcy and ruin my credit. I always pay my debts."

"But you have no money, Becca. You have to get serious. Eugene Hardy doesn't care that you're a woman, or that you're a pregnant woman. All he sees is someone who owes him money."

"I can handle it. I'm going to re-mortgage the vicarage."

Trent looked around her and shook her head. "They'll laugh you out of the bank if you try to use this place as security. There's a reason why you got it so cheaply."

Becca's anger was starting to turn to hurt. "You don't have to be hurtful, just because I won't follow your advice. I've already applied and I'm waiting on an answer."

"The last thing I want to do is hurt you. I apologize." Trent took her hand. "Please forgive me? You know I'll always love you, don't you?"

❖

Dale whistled as she emptied her bags from the back of the van. Who would have known that doing such mundane tasks for people you cared about would be so much fun? While she was getting Becca's prescription, Dale popped into the supermarket nearby and got some food and drinks for Becca and Jake.

She closed up the van and started to walk to the back door, laden with bags like a packhorse. A bunch of supermarket flowers, her most precious purchase, was safely tucked under her arm. The supermarket called them an autumnal mix. They weren't from a florist or anything fancy, but she hoped Becca would appreciate the thought.

There was one more reason why Dale had a spring on her step. She had told Becca her truth, and Becca hadn't laughed or judged her. Deep inside herself, Dale had always harboured the worry that there was something wrong with her, and that was the reason her mother didn't want her, but loved her other children.

Becca hadn't seen it that way. She had comforted her the way no other person had, not even Val or Sammy. When Dale had looked into Becca's eyes and seen want, she was certain this was the woman for her. Regardless of the children they shared, Dale wanted Becca, and whether Becca knew yet or not, Dale was determined to win her heart.

She got to the back door and didn't bother knocking since

Becca was up in bed. It was tricky turning the handle with all the bags, but she managed it eventually and gave the door a soft kick open with her foot.

When the door opened, she saw the last thing she expected, Becca being held intimately in another woman's arms. Her stomach clenched in anger and jealously.

Becca's eyes snapped open and she let go of the woman immediately.

"Dale? I wasn't expecting you back so soon. Trent came around to give me some legal advice."

"Clearly," Dale said with irritation in her voice.

"Dale?" Trent said. "Becca is this *the* Dale McGuire you were telling me about?"

Becca nodded. "Yes, she's been—"

But Becca didn't get chance to finish her question before Trent stood and confronted Dale.

"Who do you think you are, bursting into Ms. Harper's home?"

Dale ignored her and went to place her bags on the countertop.

"She's been helping me, Trent," Becca said, trying to defuse the situation. But to make things worse Jake came running downstairs and into the kitchen when he heard the noise.

Trent. The ex. That's just what I need when Becca and I are getting closer, Dale thought.

Trent looked at Becca in disbelief. "You let her talk you into allowing her into your life? Are you insane, Becca? You know what you have to lose."

"No, I'm not insane. I'm tired of looking over my shoulder and hiding. I want to learn to trust. Dale doesn't want to take my children—she wants to help us."

Trent rounded on Dale. "I don't know what you've said to convince her, but you should know Becca is not unprotected. She has me to rely on when she needs anything."

Dale had enough of this pompous idiot. "Aye, you're helping her so much that she's living alone in a cold, broken-down house, with no one to care for her."

"That's not my fault, it's hers. She had a dream life before she decided she had to have a child."

"His name is Jake," Dale said through gritted teeth.

Jake had run to her side and cuddled into her hip. Becca got up and stood between Dale and Trent.

"Dale, take Jake to the garage and let me talk to Trent."

"Fine." Dale took her bunch of flowers and dropped them on the table next to Trent's huge bunch.

"I thought you might like these, Becca, but supermarket flowers obviously can't compete with those. Come on, Jake."

Dale was fitting the tyres back onto Becca's car while Jake watched her.

"Trent doesn't like me, Dale."

"I wouldn't take it personally, wee man. She doesn't like me very much either. Pass me the wrench, would you?"

He opened Dale's toolbox and saw an array of different wrenches. "Which one?"

"The big long one," Dale said.

Jake held up the longest one he could see. "This one?"

"That's the one." Dale tightened up the wheel nuts and then moved onto the next.

"What if Trent makes Mummy send you away?"

That's what Dale was afraid of, but she tried not to show Jake she was worried. "I doubt your mummy would be influenced like that. She's a very independent woman, but if she did change her mind about me coming around, I'd try my best to make sure we could still see each other. Remember, I always keep my promises."

Dale and Jake both heard the crunch of gravel on the driveway. They walked to the garage door and saw an angry looking Trent walking towards her car.

When Trent spotted her, she stormed over. "You really have done a number on her, haven't you?"

"I've done nothing but help her. She's a woman all alone in the world, and it took some heavies coming and stirring up trouble to get you from behind your desk in London."

"You have no idea what you're talking about. I've kept Becca safe in all sorts of ways you will never understand, McGuire. I know your reputation, and if you think you can use Becca like the usual women you fuck about with for an hour or two, then you have another think coming. Becca has more class than that."

"Don't talk that way in front of Jake. He doesn't need to hear that," Dale warned.

"I will always love Becca, McGuire. And I will not sit and watch anything happen to her. She is in a lot of trouble, as you probably know. She doesn't have time for someone like you messing her around."

Dale put her arm around Jake's shoulders and decided to make her position clear. "If Becca doesn't want me around, then I'll go, but until she tells me that, go back to your office and leave me to *my* family."

Trent walked off and slammed her car door, and screeched out of the driveway.

"Jake, why don't you go and see if your mummy's okay, and I'll finish the car."

"Okay, but don't run away."

Dale kissed his head and gave him a squeeze. "I promise I'll never run from you, wee man."

Chapter Thirteen

Becca pushed herself up from the seat slowly. The stressful exchange with Trent had left her exhausted. She picked up Dale's supermarket flowers and inhaled their fresh, sweet scent.

A smile spread across her face and the baby kicked softly inside her. She rubbed her hand across her bump and said, "I hear you, little one. Sometimes the more modest package is the best."

Becca got a vase for the flowers and arranged them nicely. She looked around and tried to think where to put them, and saw the perfect place on her kitchen windowsill. Now every time she was busy at the sink, she'd be reminded of Dale and her simple kindness.

It was strange. She'd never seen Trent so territorial before. They hadn't been together in such a long time, but then again she'd never had another relationship since Trent.

It suddenly hit her what she had just thought.

I am not in a relationship with Dale, Becca told herself firmly. But then why did it feel like it was going that way?

Her gaze was drawn to the supermarket bags on the side, and she realized that it was because they were behaving like they were in one. It wasn't forced or artificial—they had just gradually began to knit their lives together. Dale was running errands, bringing groceries home, working in the garage while she pottered in the kitchen, and the thought gave Becca a warm glow inside. Not as hot as when she thought Dale was going to kiss her, but comforting warmth all the same.

She picked up her meds and took a dose. Hopefully she could start to feel like herself again.

Jake came running in the door saying, "Mummy, are you okay? Dale wanted me to check."

"I'm fine. Why don't you ask Dale to come in for tea, and we can talk."

Jake had a panicked look on his face. "You're not going to send her away, are you, Mummy?"

"No, I won't do that. We just have to talk."

"Trent wasn't very nice to her at the garage, and Dale just wants to help us."

Becca sighed. "Okay. Go and get her, Pooh Bear."

Trent would always be an important part of her life, and the one who had stood by her since she had found her crying on the drawing room floor of her family home, surrounded by the press hovering outside.

She had to make it right with her, and Becca promised herself to call her later. But first she had to get these groceries put away. Dale seemed to have bought a lot. She saw several pizza boxes sticking out of the bags, and they made Becca smile.

Cleary Dale thought pizza was a household priority since Jake liked it. Becca emptied the bags of pizza, milk, cheese, crisps, and lollipops, clearly another McGuire priority.

She got to the last bag and found it full of at least a dozen jars of hot jalapeños, and boxes of crackers.

Dale remembered.

All her emotion and stress were not going to be held back after seeing this sweet act of kindness, and she began to sob.

"Hi, Becca, Jake said—" Dale pushed through the door when she heard Becca crying. This was not what she expected. Jake said his mum was okay, and just wanted a chat.

"Becca, what's wrong?"

Becca turned around and hurried across the room and into her arms. Dale held her tightly and stroked her hair. "Shh…it's okay. Tell me what's wrong."

Becca spoke but Dale couldn't understand what she was saying because she was crying so hard. She looked over to the windowsill and saw her flowers, pride of place, whereas Trent's were still on the table. *Yes! One-nil, team McGuire.*

Dale took a step back and cradled Becca's head gently. "Take a breath, hen. Take a breath and tell me again."

"Jalapenos and crackers," Becca managed to say.

"What?" Dale was lost as to why jalapeños and crackers would make a woman cry. She thought she had been doing the right thing. "Maybe chocolates would have been better. I wasn't really sure what to get."

"No." Becca had calmed a bit and placed a hand on Dale's chest. "I'm crying because getting me jalapenos and crackers was the sweetest thing anyone's ever done for me."

"It was?" The adoring look Becca was giving her made her heart flutter. Who knew chilli peppers had this kind of effect on women? Someone should really write this stuff down.

"Dale, I told you one time, in a throwaway comment, that they were my craving. You remembered and brought me not just a few, but over a dozen. No one else would have thought of that."

Becca reached up and gave her the sweetest kiss on her cheek. Electricity spread from her cheek and down her body.

Dale wanted to kiss Becca so badly, and it got even worse when Becca grabbed her hand and pressed it to her stomach. "Your wee yin is kicking."

"*My* wee yin?" Dale questioned.

Becca smiled and nodded. "Our wee yin. You've done so much for us, Dale, and I trust you, and I would like you to be part of their lives. If you want to?"

Dale felt her own tears coming, but she gulped them down. She had gotten in the door, and gained Becca's trust. Nothing could make her happier, nothing apart from kissing her.

"Thank you, Becca. I won't let you down. All I want to be is a support to you, and someone the kids can rely on."

On cue the baby started kicking again. Dale slipped her hand under the edge of Becca's blouse and tenderly stroked her stomach. As she did, she noticed Becca's breathing quicken. She was clearly enjoying Dale's touch, and that excited Dale so much.

"You're so beautiful, Becca."

Dale leaned in, her lips aching to touch Becca's.

"I'm not. I'm a huge pregnant woman."

"Then you can't see what I see. Maybe I can show you?"

Becca nodded and her lips were inches from touching hers when Jake came bundling in the door and they broke apart.

Becca's cheeks went bright red.

"Mummy, have you finished talking? I want Dale to come and see my computer program."

Becca cleared her throat nervously. "Can you give us a minute, and I'll send Dale up?"

"With lollipops?" Dale said with a wink.

"Yes!" Jake shouted excitedly and ran off up the stairs.

They stepped apart, and Becca said, "I've never seen him so animated as he is with you."

"Eh, thanks. It's probably just my stupid jokes."

"No, it's more than that, but we can add that to the million other things we need to talk about, and I mean we need to talk. I want to tell you about my past before…" Becca hesitated.

And Dale finished for her, "Before we go any further with our relationship?"

"Yes, exactly," Becca said.

Dale took another chance and held Becca's hand. "There's nothing that could stop me wanting to be here for you. I want to help you."

"You know I'm Victoria, but you don't know the real story, only the one the media sold."

Dale smiled. "We've got lots of time, because you've got to understand one thing. I'm not leaving you and Jake alone tonight after what happened."

"We'll be okay. Trent negotiated two weeks for me to pay him. His thugs won't be back till then."

Dale placed her hand on Becca's baby bump and said softly, "You were puking your guts up this morning. You need rest, proper rest. Tell me you wouldn't sleep better if I was in the house?"

Becca let out a long breath. "Okay, but I don't want you to ever feel like you have to be here."

I want to be here, Dale thought.

"I promise I won't, and I always keep my promises. And I brought pizza so you don't have to worry about dinner."

Becca laughed. "That's one thing you're going to have to learn about being in a family, Dale. You can't just give your kids pizza all the time because they like it, or lollipops."

Dale felt like her heart might just burst after what Becca said. *Your kids.*

Oh man, I want them to be my kids.

"You can't? Okay, well maybe you could teach me," Dale said with a smile.

"Maybe. You better go and see Jake now or he'll come back and pull you upstairs."

"I'm going, hen. Don't lift or do anything, will you?" Dale said while walking backwards to the kitchen door.

"I'll put the food in the fridge and then pig out on some jalapenos. Is that acceptable?"

"Perfect." Dale was halfway out the door when she turned back and said, "Hey, Becca. Why did the jalapeno put on a jumper?"

"Do tell," Becca said.

"Because he was chilli. You get it? The *chilli* was *chilly*?"

Becca shook her head and smiled. "That was terrible, McGuire. But in a good way."

❖

Dale sat at Jake's computer desk and watched with awe as his fingers whizzed across the keyboard, and he explained what he was doing.

"The game is a story mixed with maths problems. If a child gets the problem wrong, then the story takes a bad path, and they know they have to go back and fix it, but if they get it right, the hero moves on to the next puzzle."

"That's amazing, Jake, and really kind of you to think of other kids."

Jake shrugged. "I wanted other kids to know how cool numbers are. They're not scary like most kids think."

"So this will keep you busy enough that you won't hack into any more websites?" Dale said firmly.

Jake put his head down. "I hadn't done that for a long time, and then it was because I was bored. This time I just wanted to find you."

Dale stroked his head and smiled. "I'm so glad you did. You know, I love numbers too. I was really good at maths at school," Dale told him.

Jake smiled excitedly. "You did? I'm just like you then."

"No, you are so much more intelligent than I was, and braver. When I got to high school, and got involved with my friends, cars, and going out, I gave up on my studies. I was too concerned about fitting in with the crowd."

"What was your school like?" Jake focused intently on Dale while sucking on one of the lollipops she had bought.

"It wasn't the best of areas I lived in, but my primary school was a great place—and then I went to high school. I was kind of naughty."

For some reason, this made Jake laugh. "Tell me, tell me what you did."

Dale went on to entertain him with some censored exploits of her times at school, and Jake loved hearing every second of it.

After she finished her last story she said, "Don't tell your mum about that one, okay?"

"Okay. That was so funny."

Dale had been thinking about ways to get Jake interacting with other kids, but in a way that would stimulate his razor-sharp mind, and she thought she had found the perfect answer.

"Jake? Do you know how to play chess?"

❖

After a nice dinner, Becca got Jake ready for bed and left him reading a book on chess on his iPad. Ever since Dale had told him how she enjoyed the game, and suggested he go to the school's chess club, he'd become determined to learn everything about it.

It was sweet that he had come to hero worship Dale in such a short space of time. It wasn't surprising though—Dale just had that sort of enthusiastic personality that drew you to her. Becca was getting closer and closer herself.

Becca settled herself on the living room couch while Dale attended to the fire. The roaring fire and the low lights gave the room a warm glow. Becca hadn't sat with someone like this for a long time, and it was nice.

"Thanks for getting Jake to go to chess club. That was a great idea."

"Well, I thought it might interest a boy as intelligent as Jake. Plus he'll have to play and mix with the other kids. Hopefully it'll help him. I know I loved it."

"You, Dale McGuire, went to chess club?" Becca laughed softly.

Dale's cheeks went a little red. "Aye, up until my first year at high school, when I foolishly bowed to peer pressure and gave up chess and maths clubs. I was getting made fun of, and I realized the girls were more into the cool boys that played sports and worked on cars. All my mates were boys, and I wanted attention from the girls, just like them."

"I can just imagine you chasing after girls when you were young. So? What did your parents say?" Becca realized what she had said and backed up. "I'm so sorry—I didn't mean to mention them."

"Hey, don't worry. You were right. They were my only parents. Ma and Da loved me so much. I sometimes wish I had never found out. Anyway, my ma wasn't too pleased, because she always had this dream of me being the first McGuire to go to university to become a doctor or lawyer. Da, on the other hand, was secretly pleased, I think. He worked all his life in the Glasgow shipyards as a welder. So he wanted me to have a trade."

Becca wasn't surprised by Dale's story. It all made perfect sense. "Did you give up on school then?" Becca asked.

"Pretty much, apart from sports and tech classes. I didn't stay on at school past sixteen, but I did leave with qualifications in maths and physics." Dale smiled mischievously. "You know why?"

Becca shook her head in reply.

"My maths and physics teachers hated me. Who knows why? Well maybe because I left a fish behind the heaters in both their classrooms over the summer…"

Becca burst out laughing. "You did not."

"Uh-huh. They had to get the place fumigated. I was an idiot trying to impress her idiot friends. Anyway, that's beside the point. They both told me there wasn't any point in me taking the exam, because there was no way I'd pass it."

"A teacher said that to you? So I suppose you took that as a challenge?"

"Oh yes. I got A plus in both subjects, and then left school with the most arrogant smile on my face. I'm surprised one of them didn't kill me. Looking back now, I wouldn't have blamed them."

Becca felt just the opposite. "I don't think so—they should have tried to engage you more, and interest you with work, and then you wouldn't have had time to cook up fish plots."

Dale laughed. "Maybe."

There was a lull in the conversation, as they each took a drink of tea. Becca felt the nerves start to twist in her stomach, because she knew it was her turn to talk. It was right that she tell Dale, but she hadn't done this in such a long time.

"You look stressed, hen," Dale said. "You don't have to tell me if you're not ready."

Becca placed both palms on her baby bump. "No, I want to, I need to. I'm so sick of hiding."

"You don't ever have to hide from me. We share egg stuff, remember?" Dale said with a wink.

The comment made her relax immediately. "You were right. My name was Victoria Carter. What did you find out on the internet?"

"I only looked quickly before I left to come here. I read that your dad was a doctor and involved in a big fraud scandal."

"That's just a part of the story. My father was a doctor. He worked for the National Health Service as a consultant pain specialist, and he had a private practice on Harley Street."

Dale's eyes went wide. "Wow, he was an accomplished guy."

"Academically, yes, but not as a man, husband, or father." Becca started to shiver slightly with the cold and reliving the story.

Dale noticed and got up to get a blanket from the chair and tucked it around her. Dale was so kind and considerate. Becca knew she was doing the right thing in placing her trust in her.

Becca continued, "As I was growing up, I never thought we were different from other people. I thought my life was normal, that all doctors lived as lavishly as we did. We had a large house in Belgravia, and relied on staff to look after us. Nanny, cook, that sort of thing. It's a sad fact that I had to teach myself to cook when I went to university."

Dale lifted Becca's blanket-covered feet and placed them on her lap. "Hey, don't feel bad. You had a cook and staff. I had a ma who did everything for me, and I mean everything. When I moved in with Sammy and Val, Val quickly gave me a crash course on household tasks, like how to use the washing machine and iron, because she certainly wasn't doing them for me. So we're similar at different ends of the scale."

Becca chuckled, imagining Dale wrestling with domestic appliances. "So can you use a washing machine now?"

Dale looked down sheepishly. "Well since we're sharing secrets, I'll tell you. Every time I've gotten a new washing machine for my flat, Val sticks a yellow label next to the washing programme I'm meant to use. Pathetic, huh?"

"No, as you say, we were both spoiled, just at opposite ends of the scale. My own mother wouldn't have known where our appliances were."

"What was your ma like?" Dale asked.

How to explain Carlotta Carter? "It's difficult to explain. My mother Carlotta wasn't in any sense of the word a mother. I don't want you to think she was a bad mother who didn't care about me, she did, and I loved her a lot, but she was more like a big sister. A glamorous, much older sister who regaled me with stories of her and my father's nights out in London society circles. She was a former model, much younger than my father, and he was delighted with her. Delighted to have her on his arm."

"Like a trophy kind of thing?" Dale asked.

"Yes, exactly. He wasn't cruel to her, but he wasn't affectionate. It just wasn't him, and she was used to being given lots of love and attention during her career. I found out later she used drugs and alcohol to compensate for that lack of love. Father was rarely home as she got older, and I would often find Mother in drug-induced stupors."

"Man, that's a shame," Dale said.

"It was. Little did I know she was being supplied by my father and his friends."

Dale did a double take. "Your father? I thought it was fraud he was done for?"

"It was, prescription fraud. Eugene Hardy was in partnership with my father, Thomas. My father invented phantom patients and used the prescriptions to procure drugs, which Eugene would then sell on the streets for big money. Everything that I ever had was bought with ordinary people's desperation for drugs," Becca said, still feeling the guilt deeply inside her.

"You can't think like that, Becca. You didn't know," Dale said, while she rubbed her feet to soothe her.

"It doesn't make it any better though. Then everything came crashing down. I was in my first year at uni. I still lived at home, and the police raided our house at five a.m. one morning. It was terrifying. They took nearly everything for evidence, arrested my father, and froze all our bank accounts. Mother and I were in a bad way. The press was camped outside the house, so we couldn't go anywhere."

"That must have been a scary time," Dale said.

"It was. The press vilified my father, and I don't blame them. He and Eugene stole three hundred million pounds over the years. It was a huge scandal—there were government committees, inquiries—and all the time my mother was struggling. Her addictions had gotten a whole lot worse, and then I made a mistake that…" Becca struggled to say the words. "The mistake that killed her."

❖

Ash looked at her watch. *He's late.*

Her informant at McGuire's Motors had texted her to say he wanted to meet. So they decided on a pub not too far from the garage. It was Saturday night and the pub was busy, so it was hard to keep track of who was coming and going.

There are so many ways I could be spending Saturday night, but if I can find you, Vic, it'll all be worth it.

"Ash?"

Mike had arrived at the table without her even noticing. "Mike, sit down. It's good to see you. I got you a pint and a whisky chaser."

"Thanks." Mike looked nervous, and he showed it when he downed the whisky in one.

"You said you had something for me?"

Mike's eyes darted around the room. "Are you sure this will be confidential?"

"Of course. You can trust me. I always look after my sources."

Mike tapped his fingers on the table. "I asked the other lads in work about what was going on, and there are rumours."

"Oh? About Dale McGuire?"

"Yeah, she's hardly ever here these days, and that's not like her."

"Maybe a woman?"

Mike laughed nervously. "Dale's women don't last weeks at a time."

A woman after my own heart.

"So? What are the lads saying?"

"That she's taking care of some kid or something. It's strange. Someone overheard her talking to Val, my boss, about a kid that she's responsible for and this woman you were asking about."

"A child?" Could it be Vic's? There was clearly something strong linking McGuire to Vic, and she had to find out what it was, and quick.

"Did you get the address for me?"

Mike nodded. "You have no idea how hard it was to get this from the works system. Sammy, my manager, caught me, and I had to make up some stupid excuse. Now she thinks I was trying to buy parts for myself on the company account. I've been given a warning."

Do I care?

"Can I have it?"

"Money first," Mike said firmly.

"And here I thought we trusted each other." Ash pulled an envelope out of her pocket and handed it over. "It's all there, I assure you."

Mike counted it quickly, then gave her a slip of paper.

Rebecca Harper, The Old Vicarage, Plumtun.

❖

"What?" Dale sat up quickly, stunned at what Becca had just said. "How could anything you do cause that?"

"I trusted someone. I confided in them and they sold every intimate detail of our lives to the newspapers. The papers published stories about how we lived, holidays, luxury items that we had, paid for by my father's victims. Not only was my father vilified, but now my mother and I were too. Carlotta couldn't take it and she took an overdose."

Dale watched Becca closely as she told her story. Her eyes had started to glaze over and a few tears streamed down her face, as if she was reliving the moment somehow.

"When I saw the news on TV and online, I hurried to my mum's bedroom and found her unconscious. The paramedics came, but it was already too late."

Dale couldn't just sit and watch Becca's pain, so she knelt on the floor beside her and took Becca's hand. "I'm so sorry, Becca. I can't imagine what that must've felt like."

"I trusted someone I thought I was falling in love with, and I couldn't have been more wrong."

"What happened then?"

"My father's lawyer was Trent's father. I had seen Trent a few times over the years at functions and social gatherings. She came around to check on me, and found me on the floor in a terrible state."

Despite the cross words she'd had with Trent today, Dale was glad Becca had had her at a time when she'd needed someone.

"Once the trial was over, Trent helped me create a new identity and switch universities. I've been trying to hide ever since."

Dale took Becca's hand and kissed the palm. "I'm truly, truly sorry about what you had to go through then, and since. It must have taken a real strength to survive."

Becca managed the smallest of smiles. "That's why I had Jake. I had no other family, nothing else to stay strong for. Jake's given me a reason to get up every morning, a reason to keep going."

"Does Jake know?"

Becca shook her head vigorously. "No, and I don't want him to ever know."

"You have my word I won't tell anyone. Is your father still in jail?"

"No, he died last year. He hanged himself in his jail cell. It hit me hard, even though I had never been close to him. That's when I got pregnant again, when I moved out here. I needed to build a new family, so I thought at the time, but really I put Jake's future at risk. I had just taken on this huge project, and it was all bad timing."

"Hey, you wouldn't change having this wee yin, would you?" Dale handed her a tissue from the box on the coffee table.

Becca dabbed her eyes. "No, never. I just feel so guilty that I made things difficult for Jake. I made things so bad that he went off to find you."

"That was the best thing that's ever happened to me, Becca. I was drifting, trying to find a purpose outside work, and I've found it."

Becca looked down at their clasped hands now. "Thank you for being here. I don't think I've said that."

"Thank you for letting me in."

They sat together for a little while longer, until with all the emotion of the day, Becca fell asleep.

Dale lifted Becca in her arms and carried her up to bed. She settled her down to sleep and made sure she had plenty of blankets to keep her warm, and then she checked on Jake, before walking around, making sure the vicarage was secure.

Becca had given her a blanket and a pillow earlier, and so she made herself comfortable on the couch. She watched the flames dance in the fireplace and counted herself lucky that Becca had trusted her and let her into this family.

She vowed that she was going to do everything in her power to protect them, even if that meant making an alliance with her new nemesis.

Chapter Fourteen

A week later, Dale was at her office in the garage working out some of her finances.

Val popped her head in the office. "Dale? Are you finished with payroll?"

"One sec." Dale moved from her banking website to the payroll document she had been working on and clicked send. "All done."

"Great. Remember, you and Sammy have the premises to look at this afternoon."

"I cancelled that," Dale said quickly, returning to her banking site.

"You cancelled? What for?" Val came and sat at her desk.

"I've got another appointment I need to take, and besides, I'm not sure this is the right time to expand." Dale kept her eyes on the computer screen.

"Dale? Look at me."

Dale suddenly felt seventeen again, trying not to answer a difficult question, but she looked up.

"Why suddenly is it not a good time? You were excited about it. It's because of Becca and Jake, isn't it?"

"Maybe I just need to concentrate on them and my life just now. Expansion can come later." Dale didn't mention spending money on a new premises wouldn't help her plans for this afternoon. She could see the tension on Val's face—she was dying to say something. "If you want to say something, just say it."

"You're turning your life upside down for them."

"What's wrong with that?" Dale said defensively. "Why shouldn't I turn it upside down. I was unhappy the way it was anyway. Apart from the business, and you guys, my life was empty. Why is it wrong, Val?"

Val sighed and leaned on the desk. "Because you are investing in a woman who could tell you never to come back tomorrow, and you would be devastated."

"She won't do that. We've reached a point of trust, and it took hard work to get to this stage. I'm not turning back now."

"You're falling in love with her, aren't you? Or are you falling in love with the idea of being a family?"

Dale rubbed her forehead as she tried to form her thoughts correctly. "Both. I can't help the way I'm feeling. She's just...I don't know, like she was meant to be mine. I told her about Nora."

Val looked very surprised. "You did?"

"It was part of getting her to trust me, but I'm glad I did. I felt better after telling her," Dale said.

"Did she show you the same trust?"

Dale nodded. "She told me everything, and from someone as careful as she is, that's a big leap."

"I suppose you're right." Val smiled at Dale. "I can't help thinking you're still the same baby butch we took under our wing, all those years ago."

Dale laughed. "I hope I'm not a baby any more, but I understand. It's nice to know there will always be two people who'll watch out for me."

"Always. So how is she feeling now?"

"Much better. The new medicines are making a difference and her doctor is pleased with her. Hopefully the vicarage will be more comfortable for them this week, since the new boiler is getting fitted tomorrow."

Val sat back and crossed her legs. "How did you get her to agree to that? I know you've said how independent she is."

Dale looked down sheepishly. "Ah, well...she thinks the fitter is a mate of mine, who owes me a big favour if I just slip him a few quid. She said okay only if she takes new pictures of us and the business for the website."

"Well it is true they need to be updated. Is she up to it?" Val asked.

"Probably not, but she's insisting. I'd like you to meet her, and Jake. I think it would be nice for Jake to know Mia."

"That would be lovely. How about next Saturday? You and Sammy don't have a race that weekend."

"Sounds good. I'll ask." Dale looked at her watch and hit her forehead. "Shit! I need to get going." She grabbed her jacket from the hanger and said, "I'll just be a few hours."

❖

Dale ended up parking nearly a mile away from her destination, so she had to run to try to make her appointment on time. She followed the map on her phone as she went, trying to find her way. She stopped outside the building and looked at the nameplate on the wall next to the door.

Trent, Trent, and Masters.

Trent's offices were just as she'd imagined—old, posh, and intimidating to the public. *Let's do this.*

Dale went through the door and saw a receptionist at the desk. She immediately felt underdressed when she saw the rest of the clientele in the waiting room, suited and booted. Looking down at her designer jeans and her stylish but casual army jacket, she wished she had worn her suit.

Fuck it. They can take it or leave it.

She walked up to the desk and saw the glamorous receptionist hungrily check her out. "All right, darlin'. I've got an appointment with Trent today. Dale McGuire."

Dale's charms obviously still worked, because the receptionist blushed. "Please take a seat, Ms. McGuire. I'll let Trent know you're here."

"Thanks."

She took a seat and got some funny looks from the very proper looking people around her. It was a funny thing. Probably at least one or two of these people took their cars to be serviced or repaired at McGuire's Motors, but they would never think the owner was sitting next to them in jeans and boots, with messy hair. Dale chuckled to herself. She liked to exceed people's expectations, just as she had all those years ago with her schoolteachers.

Dale waited patiently for about fifteen minutes before Trent called her in. They didn't shake hands. It was clearly going to be a frosty meeting. Dale sat and Trent took her seat behind her desk and silently stared at her for a few minutes.

So Dale broke the silence. "Thanks for seeing me, mate."

"One, I'm not your mate, and I only agreed to see you because you said it was about protecting Becca."

"Hey, there's no need to be hostile—as I said, this is for Becca."

"Just talk," Trent said sharply.

"Okay, if you want it like that, then fine. You may not like me, but we share something in common. We care for Becca."

"I don't just care for Becca. I've always loved her. I just wasn't ready for what she wanted."

"Well, too late. You had over ten years to work out you still loved her. Funnily enough, that happened only when I came into the picture."

Trent looked really angry. "You would be just a bit of rough to her, not a lifelong partner. Say what you want and go."

"Look, we both care, and we both know that Eugene Hardy needs to be paid as quickly as possible."

Trent sat forward and clasped her hands. "On that we agree. The Hardy brothers don't mess about."

"We also know the bank is not going to give Becca nearly enough, if anything, on the vicarage. So I think we have to sort it out."

"Oh, I see, you're going to ride in like a knight in shining armour and pay it off?"

"I'm a medium-size business owner. I don't have that sort of money hanging around in my accounts. It's tied up in the business."

"So what do you suggest?"

"I can take out a loan against one of my properties, pay Eugene off, and pay it back at my own pace."

Trent looked sceptical. "And you're willing to do all this just for the sake of a roll in the hay with Becca?"

Dale shook her head. She was really getting pissed off now. "You really don't think much of me, do you?"

"I've heard about your reputation, and I don't want that for Becca," Trent said firmly.

"Oh, and I suppose you've been fucking celibate since you split up with her? My ma always used to say, people in glass houses shouldnae throw stones. Put away your personal feelings about me and think of Becca, Jake, and the baby. I'm trying to protect my kids and their mother. Whether I'm in their life or not, I don't want this debt hanging over their heads."

Trent sighed. "What do you want from me?"

"Becca says you have a way of contacting Eugene. Make the connection for me. Pay it and draw up any legal documents you need to prove the debt is paid."

"She won't accept charity, you know. I tried to offer her something to help."

"That's why she can't know I paid it, and that's where you come in."

Dale laid out her plan, then offered Trent her hand. "Deal?"

Trent tapped her fingers on the desk for a few seconds, clearly contemplating her answer, then stood and took Dale's hand. "You have a deal, McGuire."

❖

Becca was driving home from the local shop, humming along to the radio. She hadn't felt as good for a long time. She had felt so chirpy that she'd stopped at a local beauty spot to take some pictures of the birds and scenery. Her symptoms were much reduced on the new medication, the car was running well, and Jake was happy, all because Dale had come into their life.

She started to giggle when one of Dale's favourite Britney Spears songs came on the radio.

The one thing that had changed since Dale came into their life was laughter and light, where there had been darkness and worry. Dale was a positive, happy-go-lucky person, not the arrogant player she'd first appeared. She did like the ladies, but Becca couldn't imagine her being cruel to anyone. It just wasn't in her.

And Dale had brought qualities out in her that had been long buried—a sense of humour, excitement, and a long-lost libido.

She pulled into her driveway and saw an image that nearly made her drive off into a tree. Dale was leaning against her Jaguar in a pair of jeans, a simple tight white T-shirt with the sleeve tightly gripping her Celtic tattoo, looking like the lesbian version of James Dean. And to make matters worse, she was sucking on her ever-present lollipop.

Becca felt a rush of arousal that made her ache deep inside. *I wish I was that lollipop.*

Just as she was chastising herself for that thought, another one floated across her mind. A thought that made her hungry for Dale.

I'm carrying her baby.

Becca wanted her badly, but that was such a bad, bad idea. Wasn't it?

When Dale saw her car, she started to walk towards her, and Becca somehow managed to park.

Dale opened her door and said, "Hi, hen. I hope you don't mind me turning up to see you?"

"No, it's a nice surprise," Becca managed to say coherently while her eyes roved over Dale's body.

Dale took Becca's hand and helped her out. Dale noticed that Becca didn't let go of her hand and had a dreamy expression on her face. "How's the wee yin today?"

"She's good."

She was surprised when Becca took her hand and placed it on her stomach. It was such an intimate act, it seemed only natural to kiss Becca passionately in response. The urge was so strong, but she brushed Becca's cheek with her lips instead.

"I thought you were busy today."

"I got finished earlier than I thought, so I popped by with dinner—and don't worry, it's not pizza. It a big lasagne, freshly made at my local deli."

Becca smile and raised an eyebrow. "Sounds delicious, but not quite at the parenting healthy dinner level yet."

"I'm working my way up to it. Next stop is mince, neeps, and tatties. I think Jake would appreciate tasting some Scottish delicacies."

"I take it that's minced beef, turnip, and potatoes?"

Dale laughed. "Aye, posh girl."

"Posh girl?" Becca said with mock anger.

"I'll take your bags if you can hold something for me."

Dale retrieved a plastic bag from her car and gave it to Becca, then walked up to the house.

Becca took out an intricate and highly polished wooden box and a checkerboard. "This is beautiful, Dale. Where did you get it?"

Dale put the bags on the countertop, joined Becca at the table, and opened the brass clasp on the box. Inside was a set of beautifully carved chess pieces. "My Granda. He was a joiner by trade, and he made these for me when I went to chess club. The club went to lots of tournaments, so I needed something to practice with. I thought Jake might like it since he's started learning the game."

Becca reached out and touched Dale's tattoo, before pulling her hand away quickly. "Um, I better get these bags of shopping put away."

Dale leaned against the countertop with her arms crossed. She saw want in Becca's eyes and she wanted her right back. Becca had nearly touched her but pulled away. Dale kicked herself mentally for not taking control and touching Becca herself.

She watched Becca closely as she put away the shopping, taking in Becca's gentle curves, her ample breasts that she longed to take in her hands, and her gorgeous bottom that she longed to caress. This feeling was different, this was new—to experience an ache in her heart as well as an ache in her sex. Both sensations made Dale's desire for Becca all the more intense.

"Don't look at me like that, Dale," Becca said suddenly.

Dale had felt the energy between them since she'd pulled up in the car, but she needed Becca to say it. "What look?"

"The look that probably makes all the girls fall at your feet."

Dale pushed off from the counter and stalked towards her, Becca's breathing getting shorter with every passing second.

Dale stopped and boxed her in against the countertop. "What about posh girls?"

Becca couldn't stop herself, not any more. She wanted to taste Dale and understand every part of her. She nodded. "Posh girls especially."

Dale smiled ever so slightly and leaned in to kiss her. The first touch of Dale's lips was unbelievably soft, nothing like she had first imagined someone like her to be. As Dale kissed her and teased her lips so softly, Becca felt like she was melting.

In fact her knees weakened and Dale supported her with one arm around her, while the other grasped and then caressed Becca's thigh and buttock. They were connected both physically and mentally, making the moment much more intense.

Dale's tongue softly ran along her top lip, and then slipped inside, making Becca moan.

Parts of Becca long dormant came alive, and alive was what Dale had made her feel. Dale had crashed into her life and wakened everything from its long slumber.

Dale pulled back and rested her forehead against Becca's, her eyes still closed. "I've been wanting to do that for the longest time."

"Posh girls—" Becca was interrupted by the ringing of her mobile.

Dale said, "Leave it."

Becca sighed. "I can't. It might be the school."

They pulled apart and Becca answered the call. "Hello?"

It was the bank, and her stomach dropped when they told her the news on her mortgage application. "Please? There must be some mistake. It's a large piece of land, even if the buildings…"

There was no point in arguing with the bank clerk. The decision was already made. She hung up the phone.

"It's over." Becca was overcome by a wave of dizziness, but Dale grasped her as she swayed.

"I've got you, hen. Come and sit."

Dale sat her down before she fell. Becca held her head in her hands and she couldn't even cry. She just felt numb.

❖

Dale made an excuse to get out of the house. She headed out to the garage, leaving a devastated Becca in the kitchen.

She dialled Trent's number.

"Trent, have you contacted Eugene yet?"

"I called, made the offer, and I'm waiting on his reply."

Dale growled in frustration. "Well chase it up. The bank has just turned down Becca's application and she's really upset. She's talking about putting the vicarage up for sale."

"Jesus Christ, look, you don't just chase up Hardy—"

"Just fucking do it, Trent. I have the money in my business account. Email me your details and transfer it."

"I'll do my best, and don't swear at me again, McGuire."

"Fine. Pretty fucking please, remember our deal."

"I'll see what I can do." Trent hung up.

Dale looked at her phone and said, "Yeah, love you too, Trent."

She heard the noise of an engine, and Jake's school bus came around the corner. She didn't know if she should run inside and warn Becca he was home or not.

Jake got off the bus and walked dejectedly up the drive, kicking loose stones as he went.

Great, another Harper in need of cheering up. Dale hurried over to him and said, "Hey, wee man. What's up?"

Jake smiled briefly when he realized who it was, and then ran into her arms, crying.

"What's the matter?" She held him tightly, worried about what was wrong, but at the same time pleased he'd run to her. Just like Mia ran to Sammy.

"I can't kick…kick…a ball," Jake stammered through his tears.

Dale had no idea what he meant. "Just tell me what happened. Slow down, okay?"

Jake nodded and wiped his tears on his jacket. "At school. We're doing football for six weeks in gym. I can't kick a ball or catch, and all the kids were laughing at me."

It hurt and upset Dale how upset Jake was. It was amazing that a boy so intelligent, much more intelligent than herself, could lack a simple, basic skill. Well, she was going to fix it.

"Jake, you go and see your mum. Tell her I'll be back in about twenty-five minutes, and then you and me are going to play football. You can do anything you want to, Jake—you just need to practice."

"Thanks. I'll try," Jake said.

Dale kissed his head and said, "Oh, and ask your mummy to show you the present I brought you."

❖

Ash walked into her lover's office, a smug sense of satisfaction showing on her face. "I think I've found her."

Nika turned around quickly. "Found who, and where have you been all day yesterday and today?"

"Working, like *Daddy* asked me to."

Ash locked the office door and walked around the office lowering the blinds, and then sat on the desk.

Nika stepped towards her. "You've got something, baby?"

Ash pulled her between her legs, and grasped her hips. "Oh, I have. What would you say if I told you I've found Victoria Carter?"

Nika gasped. "Carter? *The* Victoria Carter? But no one knows where she went. She disappeared off the face of the earth."

Ash laughed. "Yeah, well I found her, and I'm going to get an interview with her. Do you know what that would mean? An exclusive interview with the inside scoop on Thomas Carter and Eugene Hardy for the *Tribune*?"

Ash spun a smiling Nika against the desk and started to kiss and bite her neck, making Nika gasp.

"My God, Ash. This will be huge!"

"I know. A Eugene Hardy story alone would push circulation up, but the daughter of Thomas and Carlotta Carter, who's tried to hide from the public all this time? Pure hundred carat gold. I told you I would impress Daddy, didn't I?"

Ash was buzzing. After all this time, Vic had fallen back in her lap, and she had mileage for lots and lots more stories.

"I knew you would, baby. He will be so, so impressed. So impressed that I think he'll want to announce our engagement." Nika kissed her deeply.

And once I get that ring on your finger, this office will be mine.

Ash pushed Nika down on the desk, and took her lover's hand and placed it on her belt. "I think I deserve a thank you."

❖

Becca had been in lots of stressful, dire situations since her father had been arrested. Each time there had always seemed like there was hope, some conceivable way out of the situation, but today felt like she had come to the end of the road. Her situation was hopeless.

She walked over to the kitchen window and gazed out at Dale teaching Jake how to kick a ball.

Her heart warmed at the sight, despite her worries. Dale would be a perfect other parent for Jake. He clearly adored her, and Dale gave him something she didn't and was so kind and gentle with him.

Why did this have to happen now? Becca knew she had feelings for Dale. She had been slowly falling in love with her, with each passing bad joke and act of kindness. But could they explore what was between them when she was going to have to sell up and leave?

I want you, Dale, but is it all too weird for us?

Becca jumped when she saw Trent in the garden. Strangely, Trent stopped beside Dale. Dale said something, and Trent nodded before coming to the kitchen door.

She opened the door. "Trent? What's going on?"

"I've got some good news." Trent smiled.

"I could do with some. Come in and sit down." Becca pulled out a kitchen chair for her.

Trent opened her briefcase, brought out a paper, and handed it to Becca. "If you read that, you'll find that it says Eugene Hardy acknowledges your debt paid in full."

Becca stared and stared at the paper, trying to comprehend the words and what Trent had just said, but it just wasn't going in. "I don't understand. Tell me what this means."

Trent clasped her hands and looked down at the table. "I overlooked another trust set up by your grandmother. She must have made it and forgotten about it, because there was only one piece of paperwork on it. I checked the original files from before the office was computerized, and there it was, large as life. But the main thing is, it was enough to pay off your debt. You're free, Becca."

CHAPTER FIFTEEN

Trent, I really can't thank you enough. You can't imagine the horrible dread I've been feeling, and you've taken it all away in an instant. Jake and I are free from the past and everything connected with it. I mean, I wish I had known my grandmother left more money."

If Becca hadn't have been seven months pregnant, she would have been doing cartwheels, she was so happy.

Trent sighed and put down her coffee cup. "Can I ask you a question, Becca?"

"Anything, Trent. You know that."

"Do you think there'll ever be a chance we could get back together? Any part of you that still loves me?"

Becca froze with panic. "Trent...I..."

Trent took her hand. "I need to know if we'll ever have a chance."

All Becca could think of was Dale. Dale kissing her. Dale playing football with Jake. They felt like a family, and somehow she felt like she was betraying Dale by even talking like this.

"You've never wanted a family, Trent. That's why we split up."

"I know, but I always had this dream at the back of my mind that when Jake grew up, you might have time to have a relationship with me."

"I can't just push Jake and the baby to the side. I need a partner who wants to be a full member of this family, not just me. I'll always love you, Trent, but I'm not in love with you."

"Dale would slot right in to your family, wouldn't she? Do you have feelings for her?"

Becca looked down at her coffee mug and nodded. "But it can't work. It's too strange, we're from different worlds, and Dale might lose interest after a while."

Trent sighed and put her cup down with a bang. "I can't do this any more, but I can't believe I'm going to tell you this."

"What are you talking about, Trent?"

"McGuire won't lose interest in you. In fact I think she's in love with you."

Becca could not comprehend what Trent was saying. "How could you know that? And I thought you didn't like her."

"I know because she paid the debt to Eugene Hardy. The whole thing," Trent said reluctantly.

Becca brain was whizzing at a million miles an hour and making no connections. "I don't understand."

"She came to see me the other day at the office. McGuire wanted me to make contact with Eugene. She took a business loan out to pay it, but she knew you wouldn't take charity, so she made me promise to take the glory of finding a fictional trust that I had previously overlooked."

"I can't believe it," Becca said.

"Believe it. She stood out there and watched you hugging me and telling me how wonderful I was. I feel like a fraud. It pains me to say it, but McGuire is a good, unselfish person, despite her reputation. She must love you."

All Becca could think of was Dale, of pulling her close and kissing her with everything in her heart. "Thank you for telling me, Trent. I know it wasn't easy."

Trent gulped down her emotions. "Yes, well. I missed my chance with you. I let the years go by when I should have been giving you my heart. I'll always love you, Becca."

Becca got up and walked over to Trent. She leaned over and gave her a kiss on the lips. It was a kiss to say goodbye. "I'll always love you, and I know you'll find someone who'll love you like I never could."

❖

Dale's character on the console game she was playing was blown up for what seemed like the hundredth time. She threw her controller onto the other chair in frustration. Since leaving the vicarage, she couldn't settle her mind at all. She got up from the couch and walked to the window.

"What have I done? I've thrown Becca right into Trent's lap. What a fucking idiot."

Becca said that she would always allow Dale to see Jake and the baby, but how hard would it be visiting and seeing Trent in the place she wanted to be, to see Trent holding and touching Becca?

"My only chance at family, and I've fucked it up. Typical."

Dale's mobile started to ring. She pulled it from her pocket—it was Becca calling.

"Hello? Is everything okay, hen?"

"Everything is fine. I wanted to call because I didn't like the way you left. I wish you would have stayed for dinner with us."

"Nah, it's okay. I wanted to let you enjoy your good news with Trent."

"Did you get something to eat?" Becca asked.

Dale looked over at the unopened bag of Chinese food that she just couldn't think about eating. "Yeah, I got a takeaway. Why are you all concerned anyway?" Dale said that just a little too sharply.

"Because I care. I thought we cared about each other?"

All that Dale could picture was Trent sitting in Becca's sitting room, in front of the roaring fire, in her place, with her family.

"And why do you sound so hostile all of a sudden?" Becca asked.

"I'm not hostile. I just don't know why you called me up to ask if I'd eaten anything. Go back to Trent, and don't worry about me."

"Trent's not here. Why would she be?"

Dale sighed. "Because she brought you good news, I suppose. It doesn't matter anyway."

They were silent for a few seconds. Dale wished she could articulate what she wanted to Becca, because it was so simple. She wanted Becca, and she wanted a family.

"The other reason I was calling you was to tell you that I have an ultrasound appointment on Wednesday."

Great, just great. Now Trent was probably going to go and share that moment with her.

"I hope it goes well then." Dale knew she sounded really annoyed now, but she couldn't help it.

Becca sighed and said, "I don't know what's going on with you, but I wanted to ask you to come with me. To meet our baby girl."

Dale nearly dropped her phone. "You want me to come to your scan?"

"Of course. Who else would I want with me?"

"I thought maybe Trent…"

"Dale, let me make this really clear. Trent is never going to be with me, or substitute for Jake and the little one's other parent."

Dale's shock started to turn into excitement. She paced around the floor, full of energy. "Oh, I'd love that, hen. That would make me so happy. Thank you, Becca, thank you. I can't wait to see the wee yin."

"Dale, we may be an unusual family unit, but that's what I'd like us to be. You give Jake so much, and you'll do the same for our little girl."

"You don't know how much this means to me," Dale said.

"I do know, and that's why I want you to be part of this, because I know you will never turn your back on your children, or walk away."

"Never, they mean everything to me." *So do you, Becca.*

❖

Wednesday couldn't come quick enough for Dale. She was so happy Becca was allowing her to be so involved.

Dale pulled in to the vicarage driveway and saw Becca waiting for her by the front door. She got out quickly and greeted Becca with a kiss on the cheek, then offered her arm.

"Where's the Jag?" Becca asked.

"Val told me under no circumstance was I to take a pregnant woman for a scan in my Jaguar. So I hired this family car."

"Dale McGuire in a family car? Wonders will never cease," Becca joked.

"This is much more fun than any sports car, believe me." Dale got her in, and nearly ran around to get in the driver's seat. She was so full of energy and excitement she could hardly contain herself.

Dale got in and reached into the back seat. "I bought this for the baby." She took a soft plush teddy bear from the bag, with *Baby's First Teddy Bear* embroidered on its paw.

"Oh, it's adorable," Becca said, clutching the bear to her chest.

"I wanted the baby to know when I met her, how much she was wanted, and that I'll always be here to give her what she needs." Dale's voice cracked, and she quickly tried to regain control of herself. "My God, I'm such an emotional idiot."

Becca clasped her hand and smiled. "No, you're so sweet, and that's why I wanted to share this with you."

Dale wanted to ask something that had been bothering her since she had spoken to Val about the scan. "Becca? Is there something wrong with the baby?"

"Of course not. Why would you think that?"

"Val told me it was unusual to have a scan at this stage in pregnancy. It made me worry that they were monitoring the baby or something."

"Oh no, she's fine. I need to be monitored for my blood pressure, but she's fine. This isn't a regular scan." Becca reached into her bag and brought out a glossy brochure. "I'll explain everything but first I want to talk to you."

As soon as Becca found out what Dale had done for her, paying off her debt to Eugene Hardy, she racked her brains to think of a way to pay back Dale's kindness. She couldn't hope to pay the debt back, for a very long time anyway, so she had to think of something else, and this was the something else.

"Were you ever going to tell me about the money?"

Dale looked rather nervous. "What? I'm not sure what you mean."

There was something so adorably sweet about Dale, even now when she was trying to cover her tracks. It reminded Becca of when Jake was younger and he tried to deny taking that one extra biscuit from the biscuit tin.

It would be quicker if Becca just cut to the chase. "The money for Eugene Hardy. You would never have told me about it, would you? You stood and let me hug and generally make a fuss over Trent, while it was you all along."

"Ah…how did you find out?

"Trent told me, and before you say it, I know she swore she wouldn't, but that night she asked if there could ever be a chance for us again."

She saw Dale gulp hard with worry. This thing that was between them, this magnetic pull, chemistry or whatever, was clearly felt by both of them. But as Becca had been constantly turning over in her head, was it real or was it a biological need to couple up with the other parent of her baby?

"What did you tell her?" Dale asked.

"That there was no chance. My time with Trent is long over. I love her as a friend but I'm not in love with her, and because of that she thought I should know how much you care."

Dale let out a long breath.

Becca put her hand on Dale's knee. "Why did you stand there and let me fawn over Trent?"

"Because protecting my family is more important than me."

Becca cupped Dale's cheek with her hand. "Oh, Dale, you are one of the most unselfish, noblest people I've ever met."

"Nah, I'm just a grease monkey."

Becca shook her head. "No, you are so much more than that. You're kind, generous, and unselfish. I couldn't have chosen a better other parent for Jake and this little one."

"Thank you, Becca. That means the world to me."

Becca handed Dale the brochure in her hands. "This is one way I thought I could show the same kindness as you did to me. You missed out on my hospital scans, so I thought I'd book us a private scan so you could share that joy."

Dale's eyes lit up as she flicked through the pages. "A 4D picture?"

"Yes, the company call it a bonding scan, and I want you to bond with the little one."

Dale pulled Becca into her arms for a hug, and simply said, "Thank you."

❖

Dale watched on from a chair by the side of the hospital bed, while the member of staff prepared Becca for the scan.

She had never felt so nervous in her life, and she'd done some scary, stupid stuff when racing, but this was a whole different level. She was about to come face-to-face with her unborn child. Dale just prayed that she could be worthy enough.

The room wasn't what she'd expected. It was more of a comfortable hotel room than hospital. On each wall there was a TV screen, and immediately in front of the bed was the largest screen, all ready to show them the baby.

As the baby's picture appeared on the screens, in all the different angles, Becca reached out and took her hand. "Meet your little girl, Dale."

Dale sat in stunned silence and watched as the assistant took them through every angle, and pointed out features as they went.

"Now I'll switch the scan to 4D and you'll see baby's face clear as day," the assistant said.

Both Dale and Becca gasped. On-screen the baby's head and face were clear.

"Look, Dale," Becca said. "She's sucking her thumb."

Dale clutched the teddy bear she had bought and felt tears start to roll down her cheeks. She never thought children would be a part of her life, but since she'd met Becca and Jake, there was nothing she wanted more. She had helped make this child inside Becca, and no matter what, she would never turn her back on her.

"Hi, wee yin, I can't wait to meet you."

Becca squeezed her hand. "She can't wait to meet you."

The scan was one of the most emotional experiences she had ever had, and they both felt a little drained, so they decided to get some lunch and eat it back at Dale's flat.

"This is exactly how I imagined your flat. Modern, minimalist, although I half expected a pinball machine somewhere."

Dale rubbed her neck bashfully. "It's in the second bedroom."

Becca threw her head back and laughed. "I thought so. The perfect bachelor pad."

She walked up to Becca and took her hand. "I never knew I could have anything else."

Becca walked into her arms and hugged her. "Thank you for today. I'll remember it for the rest of my life."

She snuggled into Dale's chest. Becca felt right, wrapped in Dale's strong arms. Everything about her was right. The way she held her, the way she smelled, the way she felt lighter when she was with Dale.

"Thank you, Dale. Thank you for being there for us, for taking care of me."

"I want to take care of you all. My life was empty before Jake found me, and it…"

Dale's hesitation and the tension in her body made Becca pull back from her slightly. "What?"

"It makes me scared that I'll wake up and suddenly this will all have been a dream."

Becca gazed lovingly into Dale's eyes and said, "You're not going to wake up. We're here, and we're real."

Dale closed the distance between them and kissed her. Becca gave in to an urge she'd had from the very first, and slipped her fingers into Dale's thick unruly hair. The kiss became more fevered.

"Dale? I want you to touch me." Becca couldn't get enough of tasting Dale's lips and neck. She wanted her so badly.

"Are you sure? Is it safe?" Dale asked.

Becca replied by taking Dale's hand and saying, "Where's your bedroom?"

Dale led her through to her bedroom and closed the door and curtains, leaving them in the dull afternoon light. Surprisingly Dale looked nervous. Becca imagined Dale had never been nervous about sex, but she looked it now.

Becca put her hands flat on Dale's chest. "Are you okay?"

"I'm nervous—for the first time in my life I'm nervous about touching someone."

"Why? Is it me?" Becca wondered if it was because of the way she looked. "I know being pregnant I—"

Dale silenced her with a kiss, and then whispered close to her lips, "Nothing like that, you're beautiful. I'm scared that once I touch you, I'll never be able to stop, because I need you so much."

Becca was bold and started to unbutton her blouse slowly. Dale's breathing shortened and her eyes never wavered from looking at the skin Becca was exposing.

She threw her blouse to the side, took Dale's hand, and placed it on her bra-covered breast. "It's been so long since someone touched me. Will you touch me, please?"

That plea seemed to help Dale's confidence, and she kissed Becca deeply. She turned her around and kissed the back and side of her neck, while unclasping her bra.

When the bra was off, Dale immediately took her large breasts in her hands and both of them groaned.

"I've dreamt about this, Becca."

Becca was so wet already. She had forgotten what it felt like to be touched, although Trent's touch had never felt hot, desperate, and needy like this.

Becca covered Dale's hands with her own, and allowed herself a gentle squeeze. "Oh, that feels so good."

Dale continued to kiss her neck, and she gently bit Becca's earlobe. Becca moved her lover's hands down onto her baby bump, and said, "I'm having your baby, Dale."

"Yes, mine."

Dale pulled off her T-shirt and sports bra so they were skin to skin. Instinctively Becca pushed her bottom back into Dale's groin. She heard her moan, and felt her thrust softly back.

"I need to be closer, Becca."

Becca unzipped her skirt and let it fall to the floor. She turned around and Dale lifted her into her arms and carried her to the bed, kissing Becca as she went.

Dale lowered her onto the edge of the bed so she was sitting. Becca reached for Dale's belt and unfastened it. Dale stopped her and said, "Let me take care of you. That's all I've ever wanted."

Dale took off her jeans and boxers, giving Becca a full view of her toned body. Her biceps were strong from years of manual labour, and her Celtic tattoo made her biceps look more pronounced. It was no wonder women loved her.

Becca was surprised to see a long scar that ran down her thigh. She traced her finger down it and asked, "How did you get this?"

"I had a crash at one of my races."

"It must have been bad. Do you have any more scars?"

Dale pointed to her heart and said, "Just one, but I think it's healing every day I spend with you."

It was true, no one had ever come close to helping her heal, but Becca and what she gave her, what she was giving her, was making her life make sense and mending her broken heart.

Dale dropped to her knees and carefully and slowly took off Becca's tights, kissing Becca's skin as she went.

Becca used her hands to cover up some stretch marks and the caesarean scar on her growing stomach, and Dale immediately pushed them off.

"I want to see all of you. Everything that you are, everything that helped nurture and protect our children." Dale cupped her cheek and said with great sincerity, "All I need is you."

Dale pushed Becca back on the bed and took her underwear off. She could see how wet Becca was and it made her mouth water. Dale leaned forward and kissed Becca's stomach tenderly while grasping one of her breasts.

"God, you're so beautiful, Becca. I love these." Dale gently squeezed Becca's full breasts, and her mouth watered at the thought of taking her hard nipples into her mouth. She kissed and licked her way over her breasts. She felt Becca's fingers grip her hair almost painfully, and Becca's chest rose just slightly as if to encourage Dale to take her nipple into her mouth, and so she did.

Dale hummed in pleasure, and Becca cried out, "Yes, oh God."

She was careful not to rush. Becca hadn't had anyone touch her in a long time, and Dale wanted to show her how much it meant to her. Dale licked all around her nipple while squeezing the other with hand. She held Becca's nipple between her teeth while flicking the tip with her tongue.

This made Becca's nails dig into her back, and her hips move, seeking the release that Dale would give her. After one last big lick over her puckered nipple, Dale looked up at a flushed and hot looking Becca, and said, "Can I taste you?"

Becca raised herself up on her elbows and met her eyes. "Please. Make me feel again."

Dale didn't need to be asked twice. She kissed her way down Becca's stomach and placed her legs over her shoulders, giving herself complete access to Becca's sex.

She teased Becca by kissing her thighs, and licking around the lips of her sex. "You're so wet."

She felt Becca's hand in her hair encouraging Dale to quicken the pace. "I need you."

Dale couldn't wait any longer. She opened up Becca's sex and slowly at first circled her tongue around Becca's hard clit.

Becca's hips bucked, and she cried out at Dale's touch. "Oh, that feels so good. Just like that."

Dale lapped at her sex, hooked on Becca's taste from the first touch of her tongue. Becca's throaty moans were something she'd never get tired of hearing.

"Yes, right there," Becca cried. "I need to feel you inside."

Dale took two fingers and slipped them into Becca's velvety warmth. "You're soaking wet for me, babe."

"Yes, fill me up."

Dale returned her attentions back to Becca's clit while she thrust her fingers inside her, not too rough, just slow and loving.

She started to feel Becca's walls flutter, her moans and shouts grow higher pitched, and her hips thrust harder.

"That's it, babe. Come for me. Are you going to come for me?"

"Yes, God, yes," Becca cried.

Dale watched as she threw her head back and screamed her release, while the walls of Becca's sex gripped her fingers tightly.

As Becca recovered her breath, Dale kissed her thighs, and thought, *I love you.*

"Dale? Please come here," Becca pleaded.

She got on the bed and lay down by Becca's side.

"That was so good. No one's ever touched me like that," Becca said.

Dale stroked her cheek with the back of her hand. "That's because I was meant to touch you. You're the mother of my children."

"Yes, I am, aren't I?" Becca gazed into Dale's big brown eyes and stroked her fingers through her hair. She thought about the many times since she had gotten to know Dale better that she had allowed herself to fantasize about touching Dale, and felt her passion to have Dale surge through her.

She pulled Dale to her by her hair, gave her a long deep kiss that made Dale moan, and then pushed her away.

Dale was a little dazed and Becca took her chance to push her on her back. Becca was amused at the look of confusion on Dale's face.

"Becca—"

Becca lay on her side, with one of Dale's arms under her, held captive, and so she grasped the other one and held it above Dale's head.

She whispered, "I love your body, Dale. Do you know how many times I've watched you and then fantasized about it later?"

"You? You fantasized about me?" Dale said with surprise.

Becca released her grasp on Dale's wrist, confident that she would keep it where it was. "Uh-huh."

She trailed her fingers down Dale's shoulder and arm, circling her tattoo. "Yes, you woke up feelings inside me that I thought I'd never feel again. I thought about how gorgeous you were in your overalls."

Becca trailed her fingers down Dale's chest, circled her hard nipples, then made circles on her lower stomach.

Dale's breathing had shortened, and her eyes were glued to Becca's.

"I thought about how I'd like to come down to the garage in the afternoon, and have you lift me onto the car and—"

Becca saw the hungry look in Dale's eyes and knew she was about to take the initiative again. She placed a hand on her chest, and said, "No, let me. I've wanted to touch you for so long. You make me so wet, Dale. I've just come and it's still not enough. I need so much more of you."

Dale grasped her hand and said, "Show me."

Becca smiled and slipped her fingers into her own wetness, and allowed herself a few strokes of her clit. She pulled her fingers back, now covered, and showed Dale. "That's how much I want you, Dale. I want to show you how much I feel for you. I want to make you come."

Dale grasped her wrist, and Becca thought she was going to suck the wetness off her fingers, but instead Dale pushed her hand down to her sex.

"I want to feel you all over me."

Becca thought she had never felt anything more erotic in her life and slipped her already wet fingers into Dale's sex.

"Fuck, make me come, Becca," Dale said desperately.

Dale was hot and throbbing, so ready for her. She split her fingers around Dale's clit and stroked her softly at first, wanting this to last.

Becca saw Dale rise up on her elbows so she could watch what Becca was doing. Dale surprised her by saying, "Tell me the rest."

"The rest of what?" Becca asked.

"Your fantasy." Dale breathed hard.

"You lift me onto the car—"

Their eyes never left each other, and they were both living Becca's words. "What kind of car?" Dale asked.

Becca could have laughed out loud, but she didn't. Only Dale McGuire would worry about the make of a car in a sexual fantasy.

On a hunch Becca said, "Your Jaguar."

Dale groaned and her hips thrust against Becca's fingers. "Fuck, yes. More."

"I don't have any underwear on and you touch me and see how wet I am," Becca said huskily.

Dale cupped her cheek with her hand and kept her eyes focused on her.

"I open up your jeans—"

Before she had a chance to say anything, Dale said, "And you take out my strap-on."

Dale's eyes looked unsure as she added that into the story. Unsure as to how Becca would feel about that, she guessed.

She rewarded Dale with a sexy smile and moved closer to her lips. "Oh yes. You push your way inside me, and I feel so full, and you thrust so hard inside me—"

Dale's hips were bucking so fast now. "Yeah, yeah, I'm going to come." She grasped Becca's hand and held it as she threw back her head and gave a painful cry. "Ah, I need you, need you, Becca."

As Becca watch Dale come so freely and passionately, Becca knew that she was losing her heart to Dale, and nothing would ever feel as right as this.

❖

Dale woke from her sleep and found that she was wrapped around Becca, her hand lying protectively on her baby bump. She couldn't help the grin than erupted on her face. Last night had been magical, different and perfect. Making love and giving everything you had to the other whole person, and showing them how much you cared, was so different from the sex she'd had over the years.

She leaned on her elbow and gazed down at Becca, who was sleeping with a look of utter contentment on her face. The thought hit Dale, *She's the mother of my baby*. Dale trailed the tips of her fingers along Becca's cheek and jaw, and Becca's eyes fluttered awake.

"Morning, babe. How are you feeling?"

"Relaxed and happy in your arms. You make me feel safe."

"That's all I ever want to do. From the first moment I saw you, all I wanted to do was take care of you."

"Me or the baby?" Becca asked.

"Both. You know there's something been drawing us together from the start. It's like fate meant me to meet you."

Dale noticed Becca's eyes glaze for a second and her mind drift.

"What are you thinking?"

"I'm just a little scared what we have growing between us is just...chemicals, a primal urge to be close to each other because of the baby."

Dale smiled. "You make me have lots of primal urges, and they aren't going away. I've never wanted anyone like you."

Becca reached up and stroked her cheek. "I wish I had my camera. You look so happy, so content."

"I am, with you."

"I never thought I'd trust anyone ever again. I just didn't think I had it in me any more. The last time I trusted someone and gave them my secrets, she destroyed me."

"The person who sold your story to the newspapers?"

Becca nodded. "Ash. She was in her last year of journalism at the same university as me, and she came across me sitting on a bench outside, crying. She held me, looked after me, and made sure I was all right."

A tear escaped down Becca's face, and Dale wiped it away with her thumb. "You don't have to talk about this."

"I do. I need you to understand why I was so cold and guarded towards you, and what a big risk I'm taking now."

Dale nodded. "I understand."

"I thought she was my knight in shining armour. She protected me from the press who turned up at my university, and at my home.

I was so grateful, and so naive. She wasn't protecting me—she was protecting her interest in the story."

"What about Trent? Was she not around then? I'm sure she would have seen through her."

"Trent was just a friend then. She had just started working with her father at the law firm that represented my father. She did warn me to be careful, but I was desperately hanging on to someone who I thought would love and protect me. I told her everything. The parties, the money, the holidays, the Hardy brothers, I even took her home to help me with Mother. She saw everything. And one day I woke up and my story was all over the newspapers."

"Fucking bitch," Dale said, then started to backtrack. "Sorry for the language."

"You're right, she is."

Then the name finally dropped. "Wait, do you mean Ashley Duval? The over-opinionated woman who's on TV sometimes, or making pronouncements on social media?"

"That's her. She made a fortune off my family's misery and shame. She even wrote a book on us. That was the last straw for Mother. I found her dead after taking an overdose. Trent found me and picked up the pieces."

Becca started to cry and Dale pulled her into her arms, and kissed her hair. "Your debt is paid, and nobody knows where you are. You're free now, and your past can't hurt you any more. Whatever problems we have, I'll fix them. I won't let anything ruin what we have."

Ash had waited with her photographer for hours in a car across the road from Dale McGuire's, waiting for any sign of life. Dale and Victoria finally came out, and they appeared exceptionally close. Dale kissed Victoria tenderly before helping her into the car. Her photographer flashed off some shots of the kiss.

"Well, well, well," Ash said. "Looks like Vic's succumbed to her weakness yet again. Some smooth talking and McGuire's got her into bed." *You always were easy to manipulate, Vic.*

She turned to her photographer. "Tell me you got that kiss, Kev?"

"Yeah, I go it. Good shots too."

"Fabulous. I know McGuire's background now. I just wish I knew what her connection was to Vic and her kid."

Ash took out her phone and dialled Lisa's number. "Hi, I want you to get down to Belles and try and find out what connects McGuire to this woman and her kids."

"We've already tried that, Ash. No one knows."

"Someone knows something, Lisa. The bar manager—Mac— I'm sure knows something. It's the last piece in the puzzle. Do it for me, angel? Good girl."

She was going to find out, one way or another. *You could never hide anything from me, Vic.*

CHAPTER SIXTEEN

Dale whistled through her fingers to bring everyone to attention. "Okay, gather around, everyone. Val and Sammy are giving out fresh uniforms. We're taking these pictures for the new website, and it'll probably take a couple of hours, but I'm paying you and we'll have some food delivered for you, so be on your best behaviour. The photographer is my really good friend, and she'll be bringing her ten-year-old son. So nothing inappropriate, okay?"

"No dirty jokes then?" one of the mechanics joked.

"Not if you don't want your balls booted, mate. These two people are everything to me, so best behaviour for everyone. Imagine the Queen is coming, okay?"

Dale noticed Mike was away in a world of his own. "Hey, Mike? You got that."

"Yeah, yeah," Mike said nervously.

Sammy then added, "Go and get ready, and come back ASAP."

Dale saw Becca's car pull up in the car park. "Shit, they're here."

Val rubbed her back. "I know you're nervous, but try to stay calm. Everything will be fine."

"I don't know why I'm so nervous. I just want to make a good impression."

"You're in love, that's why. Now go and get them. I can't wait to meet Becca."

"Okay. I'll just be a sec."

Dale ran over to the car just in time for Jake to get out and jump into her arms. "Hey, wee man. How was school?"

"It was great. I scored a goal at football," Jake said excitedly.

"Yes!" Dale twirled him around. "Didn't I tell you that you could do anything? You just need to practice."

Becca walked around to join them. "He's been as high as a kite since I picked him up. Thank you for helping him."

"No problem." Dale gave her a soft kiss on the cheek. They had both agreed not to show too much affection in front of Jake, until they worked out what their relationship really was. To be more precise, Dale had agreed, but she already knew that she wanted—Becca and a relationship. She was just giving Becca some time.

"Why don't I take you two in to meet Val and Sammy, and then I can get your cameras and things?"

"Sounds good," Becca said.

Becca's heart started to beat a little bit faster. She'd been nervous about meeting Sammy and Val. They were Dale's only family, and she had no idea how they would react to her. It was Val who had recognized who Becca was, and so she knew the whole dreadful tabloid story. Who knew how they would judge her.

Dale squeezed her hand and said, "Are you okay, hen?"

"Yes, I'm fine. Just the little one doing backflips. Must be excited to see your business."

They walked through the large shutter doors into the big garage workspace. Off to the left was a separate waiting room and reception area.

"This is much bigger than the one I took the car to," Becca said.

"Aye, this is the biggest, and my first garage. I knocked down the original building and built this place when I could."

"It's wonderful, Dale. You should be very proud."

"Thanks," Dale said bashfully.

She didn't take praise very easily, one of the many traits Becca was beginning to adore about Dale. And she was beginning to adore Dale. A relationship and all its problems went against every rule Becca had, and everything about exploring these feelings with Dale was terrifying, yet she couldn't help herself.

Sammy and Val walked to meet them. "Sammy, Val, this is Becca, and you've met Jake."

Val took her in for a few seconds and then opened up her arms to Becca, with a big smile. "Becca, so nice to meet you at last."

Becca wasn't used to such warmth and was surprised when both Val and Sammy hugged her.

"It's lovely to meet you both. I've heard so much about you," Becca said.

"Likewise," Val said. "How are you feeling now? You have the beautiful glow of pregnancy from what I can see. Doesn't she, Sam?"

"Absolutely. You look beautiful, Becca."

The whole time Dale beamed with happiness beside her.

They greeted Jake, and he said, "Is Mia here? Dale said she would like to play computer games with me."

Val stroked his head. "I'm sorry but she had football practice tonight. She plays for a local girls' team, so her grandma took her to that."

"Oh," Jake said dejectedly.

Dale put an arm around him. "Don't worry, wee man. We'll all get together soon. In the meantime, you can check out my computers in the office. I'm sure you can do something to make them work faster."

"Yes, let's go." Jake pulled Dale by the arm, and she said to Becca, "I'll just be a few minutes."

Becca had her camera and equipment all set up and was taking the group photograph. She had already taken some action shots of the mechanics working on the cars, and equipment, and now it was just the team photo to do before Dale's employees could leave, so they were quite restless. Jake had grabbed several slices of pizza and run off to mess around some more with Dale's office computer.

The staff were making an arch while Dale, Sammy, and Val stood in front.

"Okay, everyone. Are we ready?" Becca said as loud as she could, but there was still murmuring and laughter going on.

Before Becca had a chance to say anything more, Dale turned around and roared at the top of her voice. "Shut up!"

Everyone went immediately silent and she turned back around and winked at Becca.

Becca fluttered inside. Dale was gorgeous, and confidence and swagger were two big parts of that attractiveness. They hadn't made love again since that day after the scan, but if Dale touched her, she didn't think she could say no.

She finished up the shots and the staff drifted home, leaving just Dale, Sammy, and Val.

While Becca packed up her things, Val walked over to chat. "Hi, I wanted to have a quick chat with you without Sammy and Dale around. How are you feeling really? It must have been a huge shock to have Dale bounce into your lives."

Becca laughed at that description, because it was entirely accurate. "Yes she did bounce in, just like Tigger, but she's been wonderful." Becca hesitated. "Dale says you know a bit about my history."

"Only what I've read, but I'm sure that's very far from the truth, and I know someone betrayed you."

Becca nodded. "The last woman I trusted betrayed me, so it was hard to trust again, but Dale was persistent."

"I can quite believe it." Val touched her arm in a friendly gesture. "I've known Dale since she was seventeen, and she may look like your typical bad boy, but she has a heart of gold, and is so loyal to the ones she loves. If you let her in, she'll never leave your side, but if you think a relationship is all too much for you, please tell her now, because it'll break her heart."

Val was certainly like a mother to Dale, because that was a mother's warning. "I don't intend to hurt her. We just need some time to see if this can work, for both of us."

At that moment, Jake came running out of the office with a laptop under his arm. "Mummy, look what Dale says I can borrow."

Becca smiled and turned to Val. "One thing is for certain. I'll never stop her seeing the children. She is going to be an important part of their lives."

❖

"This laptop is so fast, Mummy, my coding is going to be so much quicker," Jake said, as he played around with the laptop at the dinner table.

Dale nudged Jake and said, "Just don't hack into NASA, wee man, or your mummy is going to boot"—Dale hesitated, remembering at the last second to change the phrase—"my backside."

"I won't. Mummy's already warned me. I can't wait to show Mia my games on Saturday," Jake said. "I hope she likes me."

Dale ruffled Jake's hair. "She's going to love you. I'll bring over my Xbox for you both to play."

Becca brought over plates and started to dish out the food from the Chinese takeaway containers.

"Are you sure this isn't going to be too big a job for you and Sammy?" Becca said.

Dale had looked at the kitchen units in the garage and bided her time before suggesting she and Sammy fit out the kitchen. Now that Becca had accepted her help, Dale wanted to get it done as soon as possible.

"You don't trust my handiwork? Is the roof still leaking?"

"No. But it's a big job for you both," Becca said.

Dale sat back in her chair, crossed her arms, and gave Becca a confident grin. "Listen, me and Sammy fitted her and Val's bathroom and kitchen. We know what we're doing."

Becca chuckled at Dale's confidence. It was endearing and sexy in its way.

She handed out the food containers, and said, "Enjoy this, Jake. It's the last takeaway you're going to have for a while. We've been eating too much junk since Dale came into our lives."

Dale smiled and winked at her. "Listen, hen. Any nutritionist will tell you that the Asian diet is much healthier than our own."

Becca looked at the side orders spread around Dale's side of the table. "Yes, if you're not having salt and chilli chips, prawn toast, barbecue spare ribs, prawn crackers, plus your main meal."

Dale followed Becca's gaze around the food. "Hey, these are for sharing, not just for me. Anyway"—Dale gave Becca a smoky look—"I know what you would do for a taste of salt and chilli chips."

Becca took a quick breath, and their eyes were locked together. "Oh, you do?"

She nodded and pulled one of the spicy chips from the bag. "I might even let you put some jalapeños on them."

"That would make me feel hot," Becca said in a higher pitched voice than usual.

They were not talking about food any more, and Dale knew she had her lover aching inside. "Is it good when you feel hot?"

Becca nodded. "Can I have it?"

Dale was just about to answer when Jake said, "Dale? Who is Britney Spears and why is she lying across a car."

Dale's eyes went wide and she grabbed the laptop. "Shit."

Jake found her folder of Britney Spears wallpapers. Dale quickly deleted the folder but was afraid to look up at Becca.

When she did, she found Becca barely restraining her laughter. "I think you and I need to have a talk about Britney Spears."

Dale let out a sigh of relief. "It's okay, she's deleted. No room for her on my desktop any more."

She was rewarded with a beautiful smile from Becca.

I think I need to check through my files more carefully.

❖

After dinner Becca took Dale up to the studio to take her picture. It was the last close-up picture she needed for the website. Jake was happily playing in his room on the now Britney-free laptop.

Becca looked through her viewfinder and saw mischief in Dale's eyes. She pulled back, and warned her, "Hey, be serious now."

"I am. Serious is my middle name," Dale said with a cheeky smile.

"I'm sure." Becca looked back through the viewfinder. The light was good, but something wasn't quite right.

She turned her attention Dale's unruly, but sexy hair. "How do you manage to make your hair look like you've just come out of bed, and at the same time styled perfectly?"

"Great skill and dedication." Dale said.

"What about the day you came to see me with your suit on? It was all brushed and sitting smartly."

"That's when I was trying to show you I could be grown-up and respectable. If it doesn't work for the picture, come here and fix it for me." Dale looked at her like a wolf trying to entice its prey into its den. Becca felt hot and her skin ached to be touched, but she tried to shake the feeling away. She wanted to finish these pictures tonight and work on the prints tomorrow.

Dale beckoned Becca over with a nod of her head, and Becca's feet just followed directions. No wonder women fell at her feet.

Becca stepped into her personal space and Dale locked her feet around the backs of Becca's calves, and slipped her arms around her waist.

"So, fix my hair, hen."

Becca laughed. "You know, I thought this might be a trap."

"No trap, I just wanted to touch you. I've wanted to touch you ever since you arrived at the garage."

Becca felt Dale grasp her buttocks and squeeze. She felt a heavy beat start inside, and her body ached for Dale.

She grasped Dale's hair and started to run her fingers through it. Dale brought her lips to Becca's neck, and Becca felt her breath as she said, "You're so sexy, babe."

Then she started to kiss Becca's neck.

"I don't feel sexy. I wish I could be like the girls you normally attract...pert twenty-five-year-olds, with perfect breasts, no stretch marks, and no big stomach getting in the way."

"Have you even seen your breasts?" Dale said, in a way only she could. "I don't want a girl, I want a woman. A woman who feels like you, smells like you, tastes like you, and a woman who is the mother of my children. Not to mention that when you touch me, you set me on fire, right here"—Dale took Becca's hand and placed it on her heart—"and…here"—she placed Becca's hand on her belt buckle. "That is why you are so perfect."

Becca shivered and allowed Dale to pull her close and whisper in her ear, "Take the picture now. I want you to capture this moment, so when you look at the picture, you can see the want in my eyes and remember that this was because of you. Go."

Becca was a little dazed. No one had ever made her feel this turned-on, this wanted before. Not Trent, and certainly not Ash.

"I don't think I can," Becca said.

"Take it now, babe."

Becca took the picture and Dale immediately came over to her, and took Becca in her arms. "I want to make love to you. I want to make you moan and feel your nails scraping down my back."

Becca felt like her body was completely on fire and only for Dale. It was scary to be so dependent on one person again. She was giving Dale her heart, her body, and her children, and in some small part of her soul, there was still a little bit of fear.

"Let's go and put Jake to bed then."

Dale couldn't have been more content. She was lying in the dark, with Becca in her arms, after making love to her. The country sounds of animals outside the bedroom window were soothing, so different from the sounds of the city that she was used to. Dale played with Becca's long strands of soft hair. It was pure bliss.

"It's getting late," Becca whispered.

Dale closed her eyes and her heart sank. She got up immediately and pulled on her boxers and jeans without saying anything, getting angrier by the second. Angry and hurt.

Becca leaned up against the headboard and pulled the covers up to her neck.

"I wish you didn't have to go but—"

Dale grabbed her T-shirt and sports bra from the floor where she'd thrown them, and said as she put them on, "You still don't trust me yet."

"I just don't want Jake to come through here in the morning and find you here. He'll think that we're all going to be a happy family straight away, and then be devastated if this doesn't work out."

"Don't lie, it's because you're scared, not Jake. The only way it won't work is if you don't want it to. I know what I want, Becca," Dale said with anger in her voice.

"How can you know? You've seen the good parts. Jake's old enough to play with, he's well behaved. You don't know what it's like to wake up with a baby three or four times a night. To be puked on and so tired that the thought of sex would make you feel ill. You might wake up and decide it's time to leave."

"If you're trying to scare me away, it's not working. I would take all of that and more if it meant having you and being part of this family."

"Don't raise your voice," Becca warned. "Jake might hear you."

Dale took a big breath and tried to calm her simmering anger. "I don't mean to shout. It's just frustrating. As much as you've opened up to me and let me in to be part of Jake's and the wee yin's life, there's a part of you that doesn't want to let me in. Can I tell you what's worse than waking up three or four times a night for a baby? Having no one to wake up for, no one there when I go home. Why do you think I went out every weekend to listen to bad music and a bunch of giggling girls?"

Becca shook her head. "I don't know, because that's the kind of fun you want?"

"Because the weekend is a long time on your own. I love you, Becca, and I'm tired of not saying it. I love you. I never break my promises and I will never turn my back on you. But you've got to want me too."

"I do trust you, Dale—"

Dale pulled on her boots, and remembered her jacket was downstairs.

"You don't. If you did trust me, then you wouldn't sleep with me and then tell me to go, like we're doing something wrong, like we're having a sordid affair. I'm going to feel used, but maybe I was right, maybe there is something unlovable about me."

Dale walked out of the door hearing Becca shout after her, and it took everything she had not to turn around.

CHAPTER SEVENTEEN

A few days later Becca was clearing up the kitchen after breakfast, when Sadie popped her head around the door.

"Knock, knock."

"Hi, Sadie. Come in."

"I brought the cake you wanted me to make for your guests coming tomorrow, and a box of eggs from my chickens."

Becca gave Sadie a kiss on the cheek and took the items from here. "Thanks. Take a seat. Tea?"

Sadie pulled up a chair and said, "Oh, you know me. Never turn down a cuppa."

As Becca prepared a pot of tea, Sadie asked, "How have you been feeling? I noticed you went out to a few jobs this week."

"Yes, I did two this week, plus…" Becca closed her eyes for a second. "Plus Dale's garage pictures." Becca carried over the tea tray and set it on the table.

"I'll pour, sweetheart," Sadie said. "You sit back and take a breather. How have you been feeling? Is the doctor still pleased with you?"

Becca sighed. "Yes, my blood pressure is quite steady now. It's been getting better ever since Dale came into our lives."

Sadie must have detected her sad mood. She handed over a cup of tea to Becca. "Is there anything wrong?"

"We had a disagreement the other day, well a fight really."

Sadie put two heaped spoonfuls of sugar in her tea, and stirred vigorously. "I thought something was wrong when I saw you go to your doctor's appointment alone yesterday. She's taken you the last few times and fussed around you like some daddy bear."

Becca had to chuckle at that image. *I miss you, Dale.*

"She thinks I don't trust her and use Jake as an excuse," Becca said.

"In what way?"

Becca felt a little embarrassed talking about how the fight came about. "Well, sometimes Dale stays over, and…"

Sadie started to chuckle. "Just say it, sweetheart. Your generation didn't invent sex, you know."

Becca felt her cheeks heat up. She wasn't used to talking about these kind of things. She'd never had close friends, since she was always looking over her shoulder.

Sadie continued, "I can see the way you are together—there's a sparkling chemistry between you."

There was such chemistry and attraction. Dale could turn her on just by looking at her, and when she put her hands on her, Becca melted.

Sex had always been good with Trent, but not this desperate, in a rip-each-other's-clothes-off kind of way. Dale was the perfect package—she loved Becca and Jake exactly how Becca'd always dreamed a partner would, and she had a body that Becca adored. Dale knew she felt that way, and it had given her even more of a swagger than she'd had before. But that wasn't a bad, arrogant thing—it just made the sexual tension between them, the magnetic pull towards each other, all the stronger.

"She's stayed with me till late a few times, but I don't let her stay over in case Jake sees her in my room and thinks we are this perfect, happy fairy-tale couple, and then it all goes wrong. The other night Dale got angry. She thinks I don't trust her, and that Jake is an excuse. Then she said she loved me."

"Oh, my, and what did you say to her?"

"Nothing, and I hurt her. We haven't spoken since, although she texted to ask how my appointment with the doctor went."

"That's because she adores you, Becca. You can see it a mile off. She's like a big puppy following you around, trying hard to get your attention, and feeding on the scraps you give her."

Becca laughed cynically. "Sadie, Dale does not need to fight for the attention of a large pregnant woman in her late thirties. She can have her pick, and has had."

"Maybe in the past, but now, now she has a beautiful woman carrying her child, and a son she never knew about. Her life's turned upside down, but even still, she's run *to* you, not run away. You have to learn to trust her."

Just then Becca's phone beeped with a text. *Do you still want me to bring over the shopping you wanted for tomorrow?*

"It's Dale. She was supposed to get some supplies for her friends coming tomorrow, and help cook. I wasn't sure if they would still want to come."

"Tell her yes, sweetheart. Don't waste this chance for happiness. It may never come around again."

Becca stared at the phone. "I'm scared, Sadie."

"Everyone's scared when they fall in love. You are, aren't you?"

Becca took a breath and typed out a short reply. *Yes, I would like that. I miss you. Can we talk about us sometime tomorrow? About our future?*

Aye, I miss you too. Dale XX

The next morning when Dale arrived with the shopping, she hesitantly opened the kitchen door. Her insecurity almost broke Becca's heart.

Becca turned to Jake and said, "Go and get some of the bags from Dale's truck."

"Okay, Mummy."

When Jake ran out of the door, Dale remained standing there, as if still unsure of herself. "Hi, how are you and the wee yin?"

Becca walked towards her and took her hand. "We're fine."

She was drawn to Dale so strongly and she just had to touch her. Becca cupped Dale's cheek and said, "I missed you so much."

Dale immediately turned Becca against the kitchen counter, and as she went in to kiss her, she whispered, "I missed you so much it hurt." She placed her hand on Becca's stomach. "I missed all of you."

A gaggle of excited voices approached the back door. "Everyone's here," Becca said. "But we need to talk later."

They broke apart just as everyone came through. Mia and Jake were chattering away already, after only first meeting, and Val and Sammy gave them a knowing smile.

Val squeezed Sammy's arm. "Sorry to interrupt, you two."

Becca went over to greet her new friends with a smile and a kiss. "Come in. It's great to see you all."

The vicarage had never known as much noise in a long, long time. There was banging, sawing, and the roar of power tools. In the living room, Jake and Mia were playing on Dale's Xbox, and the music and noise from it were very loud.

Becca didn't mind one bit. Her life had been quiet for so long, and it was nice to liven it up. She sat with Val watching over the kids.

"Jake, get the key quickly...and run!"

"We did it! We did it!" They high fived each other.

Becca was delighted to see Jake having so much fun with another child.

"It's wonderful they are getting on so well," Becca said to Val. "He normally struggles socially with other children."

Val smiled. "Mia was so excited to meet Jake. Dale had told her so many good things about him."

Becca gazed over at Val's beautiful little girl, leading the play and showing Jake something they both found fascinating on the iPad.

"Mia is a lovely girl. I know Dale loves her to pieces."

"Thank you. Yes, Dale has a really special relationship with Mia. She's just great with kids."

Jake and Mia came over to them then, and Jake looked really

excited. "Mummy, can we go upstairs? I want to show Mia the game I've been coding."

"Okay, but remember, no hacking into NASA."

Jake nodded and they ran off excitedly, but Val looked at her strangely at her last comment.

"A running joke."

"It must be really challenging bringing up a gifted child," Val said.

"It has been, but it's been so much easier since Dale came into our lives. She's not the love 'em and leave 'em type no matter what people think about her. She's sensitive, loving, and just wants a family to love her, like her mother couldn't."

"Exactly." Val covered Becca's hand with hers. "There's a part of you that's still scared, isn't there?"

Becca shook her head. "There was, but when I saw her walk in the door today, I knew I couldn't live without her."

Val engulfed her in a hug. "Wonderful. You don't know how happy it'll make Sammy and me to see Dale with someone to love her. It's all she's ever wanted."

"It's all I've ever wanted too, but I never thought I'd be brave enough to look for it."

They heard feet thundering down the stairs, and then the loud voices and laughter of Dale and Sammy.

"Sounds like the little kids and the big kids are getting restless," Val said.

Becca stood up. "We better get some sandwiches made for lunch. Dale set all the kitchen things up in the living room."

❖

Becca stood back and allowed Dale to put Jake to bed.

"Will I see you tomorrow, Dale? Will you come back?"

Becca glanced at Dale and smiled. "You'll see Dale at breakfast. She's going to be staying the night here."

"Really?" Jake bounced out of bed and into a surprised Dale's arms.

"Yes, really," Becca said. "Dale is part of our family, Jake, and I hope she always will be."

Dale hugged Jake, but looked straight into Becca's eyes and mouthed, "Thank you." Then she said to Jake, "I told you I'd always be here for you and your baby sister, wee man. I'd really like to be part of your family."

Once they eventually got Jake settled and left his room, Dale pulled Becca to her and said, "Thank you, babe."

"I wanted to show you I wasn't frightened any more, and Jake knowing is the first step to that."

Dale started to kiss her neck and manoeuvre her to the bedroom.

Becca tried to cool her libido for at least a little while. "We promised we'd talk everything out first, darling."

Dale smiled. "Darling Dale?" She imitated Becca's accent. "I like it, but you are so posh, you know that?"

Becca was backed against her own bedroom door. "Are you making fun of my accent?"

Dale gave her a cheeky smile, and whispered in her ear, "Aye, I am. Can I be your bit of rough?"

Becca giggled. "Yes, but we have to talk first. The other night you said you felt like you were being used."

"I don't care. Use me. Use my body for your pleasure. I just want you."

Becca chuckled and opened her bedroom door. As soon as they were inside, Dale's hot hands were everywhere. They undressed each other quickly, so they could be skin to skin. Becca clung to Dale's neck as their kisses became feverish.

"Becca, I want to make you come so hard, and I want to watch you."

Dale jumped onto the bed and crooked her finger. "Come and sit here, babe." Becca climbed onto the bed, and with Dale's help moved astride her lover's hips. "Are you comfortable, babe?"

Looking down and seeing the hunger in Dale's eyes was more than comforting, it was red hot. "Yes, this is just perfect."

"It's perfect for me." Dale ran her hands from Becca's neck down to her breasts, where she stopped to gently squeeze them.

Becca's hips began to rock in response to the stimulation. "No one's ever touched me like you do."

Dale's hands moved down to caress her belly. "That's because no one's ever loved you like me."

Becca couldn't wait any longer. She took one of Dale's hands and pushed it to her sex. "Please, darling." Dale's fingers slipped straight inside her, and Becca groaned. "Oh yes."

She set her own pace, lifting and impaling herself on Dale's fingers. This position enabled Dale to touch her everywhere, and she did, encouraging Becca to enjoy every wave of pleasure her body could give.

"That's it, babe. Feel it, and come for me. I want to watch you come as I fuck you."

Dale raised her knees, giving Becca something to lean back on comfortably as her hips sped up.

Becca could feel the need inside her race towards its release, and all she could think of was how much she loved Dale.

"Dale, Dale, I need you," Becca breathed as her orgasm rushed over her.

When her body gave up on her, she was gathered in Dale's loving arms, and kissed and held until she fell asleep, blissful, and content.

❖

They woke in each other's arms.

Becca kissed Dale's chin lovingly. "Dale, I want to tell you why I was still scared. Even though I knew you cared, I was scared you loved me because of the children, and I wondered how I could ever know whether you loved me just for me."

Dale leaned up on an elbow and looked down to Becca. "You think I wouldn't love you on your own? Are you kidding? If I had seen a posh girl like you in a bar, or if you'd brought your car into one of the garages, I'd have been relentless in trying to chat you up, hen. You're beautiful, sophisticated, kind. I wouldn't have let you leave without getting your phone number, and I always get the girl's phone number."

Becca chuckled. "Oh, you would, would you?"

"Definitely. I got you into bed didn't I?" Dale winked. "And you couldn't stand the sight of me when I turned up."

Becca ran her hand down Dale's back, and squeezed her muscled backside. "Oh, I wouldn't say I couldn't stand the sight of you. You were pretty good eye candy."

"Oh yeah?"

Becca had never really been a giggly teenager when it came to women, even when she was a teenager, but she felt like it now.

"Yes, especially in those overalls and tight T-shirt, but I don't know if I can compare to the other woman in your life."

Dale looked confused. "What other woman?"

"Britney Spears," Becca said.

Dale looked mightily relieved at that answer. "Nah, it's okay. As soon as I knew I wanted you, Ms. Harper, me and Britney had a talk."

"Oh? And where did this happen?"

"On her calendar, in my office. I told her that I'll always remember her fondly, but I've fallen in love with the woman of my dreams. It was all very civil."

Becca couldn't help but laugh out loud. She grasped Dale's unruly hair and said, "You're off your rocker, do you know that?"

"I found that out a long time ago, but I make you laugh, don't I?" Dale said hopefully.

"You do—you're the only one that's ever been able to. Dale…"

Becca suddenly felt the need to be serious, and Dale gave her a soft kiss to reassure her. "Tell me."

This was the hard part. Saying those three words was giving someone else a power over you. Could she trust Dale with that power? The baby chose that moment to start kicking inside her, as if she was saying, *Tell her!*

Maybe she could have the happiness she had dreamed of, after so many years of running and looking over her shoulder.

"Is it the baby?" Dale asked.

"Yes, she's kicking and telling me to get on with it."

"Get on with what?" Dale asked.

Becca stroked the hair that so fascinated her fingers, and said, "Telling you I love you. I love you, Dale McGuire, and I'd like to use your body for a lifetime."

Dale was silent and then gulped hard as tears came to her eyes. "You love me? Really?"

Knowing Dale's background, it was easy to see how hard it was for Dale to take that on board.

"Yes, I love you, Jake loves you, your wee yin loves you, your whole family loves you, and we'll never turn our backs on you."

Dale kissed her deeply, and desperately. She had been waiting for a family her whole life, and the way Dale kissed her, she knew that Dale would never leave them. She would defend and give her loyalty to them forever.

"Thank you, Becca. Thank you for telling me. I won't let you down. I'll love and take care of you all, every day of my life."

Dale was almost shaking with the raw emotion she was feeling. Becca knew what Dale needed to help her process and cement these emotions between them.

"I want you to make love to me and then, only if you want to, go home to your flat, collect some things to stay, and come back to your family."

"Yes, that's what I want more than anything in the world."

Dale reached down to touch her, but Becca caught her hand. "No, not this time. I need you to come on me."

The hot, desperate gaze she got in return from Dale was instantaneous. Becca turned on her side and presented her bottom to Dale. She knew she would enjoy making love with Dale in this position, because Dale could hold her close in a tight embrace.

Dale ran her hand over Becca's curves and over her bottom. She couldn't believe how lucky she was. To have a woman like Rebecca Harper offer herself, her body and her heart, was more than she could have ever dreamed of.

Her body felt more alive than it ever had been, like electricity was sparking all over her, and the only one who could calm her was Becca, her love.

She quickly opened herself up, so that she could thrust against Becca's fleshy backside. Dale held Becca close, one arm holding herself up and the other alternating between Becca's hip, baby bump, and her heavy breasts.

Dale started to thrust. She was wet and ready before she even touched Becca. Her sex was so hot and she needed to come so badly, she knew it wouldn't take long. Becca's body made Dale feel fire in her veins. She had slept with a lot of girls, but Becca was a woman, not a girl. She was a lady, very female, very curvaceous, and the fact that she was pregnant with her child made her all the more attractive. Dale felt the deep need at some primal level, to claim Becca and her baby as her own.

"You're mine, Becca. I love you."

"I love you too, darling. Come on me." Becca reached back to caress Dale's face and neck with her fingers.

Dale felt Becca push her bottom harder, to give her better contact. She started to thrust much harder, and held on tightly to Becca's hip to keep them in the right position.

Her orgasm was seconds away, and she asked with desperate need in her voice, "Tell me, Becca. Please?"

"I'm yours, Dale. I love you."

That was all Dale needed. The heat that had been building in her sex exploded into an almost painful orgasm that swept down her legs, and up to the top of her head. "Fuck, fuck, I love you, I love you."

After a few seconds, Dale fell back on her pillow, limp and breathing hard. Becca turned around and placed gentle kisses over her cheeks and mouth.

Dale put her arms around her and held her while she tried to get her breath back. "That was so good. I can hardly breathe." She opened her eyes and saw Becca looked a bit unsure of herself. "What's wrong?"

"I'm sure you've made love in much more exciting ways than you have with me, but after the baby—"

Dale rolled her over and silenced her with a kiss. "Don't ever say things like that. Making love…sex has never felt like that just felt, and it's because it's you, your body, the woman I'm in love with. Don't ever say anything like that again, okay?"

Becca's smile was back. "I'm sorry, I'm pregnant and I've got hang-ups and hormones."

"Well, don't listen to them. I'm just a grease monkey from the East End of Glasgow, and you are so far above my league. I'm the lucky one, hen."

That made Becca laugh. "Oh, stop it. I'm the daughter of a doctor who was struck off for selling drugs."

"You're my posh girl, and you always will be." Dale kissed her lips, then said, "Sorry for swearing, by the way."

Becca ran her hands through Dale's hair. "It's okay. It's allowed during sex."

Dale laughed. "Is that the rule, is it?"

Becca kissed her nose sweetly. "As long as it's with me."

"Always and forever."

Dale started to kiss her way down Becca's body.

"I thought you were going to collect some things from your flat."

Dale looked up at her with a hungry look in her eyes. "I have to taste you first, posh girl."

CHAPTER EIGHTEEN

Jake was bursting with excitement this morning. Dale was going to take him for a drive to her flat, so she could pick up some essentials to stay at the vicarage, while Becca started to bring some of the kitchen things back to their rightful places.

"Don't do anything heavy," Dale called out as they walked out the door.

"I won't, just the little things. Hurry back, and we can have lunch."

Becca started carrying in tins and packets of food from the living room. She set the items on the countertop and looked around at her beautiful new kitchen. Dale and Sammy had done a wonderful job. Next they thought they would put down a new floor. There was hope in the vicarage now, whereas before she could only see never-ending problems. Now they she had a partner who wanted to be fully involved in their family, they could plan on rebuilding the home together. It was warm and cosy, and one day it would be as she had dreamed, except this time, Becca would have someone to stand by her side.

Becca heard the back door open, and assumed Dale had forgotten something. "Dale, you…"

Her voice trailed off when she saw Ashley Duval standing in her kitchen.

Ashley shut the door and said, "Hello, Vic. You've been a hard woman to find."

"Ash...what do you want?" All Becca's fear and paranoia came crashing back into her soul.

Ash pulled out a chair and sat down nonchalantly. "I see you've been busy." She indicated Becca's stomach. "Is that the daddy that just left? She looks butch enough to be capable of it. First Trent, then Dale McGuire."

Becca was in full panic mode. How did Ash know Dale's and Trent's names?

"I suppose after I fucked you, you were always going to be slumming it, but at least Trent was a lawyer. McGuire is as common as they come, but maybe you like roughing it, Vic."

"Tell me what you want, or get out."

"I want more of you. Your story made me, and I'm in need of just a little more. I tried to find you after your father hanged himself, but Trent hid you well. Then one day, quite by chance, I ran into a girl who was looking at a photograph of you and your son."

"I don't understand. Who had a picture of us?" Becca sat at the table before she fell down. How could this be happening? When she woke this morning everything had been perfect, and she was looking forward to life, but now her past was sitting right in front of her.

"A young reporter at the newspaper I work for. Dale McGuire fucked her and fucked off. I'm surprised you put up with that, but then you were always easy prey, Vic."

Becca's shock was turning into anger. "Get out of my house. I don't believe a word you say. I don't know how you found me, but it wasn't by some girl sleeping with Dale."

But we made no promises for so long. In fact Becca had tried her hardest not to fall for Dale's advances. Had Dale been sleeping with other people while they had been falling in love? She had no right to be jealous, but she was. The thought of Dale sharing herself with someone like they did last night hurt her.

"Well how else did she get your picture? Don't be a fool all of your life, Vic."

"Just tell me what you want and go. I've finally stopped running, and I'm going to make a fresh start for me and my children," Becca said.

Ash leaned forward. "You couldn't run from me forever."

"What did I ever do to you, Ash?"

Becca had always wondered what had made Ash go after her so ruthlessly. Surely there had to be a reason?

"You were an opportunity, a means to an end. One of life's little opportunities that gives you a chance to take and make yourself a success, if you're brave enough, but it also gave me a chance to destroy your bastard of a father."

"What did my father ever do to you?" Becca asked.

A look of deep anger came upon Ash's face. "Fucked my mother and got her hooked on drugs. The drugs that killed her, but since your mother topped herself maybe all things are equal."

Becca's breathing became raspy and she started to feel sick. "I had no idea."

Ash stood and leaned in close to her with hate in her eyes. "Do you know how it feels to watch you mother so desperate for her next fix that she's willing to be treated like a whore just to get her drugs? Your father did that to her. But you would never know how that feels. You and Carlotta were too busy enjoying your luxury holidays and spending the money made by other people's misery. I always swore I'd make him pay."

Ash sat back down, calming her seething rage. "Then I found you. You were my little goose that laid golden eggs, and I want one more."

"Just get on with it then."

"Now, now, no need to be like that. I'm not without a heart—I will give you a choice. There are two ways I can do this story. One, without your cooperation, but that would mean me having to dig a lot of dirt about your loved ones to make it interesting or—"

"What about my loved ones?" Becca snapped.

Vic took a file out of her case and slid it over to Becca. When Becca opened it she found lots of pictures and information, but the labels caught her eye. There were pictures of Dale's real mother, Nora, and her stepbrothers and stepsisters.

"How did you find this out?"

"I'm a journalist, Vic. No one can hide from me."

There were also pictures of Dale's garage, Sammy, Val, and Mia, and, most disturbingly, pictures of Jake with Dale.

"If you print pictures of my son, I'll kill you," Becca warned.

But Ash just laughed. "Oh, give me a break. You'll do nothing. You're weak, easily led, and pathetic."

It would break Dale's heart to have Nora and her past splashed everywhere. She couldn't allow it.

"Dale has nothing to do with this story. Why would it interest you to add in Dale's story to mine? There's no purpose to it."

"Of course there is. A sordid lesbian story spices up anything, especially if it shows family dysfunction. The readers of my newspaper are very conservative. They liked to be reminded how right they are in their condemnation of gay people and their lives."

"But you're gay, Ash. How could you do that?"

Ash smirked. "Every man—or lesbian—for themselves in this world. I look after me and me alone."

Becca threw the folder back across the table at Ash. "So? You said there are two ways you can write this story. What will it take to keep my family and friends out of this article?"

"A full no-holds-barred interview with you, on camera. I'll be able to make a lot of money off you again, Vic. Your family caused one of the biggest national scandals in fifty years, and I want more."

"Go to hell," Becca said.

"Is that a yes then?"

Becca said nothing. She couldn't speak, could hardly breathe. Why could she never walk free from the sins of her father? In the end, what choice did she have?

"I'll let you think it over, but don't be foolish. I can make your friends look really bad, even if they are perfectly good citizens."

Ash stood up and put the file back in her case. "I'll be in touch."

❖

Jake loved visiting Dale's flat. As he walked around looking at all her cool gadgets, Dale could hear, "Wow!" every few seconds.

Dale quickly put all her essentials in a small suitcase, knowing she could come back for other things later. She was so excited. She just wanted to get back to the vicarage before Becca changed her mind—not that she would.

She went into her bedside table and picked up her mum's Bible. *I've found my family, Ma, and I know you'd love them.*

After carefully placing the Bible in her bag, she zipped it up and went to get Jake. She found him in her home office, just about hugging her computer.

"Hey, wee man. You like that?"

He nodded briskly. "They have this kind at computer club but not as good a one as this. It's so cool."

Dale hoped Becca wouldn't be mad at her idea, but she did have a lot of child support to catch up on. "I'll tell you what. It's Christmas in a couple of months. You do some research into what would be the perfect computer for you to code all your projects and we'll see if Santa can bring it, okay?"

Jake's eyes went wide with wonder and he jumped into Dale's arms. "Thank you. It would be the best present ever, and I'd take care of it so well."

Dale squeezed him tight. How did she ever live without Jake and Becca in her life? It seemed like she had always known them.

"I know you would." She put him down and fished two lollipops from her pocket. "Let's celebrate with a cherry lollipop."

Jake unwrapped his stick and said, "Dale? Are you my mummy's girlfriend now?"

Girlfriend seemed such a temporary title. *I want to marry her.* Dale had never thought she would ever want that in her life, but she wanted it badly.

"Aye, girlfriend, or partner, hopefully something more, one day. Are you okay with that?"

Jake nodded enthusiastically. "Uh-huh. It's the best news ever. That's why I came to find you, to help my mummy and make her happy. No one's ever made her happy and laugh, except you."

This boy would melt your heart, Dale thought. "Well don't you worry any more, Jake. I'll take care of your mummy, and you and your baby sister."

Jake looked down at the floor, as if he was building up to something. "Dale, remember when we met you said I shouldn't call you *Mum*?"

Dale felt instantly guilty about what she'd said that first day they met. "Aye, I remember."

He looked up at her with eyes just like hers and said, "Can me and my little sister call you Mum now?"

She pulled him into a hug. "I would love that, Jake, as long as your mummy says its okay. Remember, no matter what, Mummy's in charge and we do what she says. We need to make her happy, and look after her. She's not so ill any more, and we have to keep it that way."

Jake took her hand, and said, "Okay, Mum, let's go home."

Dale didn't think she'd heard a more perfect sentence in her life.

❖

Dale looked in on Jake and saw he was sleeping soundly. She hesitated at Becca's bedroom door. She'd sensed something wrong since they'd returned from her flat, and she only prayed that Becca wasn't having second thoughts.

She walked through the door and found Becca already in bed, but lying on her side, with just the small lamp on.

"Everything okay, hen?"

"Yes, I'm just tired," Becca said, sounding unconvincing.

Dale got changed into her boxers and sleep T-shirt, and slipped under the covers. Becca never made a move towards her, and the bed suddenly felt very big. This was not how she'd imagined their first night living together.

It got even worse when Becca snapped off the light, plunging them into lonely blackness.

Dale didn't know what to say or do. Should she try and hug her? Should she talk?

"Dale?"

"Yeah?"

"When was the last time you slept with someone?"

Dale's heart sank. This was not a good opening to a conversation. She sat up quickly and switched her lamp on. "I don't think that's a good thing to talk about when we're just starting out on our life together."

Becca turned around quickly and gave her an accusatory stare. "Why, was it just last week? Was it while we were getting together?"

"What? No, what do you think I am?"

"I know you like sex with lots of women. When was the last time, Dale?"

Dale couldn't understand what had happened to her sweet, loving Becca. "Why are you being like this? I thought we were past that. You know that's not me."

"Please, Dale, just tell the truth. When was the last time?"

Dale shook her head, her anger rising inside. "You want to know? Fine, I'll tell you, even though it's stupid. Do you think I'd want to know when you last slept with Trent? I don't want to even contemplate anyone else touching you. It was the weekend Jake found me, and you sent me off, telling me never to darken your door again. I was messed up. I went on a weekend bender. I slept with two women. The first, I was so drunk I can't even remember, and the second was a screwball who tried to steal the picture Jake had given me. Is that good enough for you?"

Tears started to fall unrestrained from Becca's eyes.

"Hey, hey, I'm sorry. Don't cry."

"No," Becca gasped. "I shouldn't have asked."

Dale rocked her gently in her arms, trying to soothe Becca's tears. "Hen, I never even looked at another woman after that, and never went back out to the bar. My mate, Mac, the bar manager has probably put out a missing poster."

"I'm so sorry, darling. I've ruined our first night together."

"Listen, I knew I wanted you from the start probably. That weekend I just kept staring and staring at the picture and I felt connected to you, like I was missing from the picture. Since then the only woman's knickers I've been trying to get in are yours."

Becca laughed through her tears.

"See, I can still make you laugh. Now what brought all these thoughts to your head?" She was sure she could feel Becca stiffen.

"Nothing, just hormones, you know."

Dale remembered when Val was pregnant, the random bouts of crying and Sammy saying the wrong things. It was her turn now.

"Okay, then whenever you feel bad, you just tell me and I'll make you laugh."

Becca huddled into her tightly. "Why don't we go through the baby name book you bought?"

"Yes, I'd love that." Dale snapped on the light.

CHAPTER NINETEEN

Becca had a week to work out how to handle Ash, or face the media storm that would be coming her way. But as the week went by, Becca could not find a way out of her dilemma. If she told Dale the full story, she would likely try to stop Ash by any means, and the story would be a whole lot worse.

The sick feeling she had in the pit of her stomach when she'd seen Ash just kept getting worse. It took everything in her power not to show how worried she was to Dale. When Dale did question her on why she was being so quiet, she blamed not feeling well. Which wasn't a lie—her headaches were back, she'd had some dizzy spells, and according to the doctor, her blood pressure was starting to elevate again, and that was on the strong medication.

One thing that helped her hide what was happening was the fact that Dale was keeping herself so busy. Now staying at the vicarage most nights, and part of their family, Dale had given herself free rein to do all the jobs she wanted to on the house. Plus Jake mostly followed Dale around, frightened that she would somehow disappear.

She might after her whole personal life is exposed by Ash.

Her mobile beeped with a text and she nearly jumped out of her skin when she saw the screen. Somehow Ash had managed to get hold of her number. She held her breath as she read the message. *Tick, tock. Time is running out. Saturday or I do this myself. Do you remember what it was like to have the press pack circled around your house?*

Becca's memory replayed the scene of finding her mother dead, with half of Britain's press encamped outside, and the claustrophobic feeling of being trapped started to take over. Her vision narrowed until all she could hear was her thunderous heartbeat in her ears.

She was trapped, she couldn't breathe, she was going to suffocate. Panic was taking over. Then Becca could hear someone calling her name. "Becca? Babe, take deep breaths."

Becca's vision started to clear and she saw Dale kneeling in front of her, cradling her face tenderly.

"Babe? I'm here. Don't panic, I'll take care of you."

"Dale?" Becca latched on to her lover's neck like a limpet. "I was so scared. So scared."

Dale squeezed tightly and rubbed her back. She had no idea what brought that on this panic attack, but it was terrifying to find Becca gasping for air, clutching the bedcovers so tightly, her knuckles were turning white, but she had to make this better because this kind of stress wasn't good for Becca or the baby.

"I'm here, hen. No one or nothing can ever frighten you when I'm here."

"I love you, Dale. I don't want you ever to feel pain like Nora gave you again," Becca said.

Dale pulled back and looked at Becca questioningly. "What do you mean? I'm the happiest I've ever been in my life. What brought this on?"

Becca was eerily silent.

"Becca? Tell me. I can't help it if you don't tell me."

"I think my blood pressure is a little high. I feel some of the symptoms coming back, and I had a dream that something badly wrong is going to happen…at the birth."

Dale kissed the back of Becca's hand. "Nothing is going to happen. It's just a stress dream. We'll get the doctor here to look you over and take it from there, but everything will be fine, babe."

Surprisingly, Becca didn't argue about the doctor coming, which worried Dale more than anything else.

Becca grasped Dale's T-shirt and said in a panicked voice, "Promise me if anything happens to me, you'll take the children."

"What? Why are you talking like this? Nothing is going to happen to you."

Becca's eyes were deadly serious. "Please, Dale. I just need to know, if the worst happens, Jake and our little girl will be looked after. If I get Trent to draw up the papers, will you sign them?"

Dale couldn't believe Becca was talking this way, but if it made her feel more settled, then fine.

"Of course I will. I told you I will never turn my back on my family. Now let me call the doctor and we can get you sorted out."

There was something wrong—deep down Dale could feel something was wrong with Becca. She had been nervy and jumpy. She was sure it wasn't about their relationship, because if anything she was clinging more to her with each day that passed. Maybe it was just hormones, and baby stuff? *I should talk to Val.*

❖

"Checkmate!"

Dale looked all over the chess board for possible moves but could find none. She gave Jake a high five and a huge smile. "Well done, wee man. I knew you'd be great at this game."

Dale and Jake were playing chess at the kitchen table, while Becca rested upstairs. A few days ago the doctor prescribed bed rest for at least two weeks, as Becca's blood pressure was so high. Dale couldn't understand it. She had been doing so well, but the doctor explained that the last few months of pregnancy could be tricky, especially at Becca's age and with her previous difficult pregnancy.

So Dale never left her side. Sammy and Val were shouldering the burden at McGuire's Motors and were only too happy to help. Val had come over a few times to visit and brought Mia, much to Jake's delight. The two children were becoming fast friends, with Mia helping design storyboards for Jake's games. Dale had remarked that they would all be able to retire early once the kids set up their own computer software company.

Everything was going well, except Becca's health, but Dale just had to concentrate on getting her past the last couple of months of pregnancy.

"Can we play again?" Jake asked.

"Set them up, wee man."

As they were rearranging the pieces, Becca walked into the kitchen, carrying her mug from her afternoon cup of tea in one hand and her phone in the other. That was something new and strange about Becca's behaviour. She wasn't a woman who was glued to her mobile. In fact she usually forgot it, or couldn't find it, but this week it had never been out of her hand.

Becca kissed Jake on the head. "Having fun, Pooh Bear?"

"Yes," Jake said, "I beat Mum."

Dale's heart still skipped a beat every time she heard Jake use that title for her. It was like an honour had been bestowed on her. She was a mum now, and a mum given the task to take care of this little family, and she was ready to do that until her last breath.

"Good boy. If you beat your mum, you'd probably beat me in ten seconds."

Becca walked over to the sink and Dale said to Jake, "Give me a second to talk to your mummy, will you?"

"Yes, I'll practice."

When Jake said he'd learn a game and practice, he went about it in a methodical way. He had his *How to Play Chess* book, written by a grand master, and his notebook where he wrote down special moves and tips. Dale had great doubts that she would ever win a match again.

She walked up behind Becca, slipped her hands around her waist, and kissed her neck. "I thought you were supposed to be resting."

Becca leaned back into Dale's reassuringly solid body. "I'm tired of resting, and I need to put the casserole Sadie gave us in the oven."

Dale closed her eyes and inhaled Becca's sweet-scented hair. It smelled warm and loving, and most of all, it smelled like home. "Already done. Sadie put sticky notes on the dishes telling me what temperature and how long to put it in, so you don't have to lift a finger."

"I could get used to that," Becca said, turning around into Dale's arms.

"You should because I'm going to care for you like you were the finest bone china."

Becca caressed Dale's cheek. "I love you, and I want to do what's best for you too."

Dale placed a kiss on her nose, then her cheeks, then on her mouth.

"I love you too, and what's best for me is being by your side. Maybe I should pull out of the race on Saturday. I don't like the idea of leaving you alone."

Dale felt Becca immediately tense up. "No, you can't do that. You promised Jake you would take him to see you racing with Sammy, and Mia's going to be there. I'll be happy to curl up with my book and snooze…a lot."

Dale sighed. "Maybe I could ask Val to visit with you—"

Becca pulled away from Dale and said sharply, "No, I'm quite capable of staying in for the afternoon on my own. Just keep the plans you've made. Take Jake to the racetrack"

Becca started rubbing an area under her lower ribs. She'd been doing that a lot. And why was she was so insistent that Dale and Jake go out? Dale was sure something was up. "Are you sore, babe?"

"Just indigestion. I'll go and lie down till dinner's ready."

Dale kissed her and watched her walk out of the kitchen. Out of the corner of her eye, she noticed Becca had left her phone on the kitchen counter, and the screen was lit up with a text message.

She picked it up, already feeling guilty. This was invading Becca's privacy, but something wasn't right, and Dale would do anything to keep Becca safe.

When she saw the text sender was Ashley Duval, her stomach churned. *No, it can't be.*

Dale didn't have the PIN to Becca's phone, but the first few lines were previewed on the lock sceen. It said, *Saturday, 2:15. Make sure you're there.*

Dale was going to wring her fucking neck.

Chapter Twenty

A sh set up the camera and made sure it captured them both. She took a seat in front of Becca.

Becca's insides were churning. Her throat was tight, her head fuzzy and dizzy, and she'd had a horrible pain under her ribs all day. It was like this scene was happening to someone else.

"I've waited a long time for this, Vic. So why don't we get started?"

Becca reached for the bottle of water on the table to try and counteract the nausea she was feeling.

"Okay, we're recording. I'm here with Victoria Carter, daughter of notorious drug—"

Just then the kitchen door opened and Dale came storming in. "You, get the fuck out of our house."

Ash stood quickly. "You said she would be out. Is this a set-up?"

"No," Dale replied. "You had my girlfriend so terrified she had to hide it from me. Well I'm taking control now. Becca is ill, you low-life piece of shit. Get out."

"I believe this is Vic's house and she invited me here."

Becca felt like she was watching the scene through a cloud of smoke, and it was hard to keep up with what was happening.

"I'm not asking, I'm telling." Dale picked up Ash's camera and tossed it out the door.

"You fucking idiot. That's an expensive camera."

"Is it, aye? Well your bony arse is next. No one threatens or blackmails my family. Out."

Ash picked up her things and stopped in front of Dale. "You've just made the biggest mistake of your life. Your name and your family are going to be dragged through the gutter."

"No," Becca managed to say. "Not Dale's family. Please?"

Becca tried to stand up and then she started to shake and tremor uncontrollably. Then everything went black.

❖

Dale paced up and down the hospital waiting room, feeling like she wanted to claw her insides out.

When Becca had started fitting on the kitchen floor, she was so scared, but then she saw blood on her legs, and the bottom had fallen out of Dale's world. She immediately called for an ambulance and felt so useless. The woman she loved, and their baby, were bleeding on the floor and there was nothing she could do about it.

As soon as they arrived at the hospital, Becca had been rushed to theatre, and now she had to wait while other people tried to save their lives.

Sammy and Val brought Jake to the hospital after dropping Mia off at her grandma's, and then all they had to do was wait.

Dale felt Jake at her side. "Mum? Is Mummy going to be all right? You look really worried."

She had to pull herself together for Jake's sake. Dale crouched down to his level and gave him a hug. "Mummy will be fine. I'm just frustrated because I want us to see her as soon as possible. Don't worry."

Sammy stood up and said, "Why don't Val and I take Jake for something to eat? He's got to be hungry."

Dale appreciated her friend's suggestion. Jake needed his mind taken off things.

"That would be a great idea." Dale took out her wallet and

gave Jake a twenty pound note. "There's a gift shop downstairs. Why don't you go and find something nice to give to Mummy later, huh?"

"Okay, but you'll come and find me when we can see Mummy?"

Dale gave him a hug and kissed his head. "You know I will. Off you go."

"We'll give you an hour, okay?" Val said.

Dale leaned in and kissed her cheek. "Thanks. I appreciate it."

They left and Dale was alone. She sat down and held her face in her hands. She thought about her ma's rosary beads sitting next to her Bible and wished she had them with her, but instead she sent up a silent prayer.

Ma, please watch over Becca and the baby. I've just got them in my life, please don't let me lose them.

Dale's prayer was interrupted by someone clearing their throat. She opened her eyes and saw Trent standing there. *Brilliant.*

"I'm sorry if I'm intruding but the hospital called because I'm still Becca's emergency contact. I'll go if you want, but will you just tell me what happened?"

Dale sighed. "You're not intruding. Come in and sit down."

"Where's Jake?"

"My friends have taken him for something to eat," Dale said.

"What happened?" Trent asked.

Dale scrubbed her hands through her messy hair, in an effort to waken herself up. "Ashley Duval happened."

"Ashley Duval? I thought I'd heard the last of that bitch. I've been trying to keep her away from Becca, ever since she betrayed her with that newspaper story."

"Apparently she found her through me. Becca had been great, her blood pressure much, much better."

"Thanks to you," Trent conceded.

Dale shrugged. "I just tried to help. Anyway, I'd noticed some of her symptoms start to worsen again, and her mood changed. The doctor said she was getting worse again, and ordered complete bed rest, but Becca insisted I take Jake to a race at the car track we had all planned to go to. Becca wanted me out of the house so Ash could come over. I saw messages from Ash on Becca's phone and worked it out."

"What was Ash trying to do?"

"She wanted a no-holds-barred, exclusive, on-camera interview in exchange for keeping me and my sordid family history out of the story, plus Jake. Becca was trying to protect us."

Trent growled. "That fucking bitch. As if she hasn't done enough, and made enough money out of Becca. I found Becca—or Vic as she then was—the morning her mother killed herself. She was sitting in the middle of the floor, with Ash's newspaper story all around her. She was a broken woman. If Ash is back, I'm going to file charges for harassment, get a no-contact order, and file for an injunction against the story. I won't allow that woman to do any more damage."

It was clear Trent still loved Becca, but strangely Dale was okay with that, because she was confident Becca loved her and had chosen her. But Trent would still try to protect her. The more people who wanted to protect Becca the better, especially a lawyer.

"Thank you, that will be a big help. When I burst in on the interview, Becca collapsed…She was bleeding. They think it's her blood pressure. I'm not sure what's happening exactly, but they've taken her to theatre, and she's in a bad way."

"Jesus."

"You're welcome to wait if you want. I know Becca means a lot to you."

Trent nodded and they sat in silence for a minute or so. "Dale, I'm sorry for the things I said to you before. My anger was misplaced. I was really angry with myself for letting a wonderful, beautiful woman like Becca slip though my fingers, and all because I put my own needs above hers. I should have understood why she wanted a baby after the family trouble she had been through."

Dale was more than a little surprised Trent was being so open and honest. She supposed when life hung in the balance like this, the most important things became clearer. "People want different things, Trent. That's okay."

"Ten years I let slip by. I always had this thought that eventually we might get back together, but Becca never dated, so I suppose I thought I had all the time in the world. Then you came along."

Dale looked at her with sympathy. "I came along and messed things up for you?"

Trent shook her head. "No, you came along and made her happy. Something I didn't do. You're right for her, Dale. You give her the family she's always wanted, and I wish you both happiness."

Now Dale really was surprised and touched. Trent offered her hand in friendship. Dale took it immediately and said, "I'm glad she has you as a friend."

"Treat Becca well, okay?" Trent said.

"I always will. I would move heaven and earth to make her happy."

A man in doctor's scrubs entered the waiting room. "Is there a Trent here with a Rebecca Harper?"

They both stood and Trent said gallantly, "I'm Trent, and this is her partner, Dale McGuire. I'm their solicitor."

Trent took a step back and Dale patted her on the shoulder. "Thanks, mate. How is she, doctor?"

"Rebecca's placenta ruptured, and we had to get the baby out of there before she was starved of oxygen. The baby is in an incubator under observation—we're not out of the woods yet, and she is premature, but the signs are good."

Dale was terrified to ask the next question. "And Becca?"

"Rebecca lost a lot of blood, but she's in recovery now. We're hopeful she can make a full recovery."

"Hopeful?" Dale snapped. "Does that mean there's a chance she won't be?"

"Ms. McGuire, when patients lose a lot of blood, there is always a chance of problems, but you got her help quickly, so everything is positive at the moment. If you would like to see her, I'll get a nurse to take you to her."

"Yes, please. I want to see her."

When the doctor left, Dale felt her legs turn to jelly. She sat down quickly.

"Are you okay, Dale?" Trent put a comforting hand on her shoulder.

"Aye, aye." Dale quickly wiped away the tears of relief and fear. "It just hit me that if I hadn't come back today, if Becca had done that interview, she might be dead now, the baby might be dead…" She leaped up and grabbed her jacket.

Trent moved quickly and stood in front of the waiting room door. "Where are you going?"

"I'm going to find that Ashley Duval and kick her arse. She nearly killed Becca, and our baby."

Trent placed her hand on Dale's chest. "Listen, Dale. That is not going to do any good. You'll get yourself arrested, and then the first face Becca will see when she wakes up is mine. You don't want that, do you?" Trent joked.

Dale fought with the anger trying to take control of her. "No."

"Then take a few breaths and calm down. Anger is a lot easier an emotion to deal with than fear, but it's better to face fear than get lost in anger. Let me deal with Duval. She and her newspaper are going to have a huge lawsuit coming their way for harassment, and unless they want an exclusive interview published in a rival newspaper about their journalist tactics, then they'll get her under control and write Becca a large cheque. You take care of Becca and Jake, and let me do my thing, okay?"

Dale let out a long breath. "Okay, okay. I'm calm, I'm calm."

There was a knock and they both stood back to let the nurse in. "Dale McGuire?"

"Aye, that's me."

"I'll take you through to see Rebecca. Follow me."

Dale turned to Trent and said, "Could you do me a favour and find Jake? My friends took him the restaurant and gift shop."

"No problem." Trent hesitated. "When you can, will you give her my love?"

Dale gave her a smile. "You can tell her yourself."

❖

Dale had never been so frightened in her life as she was now, looking at all sorts of leads and tubes coming from Becca, and hearing the noise and beep of the machines.

The last time she had been in this situation had been when her mum had her stroke, and that one event had sparked the most painful time in her life.

This time Dale couldn't let that happen. She took Becca's hand and held it tightly.

"Becca, I know you're tired and you need to sleep, but I just want you to know that Jake, me, and the wee yin will be waiting for you when you wake up, and we all love you."

There was no response apart from the beep of the machines. One of the nurses taking care of Becca came in to check her vitals. As she worked around Becca, she said to Dale, "You're Rebecca's partner?"

"Yes, my name's Dale."

"Did someone tell you that you could go and see the baby?"

"Uh, yeah. I want to wait and see her with Becca. Is the baby still doing okay?"

The nurse smiled. "Yes she's doing well. She's a strong girl."

My little baby girl. There had been something bothering Dale, and it was making guilt gnaw at her stomach. She had been too nervous to ask the doctor, but this nurse seemed sympathetic.

"Nurse, could I ask you something?"

"It's Maggie, and of course you can."

This was so embarrassing, but she had to know because she was driving herself crazy, blaming herself.

"The last month, Becca's pressure was a lot better, and in fact she kind of began to forget about her problems. And, well, we…"

"Yes?"

"We made love over the last few weeks. Did that contribute to Becca's problems?"

Maggie shook her head. "Not at all. Rebecca's doctor was very happy with her recently, but going by her records, Rebecca had high blood pressure and nearly had pre-eclampsia with her first birth.

She's a lot older now, and I understand she'd been under a lot of stress. It's just one of those things."

Dale held Becca's hand and prayed she would open her eyes soon.

❖

Dale took a box from her jacket and brought it over to the bed. She kissed Becca's forehead gently. "Listen, hen, I've been walking around with this box in my pocket all week. I was going to ask you to marry me. I wanted to give us both the family we've been looking for."

She bent down and whispered in Becca's ear, "I hope you'll say yes. Val helped me choose it, and it's a really good diamond, so you better wake up or no diamond for you, okay?"

Becca began to murmur and move, and Dale's heart started to beat fast.

"That's it, babe. Open those eyes."

Dale smiled with joy as Becca's eyes flickered open. "Yes, I knew a posh girl would wake up with the promise of a diamond."

Becca was mumbling something she couldn't quite make out.

"What is it, hen?"

"Baby?"

Dale knelt down at the side of the bed, grasped her hand, and kissed it repeatedly with relief. "Oh, thank God, you're awake. I was so scared. The baby is fine, they've got her in an incubator and we can see her whenever we want."

Becca's voice was a little stronger this time. "Yes."

Dale was confused. "Yes…what do you mean, yes?"

Becca managed a small little smile. "Yes, I'll marry you. I want my diamond."

"Yes! I love you, babe. We're going to have a great family and a great life. No more secrets, no more looking over your shoulder. Ashley Duval will not be a problem to you any more."

Dale took the ring from the box and placed it on Becca's finger. Becca lifted her hand to see the ring.

"It's beautiful. Thank you. Where's Jake?"

Dale gave her another soft kiss on the lips. "I'll let the nurse know you're awake, and then I'll get Jake. Sammy and Val are here too, and..." Dale hesitated. "Trent's here too. She's been helpful and kind. She really cares about you."

Becca managed to croak, "Thank you for letting her in. She's always been good to me."

Dale smiled and nodded. "I'll run and get the family then."

"That would be nice."

❖

Becca couldn't have been any more happy if she tried, as she held her newborn baby girl in the neonatal unit. Dale had taken her along in a wheelchair to visit their new child. Becca was very sore, but none of the pain mattered when the nurse laid the baby on her chest. She was filled with such love, just as she had been with Jake, but this time she had someone to share it with—Dale, the woman who had saved their little family, and saved her soul. It gave Becca such a warm joyful feeling to know she was holding a little part of Dale in her arms.

Dale was kneeling beside her chair, looking at the baby with awe. They both had on plastic aprons to protect the baby from germs.

"She's so tiny, and so perfect," Dale said, as the baby held her finger.

"She is," Becca agreed. "But she's going to get a lot bigger. Most McGuires do."

Dale looked at her with a mixture of confusion and disbelief. "Do they?"

Becca smiled and nodded. "That's what I want us to be when we get married. Harper was never real, and Carter has nothing but bad memories. The name McGuire will bind us all together forever."

Dale stared open-mouthed at her, and seemed unsure how to react, so Becca joked, "Are you changing your mind already, McGuire? You did give me a diamond ring, did you not? Or maybe you don't want to leave Britney behind."

Dale smiled. "Britney who? Thank you, that means so much to me. What about her first name? Is our favourite still Grace?"

Becca kissed the fluffy wisps of brown hair on the baby's head. "Yes, that's what she and you have brought to Jake's and my life. Grace Mary McGuire. How about that?"

"Wow, that's perfect. Hi, wee Gracie, do you like your new name Mummy gave you?"

Becca chuckled. She knew from now on the baby would forever be Gracie. It suited her perfectly.

"Does Mum want to hold her wee yin?" Becca asked.

Dale looked terrified. "Ah…I'll break her or something. Maybe when she's bigger."

"Don't be a scaredy-cat." Without giving her a choice, Becca asked the nurse for another chair for Dale.

Dale sat down and the nurse showed her how to hold the baby. At first Dale was stiff with terror, but when the nurse laid Gracie against her chest, she started to relax and smile.

"Hey, wee yin. I've been so excited to meet you. I love you so much and I promise you that I'll never leave you or turn my back on you, no matter what you do."

Becca had thought nothing could compare with holding her children, but she was wrong. Watching Dale hold Grace with such love and tenderness melted her heart. Tears started to fall. "Dale, I love you."

Dale smiled and replied, "I love you too. Thanks for trusting me and letting me in."

Her partner began to talk incessantly to the baby, telling her about Jake, the vicarage, and how she was going to get them chickens, ducks, and goats.

Jake and Gracie were going to have a wonderful life, thanks to Dale, and so was she.

"Look, she's sucking my finger," Dale said. "She must be hungry. I bet she'll want pureed jalapeños in her milk, with the amount you ate during your pregnancy."

Becca laughed. "Probably."

Then Dale whispered to the baby, "Oh, Gracie, I've got a good joke for you. Why did the jalapeño wear a jumper?"

Becca interrupted. "Uh-uh. I think we better get Jake in to see Gracie before you bore her to sleep with your bad jokes."

"You love my bad jokes, but you're right. I'll go and get him."

Dale handed the baby back to her and walked out to get their son. Becca had the family she always dreamed of at last, and now she could look forward in life, not over her shoulder.

EPILOGUE

Six months later

The summer sun was shining brightly down on the vicarage's back garden. It was looking wonderful after being landscaped and planted with some beautiful flowers.

A perfect day for a barbecue for Dale, Becca, and their friends. Sadie and Val were bringing dishes of food from the kitchen out to the picnic tables, Jake and Mia were running around with water guns, laughing and screaming, and Becca was setting up her camera on its tripod.

"A little to the right, Trent," Becca shouted over the noise of the children.

Both Trent and Sammy were setting out the chairs for the family picture Becca wanted to take.

"Is that okay?" Sammy asked.

"Looks good, just let me check." Becca looked through the viewfinder, and smiled when she felt a hand slide over the small of her back. She knew that hand only too well, and got a rush as she remembered how both Dale's hands had touched her last night.

Becca turned around and found Dale standing there with Gracie in her arms. The baby reached out for her. "Mumma."

"She wanted her mummy, because Mum's tickling her too much."

Gracie giggled as Dale tickled her tummy again.

"Okay, come to Mummy, before Mum gets you too excited."

Dale handed the baby over and said, "You never complain when I get you overexcited, Mrs. McGuire."

Becca gave her a swipe on the bum. "Behave. I do have my family lawyer here, so unless you want to head to the divorce courts, then you behave."

Dale leaned over and kissed Becca so softly and tenderly, it made Becca moan. She pulled back and said with a lot of confidence, "Nah, you're never getting rid of me, babe. Isn't that right, wee yin?"

Gracie replied, "Mumma."

"See?" Dale clapped her hands together. "Okay, are we ready for this picture, because my hair is at peak awesomeness."

Becca laughed and said to the baby, "Mum is very silly, isn't she?"

Dale put her arm around them both. "Well, I make you two smile."

Becca laid her head on Dale's shoulder, and they both watched Jake and Mia run around having so much fun.

"Jake's like a different boy since you've come into his life. He has fun and doesn't live in his head so much."

"He's got a great friend in Mia, anyway. I think those two are going to take over the gaming world," Dale joked.

"I know. It's so great he has a friend, and they like the same things. Mia brings fun to his life, just like you. You came into my world and told me stupid jokes until I laughed and fell in love with you."

Dale kissed her brow. "I'm nothing if not persistent."

"I'm being serious, darling. This…" Becca indicated to the beautiful garden, and their friends chatting away happily, and then the vicarage that was now freshly painted and looking fantastic. "None of this would have happened if Jake hadn't found you. You were completely unexpected but the best thing that's ever happened to me."

"Thank God Jake found me, or I would have missed out on my family." Dale turned and put her arms around Becca's waist, leaving the baby in between. "It's like I was living in this parallel universe, working hard, going out to clubs, never knowing I had this family waiting for me. Then Jake came along and opened up the door between the two worlds."

"And what did you think when you saw us on the other side?" Becca asked.

"From the first glimpse, I knew I wanted in, but I had to convince you, and you can be one hell of a stubborn woman, hen."

"Maybe."

"But I worked hard and I got there, and I'm never going back."

Jake came running over to them. "Mummy, can we take the picture so we can eat? We're starving."

"Okay, get everyone to sit."

Becca handed the baby back to Dale and began to set the timer.

Dale took a seat in the middle and waited for Becca to hurry over. Sammy, Val, Mia, and Trent were all there and were all part of the family they had created.

Becca took her seat beside Dale and said, "Ten seconds, everyone, say *Cheese!*"

The camera flashed and caught a happy moment in time. Because sometimes the best things are unexpected.

About the Author

Jenny Frame is from the small town of Motherwell in Scotland, where she lives with her partner, Lou, and their well-loved and very spoiled dog.

She has a diverse range of qualifications, including a BA in public management and a diploma in acting and performance. Nowadays, she likes to put her creative energies into writing rather than treading the boards.

When not writing or reading, Jenny loves cheering on her local football team, which is not always an easy task!

Books Available From Bold Strokes Books

A Lamentation of Swans by Valerie Bronwen. Ariel Montgomery returns to Sea Oats to try to save her broken marriage but soon finds herself also fighting to save her own life and catch a murderer. (978-1-62639-828-3)

Freedom to Love by Ronica Black. What happens when the woman who spent her life worrying about caring for her family finally finds the freedom to love without borders? (978-1-63555-001-6)

House of Fate by Barbara Ann Wright. Two women must throw off the lives they've known as a guardian and an assassin and save two rival houses before their secrets tear the galaxy apart. (978-1-62639-780-4)

Planning for Love by Erin Dutton. Could true love be the one thing that wedding coordinator Faith McKenna didn't plan for? (978-1-62639-954-9)

Sidebar by Carsen Taite. Judge Camille Avery and her clerk, attorney West Fallon, agree on little except their mutual attraction, but can their relationship and their careers survive a headline-grabbing case? (978-1-62639-752-1)

Sweet Boy and Wild One by T. L. Hayes. When Rachel Cole meets soulful singer Bobby Layton at an open mic, she is immediately in thrall. What she soon discovers will rock her world in ways she never imagined. (978-1-62639-963-1)

To Be Determined by Mardi Alexander and Laurie Eichler. Charlie Dickerson escapes her life in the US to rescue Australian wildlife with Pip Atkins, but can they save each other? (978-1-62639-946-4)

True Colors by Yolanda Wallace. Blogger Robby Rawlins plans to use First Daughter Taylor Crenshaw to get ahead, but she never planned on falling in love with her in the process. (978-1-62639-927-3)

Heart Stop by Radclyffe. Two women, one with a damaged body, the other a damaged spirit, challenge each other to dare to live again. (978-1-62639-899-3)

Undercover Affairs by Julie Blair. Searching for stolen documents crucial to U.S. security, CIA agent Rett Spenser confronts lies, deceit, and unexpected romance as she investigates art gallery owner Shannon Kent. (978-1-62639-905-1)

Unexpected by Jenny Frame. When Dale McGuire falls for Rebecca Harper, the mother of the son she never knew she had, will Rebecca's troubled past stop them from making the family they both truly crave? (978-1-62639-942-6)

Canvas for Love by Charlotte Greene. When ghosts from Amelia's past threaten to undermine their relationship, Chloé must navigate the greatest romance of her life without losing sight of who she is. (978-1-62639-944-0)

Repercussions by Jessica L. Webb. Someone planted information in Edie Black's brain and now they want it back, but with the protection of shy former soldier Skye Kenny, Edie has a chance at life and love. (978-1-62639-925-9)

Spark by Catherine Friend. Jamie's life is turned upside down when her consciousness travels back to 1560 and lands in the body of one of Queen Elizabeth I's ladies-in-waiting...or has she totally lost her grip on reality? (978-1-62639-930-3)

Taking Sides by Kathleen Knowles. When passion and politics collide, can love survive? (978-1-62639-876-4)

Thorns of the Past by Gun Brooke. Former cop Darcy Flynn's heart broke when her career on the force ended in disgrace, but perhaps saving Sabrina Hawk's life will mend it in more ways than one. (978-1-62639-857-3)

You Make Me Tremble by Karis Walsh. Seismologist Casey Radnor comes to the San Juan Islands to study an earthquake but finds her heart shaken by passion when she meets animal rescuer Iris Mallery. (978-1-62639-901-3)

Girls Next Door, edited by Sandy Lowe and Stacia Seaman. Bestselling romance authors tell it from the heart—sexy, romantic stories of falling for the girls next door. (978-1-62639-916-7)

Complications by MJ Williamz. Two women battle for the heart of one. (978-1-62639-769-9)

Crossing the Wide Forever by Missouri Vaun. As Cody Walsh and Lillie Ellis face the perils of the untamed West, they discover that love's uncharted frontier isn't for the weak in spirit or the faint of heart. (978-1-62639-851-1)

Fake It till You Make It by M. Ullrich. Lies will lead to trouble, but can they lead to love? (978-1-62639-923-5)

Pursuit by Jackie D. The pursuit of the most dangerous terrorist in America will crack the lines of friendship and love, and not everyone will make it out from under the weight of duty and service. (978-1-62639-903-7)

The Practitioner by Ronica Black. Sometimes love comes calling whether you're ready for it or not. (978-1-62639-948-8)

Unlikely Match by Fiona Riley. When an ambitious PR exec and her super-rich coding geek-girl client fall in love, they learn that giving something up may be the only way to have everything. (978-1-62639-891-7)

Where Love Leads by Erin McKenzie. A high school counselor and the mom of her new student bond in support of the troubled girl, never expecting deeper feelings to emerge, testing the boundaries of their relationship. (978-1-62639-991-4)

Forsaken Trust by Meredith Doench. When four women are murdered, Agent Luce Hansen must regain trust in her most valuable investigative tool—herself—to catch the killer. (978-1-62639-737-8)

Letter of the Law by Carsen Taite. Will federal prosecutor Bianca Cruz take a chance at love with horse breeder Jade Vargas, whose dark family ties threaten everything Bianca has worked to protect—including her child? (978-1-62639-750-7)

New Life by Jan Gayle. Trigena and Karrie are having a baby, but the stress of becoming a mother and the impact on their relationship might be too much for Trigena. (978-1-62639-878-8)

Royal Rebel by Jenny Frame. Charity director Lennox King sees through the party-girl image Princess Roza has cultivated, but will Lennox's past indiscretions and Roza's responsibilities make their love impossible? (978-1-62639-893-1)

Unbroken by Donna K. Ford. When Kayla and Jackie, two women with every reason to reject Happily Ever After, fall in love, will they have the courage to overcome their pasts and rewrite their stories? (978-1-62639-921-1)

Where the Light Glows by Dena Blake. Mel Thomas doesn't realize just how unhappy she is in her marriage until she meets Izzy Calabrese. Will she have the courage to overcome her insecurities and follow her heart? (978-1-62639-958-7)

Her Best Friend's Sister by Meghan O'Brien. For fifteen years, Claire Barker has nursed a massive crush on her best friend's older sister. What happens when all her wildest fantasies come true? (978-1-62639-861-0)

Escape in Time by Robyn Nyx. Working in the past is hell on your future. (978-1-62639-855-9)

Forget-Me-Not by Kris Bryant. Is love worth walking away from the only life you've ever dreamed of? (978-1-62639-865-8)

Highland Fling by Anna Larner. On vacation in the Scottish Highlands, Eve Eddison falls for the enigmatic forestry officer Moira Burns despite Eve's best friend's campaign to convince her that Moira will break her heart. (978-1-62639-853-5)

Soul Survivor by I. Beacham. Sam and Joey have given up on hope, but when fate brings them together it gives them a chance to change each other's life and make dreams come true. (978-1-62639-882-5)

Strawberry Summer by Melissa Brayden. When Margaret Beringer's first love Courtney Carrington returns to their small town, she must grapple with their troubled past and fight the temptation for a very delicious future. (978-1-62639-867-2)